# Sapphire Chameleon

## by Frieda Klein

To Susan,
My dear friend!
It's always a
pleasure being with you!
Love & best wishes
always,
Frieda

DEDICATION:

This book is dedicated to my "boyfriend" Richard,
who has been extremely loving, supportive, and
encouraging of my many creative endeavors
over the past 53 years.

He has always been my "rock", my confidante,
and my best friend, and I am forever grateful
to have been so fortunate to be married
to such a special, wonderful man.
Especially a man who understands,
respects, and loves women.

IN APPRECIATION:

A special thanks and appreciation to my editor and graphic designer Lolly Kupec. Without her brilliant help, this book might never have been published.

Lolly's remarkable understanding, wit and knowledge, as well as her psychological insights, have given SAPPHIRE CHAMELEON an added more polished dimension.

I moved to Lake Tahoe in 1974. A few years later I met Lolly who had just settled in Tahoe. She came from the east coast where she had worked as a graphic designer in New York, Connecticut and Hyannis, Massachusetts. Being an artist myself, we immediately bonded.

Over the years Lolly purchased a few of my paintings. She also helped promote my work. With her help, advice, and guidance I opened a small art gallery in the '90s. My paintings had been shown and sold in many galleries, and museums since the '70s, but I wanted to have my own gallery, where I also sold my hand-made jewelry, painted clothing and pottery.

A year ago I mentioned to her that I had just finished writing a novel. She seemed very interested and asked to read it. I began emailing her a chapter at a time, and after reading each one, she kept asking for more. She called SAPPHIRE CHAMELEON a "page turner" and encouraged me to publish it.

Needless to say, I was flattered to get that kind of positive response from her. I have always respected both Lolly's artistic and literary opinions, so I decided to hire her as my editor and graphic designer – a very wise decision. Lolly has been a tremendous help and a total pleasure to work with! I couldn't have completed SAPPHIRE CHAMELEON without her help and support.

# TABLE OF CONTENTS:

# SYNOPSIS:

SAPPHIRE CHAMELEON spans the life of Julia Forrester from her early twenties up to her mid-forties.

Julia was brought up by ignorant parents, and her childhood home was a dysfunctional one. Her mother was particularly abusive.

That childhood situation, and the paradigm of the 1950s left Julia feeling timid, shy, and insecure. Like a chameleon that changes its colors to blend into its environment to survive, she learns to survive, to be an easy-going, amicable pleaser, to not "make waves" or be confrontational.

In 1958, at age 20, she marries Ralph Worthington, an attorney she meets while a student at the University of Pennsylvania. Julia is determined to be the kind of wife who "loves, honors, and obeys," hoping to be rewarded with the promise of the day: "living happily ever after."

Ralph is offered a job at a prestigious law firm in San Francisco in 1961, and enthusiastically he and Julia look forward to the change and their move to California .

During their first few years in San Francisco three children are born and Julia becomes a stay-at-home-mom. Her same daily routine turns her into a somnambulist, and makes her question why she is not "living happily ever after." Especially, when she discovers Ralph is having affairs.

To save her marriage, particularly "for the sake of the children," Julia musters up the courage to timidly approach Ralph and suggest they see a marriage counselor. He, of course, stubbornly refuses.

Devastated and disappointed, Julia turns to her first passion, painting, as an escape from her misery.

An avid reader, books, also, slowly enlighten and strengthen her. She is particularly enamored with the writings of Otto Marlton, whom she fantasizes as being her "soul mate." (Otto Marlton is loosely based on the author, Henry Miller, who was a dear friend of mine for eight years before he died.)

Serendipitously, Julia meets Marlton at an opera function and a friendship begins. Over time they fall in love. Julia divorces Ralph and marries Marlton in 1979, who empowers her with his warmth, love, and respect.

Three years later, in June 1982 Marlton dies and Julia is left to "figure out her life" on her own. Love-starved and all alone, she is terrified of what the future might hold for her.

Hence, she begins a new journey traveling many roads. Life sometimes throws her "curve balls", forcing her to make decisions and deal with people and situations she hadn't anticipated.

These unexpected "detours" turn out to be valuable learning experiences that, surprisingly, teach her to cope and take responsibility.

Julia learns there is no formula for "living happily ever after." Like all feelings, happiness is fleeting and can't be boxed or contained.

Awareness of the truth of the moment is liberating, and rejuvenates her. She realizes everything that happened to her during her life was "meant to be." It was all part of life's plan, all she could do was accept and learn from each experience.

Once Julia takes full responsibility for herself, her actions and choices, she feels a different kind of freedom – courage and entitlement. And, a renewed energy to take one day at a time.

In essence, this is a story of self-discovery, which unwittingly is taught to all of us every day, through our daily experiences and life occurrences. There is no "how to" formula. Life is our lesson and it is as unpredictable, as are our feelings.

Julia eventually realizes there is no such thing as "living happily after." Being happy just happens, or, it doesn't, depending on one's circumstances, perceptions, and attitudes.

Though SAPPHIRE CHAMELEON is basically a story about one woman, Julia's journey is a universal one – one to which we all can relate.

*Frieda Klein*

CHAPTER ONE: The Funeral

"Au revoir, my Otto, my beloved Otto. You will be in my heart forever. I will never stop loving you," Julia whispered to herself. Otto always preferred using the French version of good-bye which became a habit for Julia, too.

She tried not to cry. She needed to show she was as strong as Jackie Kennedy seemed to be when her husband was killed. No tears. Julia wanted to emulate Jackie's remarkable composure, with grace and dignity.

As Julia looked down at the ornate casket a small tear escaped and trickled down her cheek. She dug into the depths of her black leather shoulder bag for her embroidered handkerchief and delicately and discreetly dabbed the betraying tear. She studied the lid of the casket intently, adorned with roses, gardenias, orchids, and lilies. Just as she had ordered. An odd, non-traditional combination for a funeral spread, but those were Otto's favorites. He loved rich, ruby red roses, the aroma of gardenias, the soft violet color of orchids, and the thin, wispy petals that lilies yielded. Julia often arranged bouquets of these "gems" as Otto called them, surprising him with them on the dining room table. She loved creating and she loved to cook. She reminisced Otto's "oohs" and "aahs" over their beauty, while savoring the many delicious dishes she artistically prepared. He always complimented her creativity.

The morning was overcast. The sky was light gray and fog was beginning to roll in from the ocean. The outline of the Golden Gate Bridge was barely visible now. A typical summer day in San Francisco. Chuckling to herself Julia thought of Mark Twain's infamous comment – the coldest winter he ever spent was a summer in San Francisco – or something like that.

The wind was picking up too, blowing Julia's honey-colored hair. A few strands stuck to her lips. She reached up and removed them gently so her perfectly applied lip gloss wouldn't get smeared. Out on the horizon black clouds were forming. It looked as if a storm was coming in. Her ears were beginning to hurt from the cold air. She pulled her dark green wool cape tighter around her shoulders. Oh, how she wished she was home, sitting by a crackling fire where she could feel warm and cozy ... and safely away from all these self-serving gossip mongers.

People were gathering by the gravesite for the eulogy. Julia clutched her handkerchief tightly. Reporters were watching her every move. She could see their cameras out of the corner of her eye. She was sick of publicity, of every-body knowing her business. She couldn't wait until this last ordeal was over and done with, and forgotten as quickly as possible. She wanted to get on with her life, anonymously.

Ah, yes, but she had certain duties to attend to first – shaking hands with each and every one of these hundreds of people. Thankfully, it was a week day or there would have been thousands. Shudder the thought.

A line began to form. All the phonies – writers, actors, directors, artists, neighbors, casual acquaintances – they were all there, probably hoping to get some free publicity. Few of them were really Otto Marlton's friends. She knew in her heart many of them disliked Otto, and were only at his funeral as curiosity seekers. Otto had a way of saying things that often made people uncomfortable, usually because what he said was true. Julia relished the times she had witnessed people squirming while pretending to smile when Otto made one of his infamous caustic remarks. Most people never really got his facetious sense of humor.

"Julia, you poor dahling, I'm so very, very sorry ..." Betty Astor drawled as she leaned over and gave Julia a stiff hug, then a quick air-peck to her cheek.

Julia couldn't believe Betty Astor. That woman couldn't care less about me. When Otto was alive she barely gave me the time of day.

Actually, Betty had never been overly fond of Otto either. Julia was sure she had only kept in touch with him for selfish reasons. Betty was the classic social climber. Otto had a lot of connections. He knew a lot of celebrities, who could help Betty further herself as "an aspiring actress" and Betty was well aware of that.

Andre Kramer walked over towards Julia. She had been watching him out of the corner or her eye. She always had a little crush on him, had even dreamt of him a few times. Andre was in his mid-forties. The only tell-tale sign of his age was his receding hairline, though it didn't detract from his good looks. It actually added to his charm, she thought. It made him look "seasoned."

Taking Julia's hand, Andre gave it a squeeze, then leaned over and hugged her. "Julia, I am truly sorry. I was shocked when I heard the news. If I can be of any help, just call me." Then he walked away.

Julia instinctively knew Andre was sincere. She saw it in his face, his gesture, his tone of voice. She somehow felt better during those few moments with him standing next to her. Something about him made her feel stronger, safer.

Several of Otto's closest friends gathered together to announce their farewells to him. She had asked a special few to give a eulogy. No clergy would preside over the funeral since Otto was not religious. In fact, he didn't believe in organized religion. He often said it did more harm than good, citing many wars and horrors brought on by religion, "in the name of God." "Religion was an excuse from reality," he said. Otto rarely talked about God, but Julia knew he was a deeply spiritual person, honest to a fault, with a deep reverence for nature and life.

Mark Spencer was the first to speak. Bowing his head, his voice quivered as he muttered, "Good-bye dear friend. You have left me and the world a rich legacy through your friendship, and your art. You never compromised your integrity for the sake of promoting your genius. I will miss you and remember you all the days of my life."

Jefferson Allen picked up where Spencer left off. "Frail as he might have seemed in stature, Otto Marlton was a giant amongst us. He spoke out fearlessly and frankly. He spoke with humor, a joie de vivre. I and the entire world will feel a huge gap from his absence, yet his wisdom will live on. Otto Marlton will continue to inspire many for centuries to come."

David Martin cleared his throat as he began to speak. "Otto Marlton will stand with the great writers who inspired him, like Walt Whitman, D.H. Lawrence, James Joyce – who not only left us with works of art, but with many ideas that will continue to influence our culture for years to come. I salute you, Otto, a true artist in every sense of the word. I bid you adieu dear friend."

Three more people eulogized Otto Marlton in a similar vein – "unconventional ... innovative ... remarkably original ... bold ... pure ... unadulterated." Some referred to him as an existentialist because he was such a free spirit.

"Honesty" was the word most used. No one could deny Otto Marlton's integrity. He lived and spoke the truth, even when it hurt. That was what had attracted Julia to him from the beginning. She had never known anyone quite like Otto. She had tremendous respect for his rare trait of honesty. He was truly one in a million.

The gravesite assembly began to disperse, a few more people came over to speak to Julia. It was difficult remembering everyone's name. And, even more difficult responding to their inane remarks, which made her feel like a robot.

"Julia, I was so sorry when I heard Otto had passed away."

Was sorry? Really? "Thank you, John, I'm glad you were able to make it to the funeral. Otto is ... I mean, I'm sure all this would have meant a lot to him."

God, what am I saying? Otto hated this bullshit. He would have puked if he heard me say that. Julia realized in spite of Otto's tremendous influence on her, she was still a coward. She never was or could be as honest a person as he was. She was always afraid of hurting someone's feelings. Or, was it maybe she was afraid of rejection if people got angry with her?

"It's so sad now that Otto has left us," Geraldine Moyer gushed as she tried to feign sadness. Her expression didn't fit her words. Probably too many face lifts. Everything was so tucked in, it couldn't move anymore. What a lousy actress Geraldine Moyer is in real life. And she got an Academy Award last year! Julia couldn't stomach her, yet she forced a smile.

Old Mrs. Levin leaned over. Julia cringed. Mrs. Levin's false teeth often wobbled so much that she spit when she talked. Julia was waiting for another shower, and was pleasantly surprised when she gave her a peck on the cheek. I wonder if Mrs. Levin found a new fixative to hold her teeth in place more tightly, Julia thought. Mrs. Levin sighed heavily, lamenting, "Another one of my friends gone!" As soon as the words left her mouth, she limped away leaning on her cane.

What a strange phenomenon death is. People seem afraid to use the word. Not one person has said "dead" or "died" or "death". Perhaps saying "passed away", "left us" or "gone" makes death less final. It's not like people really cared for Otto. Is it their own death they are preparing for when they attend funerals?

Then, there were the curious ...

"Julia ... what happened?"

"Was Otto in pain?"

"Did he suffer?"

"Were you with him when he passed away?"

Julia felt guilty. That last question hurt. She wasn't with Otto when he died. She was not home that day. She had gone to Inverness with her friend Suzie Clemmens. They decided to spend the night at a motel when it started raining. Both she and Suzie dreaded driving in a downpour, especially when it also began thundering and lightning. Julia called Otto to tell him she wouldn't be coming home that night. Though he said it was alright, she sensed in his voice he was a bit perturbed. Still, he seemed fine. He didn't say anything was bothering him other than his usual complaints – only mentioning the rain was making his arthritis act up again.

Julia returned late the next morning to find Otto dead. Shocked, sitting by his bedside, she held his hand in both of hers for a few minutes before she called anyone. Sobbing uncontrollably she studied the peaceful expression on his face. Where was he now? What was death like? It was all too difficult to comprehend, to believe Otto was really gone forever.

The past year had been challenging for her, and even though she had felt angry with him on occasion, Julia grieved for Otto deeply.

The coroner said Otto had a massive heart attack and probably died in his sleep that morning. He most likely went quickly without any pain. He had been dead for several hours before Julia returned home to discover his lifeless, cold body.

She felt awful and blamed herself for Otto's death. What if she hadn't spent the night in Inverness? Would this still have happened? Was Otto angry with her for not coming home that night? Did that cause his heart attack? If she'd been home she could have called the paramedics. Maybe she could have saved him. She was riddled with guilt.

Otto's death caused her to relive memories of her father's death when she was just seventeen. It had left her with similar feelings of regret and guilt. Julia loved and adored her father. She also hated him at times. Her father's passivity disgusted her, and she hated he was a wimp, that he dealt with his problems by drinking. She felt ashamed of him when he was drunk, especially in front of her friends. She hated him for marrying her mother. She hated how she felt about him. Oh, well ... he was a good father, wasn't he?

Thinking rationally, she decided Otto's death had happened for the best, and, was relieved it happened suddenly. Just think, at Otto's age it could have been worse. He could have had a stroke that left him paralyzed. He could have required constant attention. Julia knew she wouldn't have had the patience, or the energy to be Otto's nursemaid. Besides, he would have hated that. He would have hated if his life depended on others. She would have hated it, too.

Julia's thoughts were interrupted, looking at the opposite side of the grave, the twins were standing there. Stephanie and Stuart Marlton Otto's kids from his first marriage. People were extending their condolences to them, too.

She had not spoken to either one of them during the last year. It was their decision, not hers. They had resented her from the first time they met her. Especially, Stephanie. Julia tried everything to warm up to them. She invited them to dinner many times, and phoned them often. Over the last year all she ever got was an answering machine. Neither one of them ever returned her calls. And, when they called to speak to their father, they were abrupt and icy towards her if she happened to answer the phone.

Was she just being paranoid? Did her feelings of rejection have any merit?

Stephanie was a cold fish. She always had been. Difficult to figure out. Julia was approximately ten years older than Stephanie. Stephanie talked about how terrified she was of growing old – at twenty-nine! Now at thirty-three, Stephanie's dark brown hair was almost all gray, and sad lines and wrinkles were already evident on her face. Julia could see Stephanie wasn't taking good care of herself. She was gaining weight and looked unkempt. She had been married for a short time, but presently considered herself a divorcee. No children, thankfully. Stephanie would have made a terrible mother, being self-centered and immature. Julia felt another pang of guilt. She should talk. Look at the kind of mother she turned out to be.

Stuart was easier to get along with. When he wasn't drunk or on drugs, Julia could actually have a decent conversation with him. He surprised her one time – only once in the few years she had known him – when he opened up to her. They sat up all night talking about honest-to-god feelings. Stuart confessed he never cried. Julia could tell he needed to cry and wanted to badly, but he wasn't able to. They also talked about other things, the fact that he contemplated suicide on occasion. His goal in life had always been to be as famous and as successful as his father. He had attempted writing, but usually had a block. Otto tried coaching him, but that only made it worse for Stuart. Sadly, he considered Otto to be his nemesis.

Julia felt sorry for the twins. What did they have to live for now that their father was gone? They had always been dependent on Otto. They basked in the limelight of his fame and importance most of their lives, and never developed true identities of their own.

Because money was freely available to the twins, they didn't realize it was an issue in the Marlton household. A lot of debts had piled up before Otto became a financially successful writer. It was a wonder his family was able to live as well as they did. Julia discovered later Otto's friends were a substantial help financially. Many had loaned him large sums of money with no interest and no deadline to pay them back. Others believed in Otto's talent so much they just gave him money, calling it an investment.

The twins had quite a bit of money from their trust fund, and would get a small inheritance now their father was dead, but Julia wondered what they would do when that ran out. Neither had ever held a job for more than a year or so. They probably didn't know the meaning of real work.

Julia never needed Otto's money. She was independently wealthy, but Stephanie and Stuart never knew that, so they never trusted her. They were always suspicious she had only married their father for his money.

She wondered if they would fight with each other now. On the surface they got along like a loving brother and sister, but she detected more sibling rivalry than either would admit. The tone of their voices revealed a lot. They were frequently competitive, and often tried to one-up each other. Especially Stephanie.

Julia knew when she married Otto their life together would not be a private one, but she never expected the invasion of their privacy to be as bad as it was. People always seemed to be butting in. If it wasn't Otto's first wife Estelle calling him and whining about her problems, it was one of the twins. The past couple of years had been almost unbearable. Otto's many fans constantly bugged him and so did the media. There were times when Julia wanted to pull the telephone cord out of the wall.

She had little time alone with Otto, even right from the beginning of their short three-year marriage. And, when they were alone, everything centered around Otto. Now, perhaps at last Julia thought, she could focus on her own life, although she didn't have an inkling of what she was going to do. It was very frightening to suddenly be all alone.

Julia was startled out of her thoughts when a reporter suddenly approached and asked, "Mrs. Marlton ... what are your plans now?"

Julia felt like smacking him. It was as if he was reading her mind. How insensitive! Besides, everyone knew her as Julia Forrester. After her divorce from Ralph Worthington, she went back to using her maiden name, which she kept after marrying Otto. How nosey of this reporter to ask her such a personal question! The implication angered her too, as if, now that Otto was dead, she might not have a life of her own, that she was helpless without him. Even if there was partially a ring of truth to it. Everything had happened so quickly. Julia barely had time to think. Otto had some medical problems over the past year, but it was a huge shock when he died so suddenly.

Instinctively, politeness overcame her, answering the reporter she said "I'll most likely get back into painting." A lie. She had little desire to pursue her art career again. It had become less fulfilling for her each time she painted. By the time she met Otto she had stopped painting altogether. For a short time, while married to Ralph, she sold her work in galleries and had close to a dozen solo exhibits. Public opinion of her work tore her to shreds, however. She wasn't thick-skinned enough. It was too difficult to paint for the approval of others. Yet, if her paintings didn't sell, the galleries threatened to drop her, which put her in a state of constant emotional turmoil. She took a defeatist's attitude and gave up painting.

In the first year of her marriage to Otto, he encouraged her to paint again. He thought she had a lot of talent and a special knack for expressing herself. He praised her Fauvist pieces, saying they were "strong", and he loved her crazy use of bright colors. The first time he saw one of her paintings he remarked, "You must have a lot of love in your heart. You paint with such wonderful colors." Julia melted. Any crumb of praise or affection from the great Otto Marlton was too good to be true. Still, she stopped painting and decided to focus on her new role as Otto's wife.

Enough of that. Julia walked over to where the limousine was waiting to take her home.

Andre Kramer was standing alongside the line of cars brought back to the cemetery by the valet parking guys. Julia smiled at him and waved goodbye. Andre waved back and yelled, "Julia, I meant what I said – if you ever need anything, call me, OK?"

Julia smiled again, "Thank you, Andre," and stepped into the shiny black Cadillac. As it sped away, she felt a little tingle inside. Had Andre awakened something in her? Something that had been lying dormant?

Andre was not like everyone else. He seemed more real, more honest. He was a chiropractor, and had been treating Otto during the last year of his life. Otto had osteoarthritis and was frequently in a lot of pain. Julia's friend Suzie recommended Dr. Kramer, claiming he was a "miracle worker".

As predicted, Andre helped ease Otto's pain, and Otto was extremely grateful to him. Otto had suffered for years, and the medications prescribed by his regular physicians only helped temporarily. When each drug ceased to work, new ones, or stronger doses were needed, often leaving Otto feeling stuporous. It became a vicious cycle, but because the prescriptions relieved his aching body Otto felt he had no other choice. That was until Dr. Kramer treated him with his "magic hands" as Otto referred to them.

When Andre mentioned to Otto that he too dabbled in writing, Otto volunteered to read some of his work and offer his advice. After reading Andre's short story, he confessed to Julia Andre's work "showed promise" but she detected that in some way Andre was a threat to Otto. She had never seen Otto react to any writer the way he had to Andre. Otto seemed uneasy when reading Andre's work. He cleared his throat a lot, shifted around in his chair. Julia knew her husband. She had memorized his body language. She knew certain movements and gestures were significant and indicative of specific feelings, especially when he felt threatened by something. Of course, she would never mention this to him. She knew he'd deny it.

Julia anticipated Otto was not going to give Andre much encouragement. He couldn't handle the competition, which she couldn't understand, since he was already the "famous writer." And, true to her insights, when Andre came to pick up his manuscript, Otto coldly announced, "It's not so bad ... But, if you worked on it more, it could be much better."

When Otto retired early one night Julia read Andre's story. She loved it. She thought it was brilliant. Being a voracious reader she knew a little about good writing.

She wondered if Otto had ever suspected her innocent attraction to Andre. If he did, he probably would have never allowed him back into the house, Otto was, after all, extremely possessive and jealous. That bothered Julia. Nevertheless, she loved him very much, and now was feeling guilty for her sexual attraction to Andre – at her husband's funeral no less!

CHAPTER TWO:  The Divorce

Long before they ever met, Julia had fallen in love with Otto Marlton
through his work. Autobiographically written, Marlton spilled out his guts
in his books. He wrote about his life, his struggles, his feelings, his philosophy. He told it like it was – the good, the bad, and the ugly. Julia thought
she found her "soul mate" in Marlton. Even her closest friends never admitted to having such intimate feelings that Marlton wrote about. Julia often
felt there was something wrong with her. She questioned her feelings, her
sanity. No one she knew could ever express what she felt in her heart. She
wanted to share her ideas and feelings with someone, anyone. She felt so
alone and frustrated. That was until she read Otto Marlton's books.

For a year Julia was obsessed with him. She read every one of his books
she could find. She even bought extra copies to give to her friends, but most
of them never understood their  importance, or what his wisdom meant to
her. She had to contain herself at social events so as not to bore the other
guests. Given the opportunity, she would rattle on and on ad nauseam about
Otto Marlton and his writings. "Otto Marlton said this ... Otto Marlton
said that ... Otto Marlton did this ... Otto Marlton did that ... Otto Marlton
went here, there, etc, etc." Otto's articulate skill of writing about his life in a
philosophical way taught Julia so much. She wanted to pass his messages on
to everyone in the world. She was deeply saddened that no one she knew
was really interested.

For some unexplained reason, Julia assumed Otto Marlton was dead.
Then one day while in Waldon Books, as she was buying his newest release,

she began conversing with the salesgirl who told her UC Berkeley had just thrown a 70th birthday celebration for Marlton.

Julia was beside herself, feeling a joy and excitement beyond belief. She practically danced all the way up the hill to her opulent Spanish-style home overlooking San Francisco Bay. Julia lived there with her husband, Ralph and their three children.

She rushed in the front door. Ralph was at his desk preparing a case for the next day. He had become one of San Francisco's most prominent and successful attorneys.

"Ralph, guess what? Guess what I just found out? Otto Marlton is alive and well!"

"Uh, really?" Ralph hated being disturbed. He hated having his thought process interrupted. He knew how important Otto Marlton was to Julia. He wanted her to think her interests mattered to him also. Though he could really care less.

Ralph focused on portraying himself as "the perfect husband," especially when it was profitable for him. Ralph was a workaholic. The only relief he allowed himself was sex. He wanted it frequently. Intuitively, he knew just mentioning the name Otto Marlton, made Julia glow. He also knew when Julia was in a good mood she was more likely to "put out".

Ralph stopped working on his transcript and pretended to be interested in another new tale about Otto Marlton. Several times he glanced across the room at the large clock on the wall.

Seeing that she was "wasting his precious time," Julia lost her enthusiasm and realized she was beginning to dislike her husband.

She wondered what had gone wrong with her marriage. She thought curiously about how much in love she was with Ralph at one time.

They met at a Sigma Chi party at the University of Pennsylvania. Ralph Worthington was a Wharton Business school student, the president of his fraternity and from a well-to-do family.

There was an immediate, mutual attraction for both of them that first night. Ralph was tall, handsome, and suave. And, an intellectual. Those were the values of the 1950s that a girl was supposed to consider when choosing a mate. Ralph was also impressed with Julia who was an art student, not one of those rich, spoiled, snobby sorority girls. He had his fill of those prima donnas. Julia was down-to-earth, natural. She was also beautiful. She had been her high school homecoming queen. Exceptionally good looks were a top requirement for Ralph. It was important for him to have a beautiful woman on his arm. Yes, for Ralph, Julia was auspicious, and would be a huge asset for him in pursuing a successful career.

Julia knew beauty mattered, and good looking people were treated with more respect. She wasn't conceited, but was pleased and flattered people responded to her favorably because of her beauty. Ever since she was a little girl she was fawned over, and told how pretty she was. When she grew older, this sometimes bothered her, thinking people only liked her because of her looks. It scared her, too. What if she stopped being beautiful? Deep down she worried if Ralph would still love her if she lost her good looks, especially after she grew old. How would he and other people treat her then? Well, that was a long way off, she reasoned, and dismissed the thought.

It was a whirlwind romance. Ralph "pinned" Julia and they dated exclusively for almost a year. Then he proposed. Less than a few weeks after he graduated from "Penn" in 1958, they were married. Ralph was 22 and Julia was 20. She continued taking art classes, but never graduated. She wanted to focus on her marriage, to always be available for Ralph. She wanted her marriage to be perfect. Not like she viewed her parents' relationship.

Their wedding was small and simple. They managed to pay for most of the expenses themselves. When Julia's father, Chuck died, her mother, Katherine, was left with a pittance. Katherine needed every penny she had to live on, so she had little to no money to contribute to the wedding.

Ralph's parents were not pleased with their son's choice for a wife. They thought Ralph "deserved better", whatever that meant, and weren't very supportive emotionally or financially.

Their other son, Lance had married Beverly, a debutante, who seemed on the surface at least to be the ideal wife. After all, Beverly came from a "good" wealthy family. She was taught proper etiquette and was a "lady". Her "type" would have been more suitable for Ralph.

After Ralph and Julia married, however, his parents grew to appreciate her. Julia was warm and friendly, and had many good social attributes. By comparison to Beverly, who was neurotic and self-centered, Julia was a welcome relief. She phoned them every week, sent them thoughtful cards and gifts on important occasions, respected them, and showed them she genuinely cared about them. She was a joy to be with. It was a delight to be in her company. Whenever they visited, Julia laid out the red carpet, treating them as if they were important celebrities.

After Ralph graduated from Penn, he was offered many lucrative positions in the business world, but decided to go to law school instead. His parents had paid for all his undergraduate expenses from a fund they had started when he was a child. He was grateful to them for that support. Even though they were financially comfortable, he didn't want to impose by asking them to pay for law school. He had too much pride. Instead, he applied for a scholarship, which he was relieved to receive.

Julia encouraged Ralph in his new endeavor. She obtained a good paying job at a local art gallery and offered to support them while Ralph focused on his studies.

Times were tough during those law school years, but their love and devotion to each other compensated for what they lacked.

Shortly after graduating from law school in 1961, Ralph, who was at the top of his class, was offered a position with a prestigious law firm in San Francisco. He immediately flew to California to take the Bar exam, which he considered to be a cinch and was sure he passed. He was right, of course. Within a couple of months he received the results, earning him the title of Attorney at Law in the State of California.

Julia stayed in Philadelphia and packed their belongings while Ralph was settling in California. When he returned to Philadelphia to get Julia, they loaded up their Nash Rambler, and began the three thousand mile journey across the country to their new life.

It was exciting to leave the east coast and venture west. Julia had always dreamed of living in California. As a teen-ager she loved reading movie magazines, and fantasized about someday living beside movie stars and palm trees. She wanted to get as far away as possible from her mother who had often abused her. Julia could never forgive Katherine. Her mother's uncouth behavior and four letter word vocabulary had always been an embarrassment to her.

Ralph was thrilled to have been chosen by this particular law firm. He had high ambitions of being a successful attorney, and this position, one that was sought after by many of his classmates, would be a huge stepping stone for him.

San Francisco seemed too good to be true. It was unlike any other city Julia and Ralph had ever seen. It was like a dream. Compared to many eastern cities, San Francisco had an exciting landscape of roller coaster hills, gorgeous Victorian and Spanish-style homes, in a variety of colors, spectacular views and remarkable sunsets they had only seen in magazines.

Julia felt as if she was in heaven when she arrived in the Bay Area. She kept hearing Tony Bennett's, "I Left My Heart In San Francisco" in her head. Now the significance of that song made sense. Within a day of experiencing San Francisco's seductive charm, Julia felt her heart was there too, and she never wanted to leave.

The people in San Francisco were different, and fascinating. The Mod Generation had begun in the early 60s. Clothes, especially mini skirts, modeled by Twiggy from London, were the fashion of the time. Nancy Sinatra's hit song, "These Boots Are Made for Walking" influenced boot wearing by women.

1960s was the advent of the Hippie counter culture. It was a take-off of the Beat Generation of the 50s. Writers like Allen Ginsberg evolved from the Beatnik movement and became the anchors of the burgeoning Hippie and Anti-war movements. The Beatniks who lived in New York's Greenwich Village moved to San Francisco's Haight-Ashbury District.

Throughout the sixties, Julia was influenced by Hippie fashions. She loved the artistic, "groovy" way of Hippy dress – wild clothes, a lot of assorted multi-colored beaded jewelry, fringes, scarves, tie-dyed tank tops, flowing skirts, and sandals. She resonated with the non-conformity and creativity that prevailed.

Ralph's attitudes and his conservatism at the time bothered Julia, but she dismissed her feelings when she discovered she was pregnant. Ecstatic with the reality she was going to have a baby, she couldn't focus on anything else except her future role as a mother. She always promised herself she would be a "good" parent, not like her mother.

Ralph was also happy with the prospect of becoming a father. They talked for hours about their future child, and eagerly awaited its arrival. Less than a year after settling in San Francisco, Bradley Owen Worthington was born in April. By then Ralph had a substantial salary, and they were able to move from their small apartment into a lovely Spanish-style home in Pacific Heights, one of the City's most affluent neighborhoods.

Almost a year after the birth of their first son, another boy, Charles Ryan Worthington joined the "happy family".

By the time a daughter, whom they named Sandra Anne, was born in the winter of 1964, a lot had changed for Julia in her marriage. Ralph had become more and more obsessed with his work. He focused mostly on his career and his "climb up the ladder" to success. He became insatiably ambitious, spending long hours at his office, or with clients. He also began having affairs. It took a couple of years for Julia to discover this, and when she did, it devastated her.

Ralph denied her accusations, of course, but eventually owned up to one affair. He claimed it meant nothing, he was just infatuated with a client, pointing out that it helped his case.

Julia forgave him his transgressions, but had a difficult time forgetting.

She thought she still loved him, and rationalized it was in his male genes to womanize. She figured he probably needed to have other conquests. She contemplated divorce, but then there was her family to consider. She didn't want their children to suffer from the stigma of a broken home. Denial came in handy, which helped bury her disappointment and anger with Ralph.

Running the house, on-going maintenance, shopping, bills, balancing checkbooks, doing taxes, taking care of the children, driving them to and from their many activities, entertaining, being the perfect hostess, the perfect wife and mother, were all beginning to take a toll on Julia. Ralph never lifted a hand to help around the house, or with the children. He brought in the money that allowed his family to live "a very comfortable life style". He felt that was enough of a contribution.

He also insisted they throw dinner parties for co-workers and clients. And, of course, he expected Julia to do all the work. Actually, she didn't mind too much because cooking and entertaining were creative outlets for her. But, what did annoy her were the boring, stuffy people Ralph chose to invite – because they were easy tax write-offs, or good clients, or an important connection, blah, blah, blah ....

Julia started feeling like she was sleep-walking through the days, wondering if this was what "living happily ever after" was really all about. For a time she accepted this fate, tried to please Ralph, maintaining the image of the "good wife" he had expected her to be when they married. Until she couldn't take it any longer.

She began to examine who she was and what she wanted out of life. She questioned her love for Ralph and whether she would ever be able to trust him again after his affairs. But, she ultimately broke down and decided for the "children's sake" she had to put all her energy into making their marriage work.

She mustered up enough courage and timidly approached Ralph suggesting they see a marriage counselor. He looked surprised, laughed, and asked, "Why? I'm comfortable ... besides shrinks are a bunch of quacks ... they have as many problems as everyone else ... I wouldn't waste my time or money."

"But Ralph", Julia whined, "I ... I ... I'm not happy."

"Not happy? Why not? You have a nice home, great kids, and a husband who provides well and gives you lots of money to spend."

"I know, Ralph, but I feel insecure in our relationship, and ... "

"Oh, Julia ... what are you talking about? Is it that affair I had years ago? I said I was sorry. You need to get over it. You're the only woman I love. That other woman meant nothing to me."

Julia was incensed. "That other woman," ha, doesn't he mean W-O-M-E-N? She knew there were others. Ralph had lied, but as usual to "keep the peace" she went along with his dishonesty and with a heavy heart accepted his apology.

To appease herself and to escape her reality, she spent much of her time exploring San Francisco. A kaleidoscope of interesting neighborhoods each having its own special, unique appeal fascinated her. Abundant restaurants specializing in every cuisine from around the world could satisfy the palate of any food connoisseur.

Union Square offered upscale shops and department stores amidst starving artists who displayed their paintings in the central park's outdoor setting. Julia loved seeing what other artists were creating and often spent hours talking with them about their work and their lives. Many were barely able to eke out a living, yet seemed carefree and happy.

Fisherman's Wharf, a magnet for tourists, was fun to stroll through. It was like a small amusement park that offered rides and games that delighted her excited children. She took them there often. They especially loved riding the Cable Car down the hill to get to the wharf. Nearby Ghiradelli Square was a highlight. If they behaved, Julia would promise to treat them to the world-famous, delicious chocolates.

When Alcatraz Island opened to the public in 1973, Julia frequently took her children and visiting guests to tour the abandoned prison. The big boat ride excursion to Alcatraz was even more of a special treat for them as they bounced across the high waves.

Often Julia just liked lying alone on the beach near Fort Mason. It was soothing to look out at Golden Gate Bridge and "trip out" watching the steady stream of traffic and pedestrians going across it. She wondered who those people were. Were they Californians? If not, what state did they come from? Where were they all going?

Being by the Bay often reminded her of Otis Redding's song, (Sittin' on) "The Dock of the Bay", which she loved. Whenever she heard Otis sing, it gave her a small respite from her "troubles".

Julia's favorite "hang-out" was "The Haight". She thoroughly enjoyed browsing the thrift stores, especially Aardvark's, where she often found unusual clothes and novelty items. The more she watched the "Hippies" and "Flower Children", the more she felt in-sync with them and aligned with their mantra of peace, love, and brotherhood. She, too, opposed the war in Viet Nam, even though Ralph tried to convince her it was "necessary for peace" – Julia found that concept difficult to understand. Ralph scoffed at "those weirdos" and how they dressed. It was becoming a war at home – everything she was believing, everything she was enjoying, everything that was of interest to her, was ridiculed by Ralph, who held an opposite view.

Shopping and exploring San Francisco was only a temporary outlet for Julia while her children were in school. But, it didn't ease the emptiness she felt deep inside. She needed something more, something substantial to revive her spirits and uplift her.

She returned to painting and reading. Some of the books she discovered were so avant-garde, they shook her like an earthquake. Little by little Julia began to feel alive again. She toyed with the possibility of believing in her self worth. She began to take herself more seriously – just a little.

Betty Friedan's radical book, "The Feminine Mystique" impacted her strongly and ignited something in Julia.

Friedan wrote:

> "... the lack of fulfillment in women's lives, which was generally kept hidden, was connected to women being the victims of a false belief system, that required them to find their identity and meaning in their lives through their husbands and children."

Friedan studied editorial decisions in magazines that were made by men who she preached enforced "occupation: housewife", and educators who thought women should be concerned only with marriage and family, which perpetuated a "sick or immature" society (according to Friedan), instead of one that encouraged women to develop their human intelligence.

Further, Friedan wrote, "that the ability it takes to do housework can be done by an eight year old child."

While reading Friedan, Julia paused and thought of her old friend Lois, a married artist who tried to establish her own bank account. When a female teller asked Lois what her occupation was, she answered, "Artist". The teller looked at her, and said, "Oh, I'll just write down housewife." Lois was furious. She was an accomplished artist and writer, and had published a few books. Still, she politely went along with the teller, so as not to create an uncomfortable scene at the bank where there were people who knew her.

Lois had been brainwashed the same as all women. Remembering that incident made Julia realize women were incredibly intimidated by main stream society's values that strived to keep them in their place.

Friedan also pointed out women's sexual awareness, that their lack of orgasms are often problems women who marry young frequently experience. "On the contrary," Friedan said, "highly educated women experience orgasms freely."

Julia had worried about herself for a long time because she rarely had an orgasm when she and Ralph made love. She reasoned she might be too old, sex was only for younger people. She was a virgin when she married Ralph. That was expected of women from her generation. Sex was never discussed, so she often wondered if she was alone. She tried masturbating a few times and easily had an orgasm, but for some reason she couldn't figure out why Ralph just did not stimulate her.

She thought back when she was just a five year old little girl and had been molested. Her uncle, who always complimented her, and kissed her and told her how pretty she was, was the perpetrator. One time he told her to sit on his lap and said he'd read her a story. Trusting Uncle Roy, she obliged. She loved having someone hold her and read to her. This one time was different though. While Roy was reading Julia felt what seemed like a lump beneath her. At the same time her Uncle's hand reached under her seersucker pinafore, and his fingers began to tickle her between her legs. Then she felt wet. She went to her mother who admonished her for peeing her pants, and told her she was lazy and should have gone to the bathroom. Julia defended herself trying to tell her mother it was Uncle Roy who wet himself, not her. Katherine slapped Julia across the face, hollering at her, calling her a liar who makes up stories and has a dirty mind. "You are a bad girl, Julia," Katherine admonished. Julia lowered her eyes in shame, and though confused, she believed her mother. That night five year old Julia sucked her thumb for the first time in years and sobbed herself to sleep.

It wasn't until many years later that Julia saw Uncle Roy again. He had moved to New Orleans and rarely came north to visit, which was a huge relief for her. Ever since he had molested her, she vowed to avoid him as much as possible. But, when she graduated from high school he showed up and presented her with a check for two thousand dollars. That was a lot of money in those days, but Roy had a thriving, successful business and lived a rich man's life. Julia was surprised by Roy's generosity, and wondered if he felt guilty for what he had done to her when she was a child. Was this his way of repenting? Nevertheless, she thanked him and gave him a stiff kiss on his cheek. She was very grateful because she had applied for a scholarship at the University of Pennsylvania and was fearful she might be rejected. Roy's gift would at least get her through the first couple of years. Fortunately, after her second year as an art major, her instructors, who were very impressed with her talent, recommended her for a scholarship, which she ultimately did get.

From that time on Julia repressed her molestation and never told another person. Now she wondered was he a pedophile? Did he molest any other little girls? She thought how much he had scarred her. Was he the cause of her sexual fears? Maybe that was why she rarely had an orgasm. Maybe that was why Ralph cheated on her. Was it because Ralph thought she was frigid? She wondered if men might feel more potent when their partners have orgasms. Maybe Ralph had to have other conquests in order to prove his virility?

Reading "The Feminine Mystique" gave Julia a sense of relief. Maybe there really wasn't anything wrong with her after all. Maybe society and her childhood circumstances had affected her sexually. She felt cheated.

As months passed, Julia's thoughts about her life began to slowly transform. It took her awhile to absorb what she was reading. She was bombarded with new ideas and new possibilities she had never fathomed. She became addicted to reading other enlightened, liberated, female authors like Germaine Greer. Her book, "The Female Eunuch", not only reflected Friedan's feminist liberalism, but also advocated the necessity of a revolution for women to become emancipated.

Basically, Greer announced "women have waited too long to demand their human rights, and in order to not make waves they have not made enough demands, and have compromised too much." Just like her friend Lois, Julia thought.

Self-help and psychology books were also an attraction for Julia. Abraham Maslow, the father of self-actualization, talked analogously about life being like a pyramid, and the basic needs an individual has – survival needs for air, water, food, sleep and shelter, were at the bottom of the pyramid. Second was safety and security with a relative absence of threat to ourselves.

Third up the tier designated love and belonging, sharing, and a feeling of affiliation. Fourth was self-esteem, confidence, achievement, and deep freedom. Topping the pyramid, Maslow said, was most important was self-growth and development and a philosophy of acting out our potential.

When Julia read Maslow she felt sorry for herself more than she ever had before. By then she was in her thirties, and was questioning what HAD she accomplished in life. And, perhaps more importantly, what did she know about self-actualization. Like every woman she knew, she quietly and submissively went along with society's standards.

In a bookstore, Julia picked up the book, "Man's Search for Himself", by Rollo May, and became really interested when she read parts of the first chapter, which were about emptiness and loneliness. Wow! could she identify with those feelings! Her marriage left her empty, lonely and frightened. Her marriage was a complete travesty!

Just as May wrote, she didn't have a clear idea about what she wanted out of life. She was alienated from Ralph and couldn't talk to him. Her children had also become distant. The boys lived away at a boarding school, and she was often at odds with her daughter Sandra. Even Suzie, her best friend and confidante, was not always available because she was frequently traveling out of the country on business.

Julia felt all alone wallowing in her misery. She was frightened, too. She felt a vacancy within herself that left her powerless, and desperately hoped May would give her answers. She thought, like a medication, he'd prescribe a formula for her to follow to alleviate her pain.

Instead, his writing opened up new avenues of introspection for her, adding more pain as she gained more insight. Yet, he motivated her to look deeper within herself. He talked about rebellion, decision making and creativity which forced her to reflect further. How was she affected by those subjects? How did she deal with them?

May said rebellion begins with the desire for independence and freedom from one's parents, although in many cases people don't really have a good understanding of the responsibility that goes with that freedom.

Julia wondered if her estrangement from her mother was a true rebellion. Well, in a way, it was. And, then no, not really. All Julia did was move away from her and have little contact with her. Julia never took full responsibility for her feelings, or acted upon her deep down feelings for her mother. Instead, she tried to bury them, leaving them unresolved. Her conflicted relationship with her mother often appeared in her dreams, which tortured her with feelings of guilt for not being the "good little girl" her mother expected her to be.

Decision making, Julia learned according to May, is a "transition based on the need to be more independent from ones parents in order to decide what to do with ones life". Julia thought she was independent of her parents, so it confused her because she rarely made decisions on her own. More often than not, it was because she didn't trust herself. She deferred to other "authorities", particularly men.

The creative life, May said, is "an authentic, adult, self-actualization. Creativity arises out of the tension between spontaneity and limitations, and imagination is the outreaching of the mind, the bombardment of the conscious mind with ideas, impulses, and images. It is the capacity to dream dreams."

Julia asked herself, "am I really creative?" Am I original? She always thought of herself as a creative person because of her artistic skill. But even when she painted, she often copied the styles of the Masters. Truly tapping into her creative source was foreign to her. And, scary. It meant believing in herself. It meant believing in her worth as an artist. It meant letting go of her inhibitions. It meant having courage. May also pointed out, "the opposite of courage in our society is not cowardice. It is conformity."

She became depressed. The one thing she had clung to, that gave her a small sense of herself, was her ability to paint. It was her therapy. And yet, it really wasn't. She agonized over each painting, worrying how it would be received by the public. It was a painful awakening to realize all she was doing was conforming to what people wanted and would buy.

Julia had hoped to get answers to her "problems", but instead the more she read the more conflicted and confused she became.

She turned to the work of Fritz Perls, the father of Gestalt therapy, who emphasized "What is, is." Huh? At first it didn't register. It seemed too simple. But, as she kept reading, she started to become aware in an entirely different way. "What is, is." helped her focus on the present which was not easy. When she realized how much time she was spending on trying to make "what is" into "what isn't" – or vice versa, did she realize how ridiculous she was to think she had control over what was happening … except for the way she reacted to it.

Perls was a no-nonsense kind of psychiatrist. He had little patience for people who were not "in the present". Yet, there was something appealing about him and his way of saying things that made Julia laugh while listening to his tapes. In his thick German accent he said, "Don't analyze – it clogs up the verks - it's how you feel now!"

That hit a nerve for her. Focus on the present. How could she? It seemed easier to ignore her present – which was not all pleasant. She believed a lot had to do with her past, and that presently she was "in a bind". She felt lost.

After she read Perls' book, "In and Out the Garbage Pail", she started to really "get" him. Garbage Pail was a therapy exercise he put himself through. Playing "top dog" and "under dog" reflects our inner conflicts, he said. Our two "dogs" are frequently at war with each other, competing and trying to drown out the other.

Julia tried to play this game with herself, which made her see how truly distraught she was. She was confused about which "dog" she was.

Sometimes she played another game Perls advocated, which was pretending to be ones adversary. By imagining oneself as that person, you then try to see where they were coming from. That game helped her a little to understand and be more empathetic towards Ralph. Especially, coming to the realization she was also responsible for the state of their marriage.

Needing a break from the women libbers and psychology books, Julia found an Otto Marlton book. In a way, it was ironic because Marlton had been stamped a misogynist by some reviewers.

What attracted her to Marlton was that his books had been banned in the United States when they were first published. At that time they were only attainable through "the black market". Marlton's books were branded "pornographic" for years, and God forbid, puritanical America did not want their families corrupted by "evil forces".

When the Supreme Court finally ruled against the ban, Marlton got better publicity than he had ever had before, and sales of his books tripled. People were curious as to why so much fuss was made over his work, which now, by the standards of the seventies was relatively mild. Films were showing explicit sex scenes and the language often used was hardly ever censored. Marlton's books were tame by comparison.

Once she read Marlton Julia felt she found her "soul mate". It was interesting, although he wrote autobiographically, he mirrored the "shrinks" she had been reading, but in a totally different way. His style of writing was a stream-of-consciousness. He told it like it was – the truth from his perspective. True, some of his descriptions and "sexcapades" were a bit too graphic for her, but they were incidental to his philosophy.

Marlton had been programmed by the same social fabric that Julia had been regarding women and their roles. He grew up in an era that stifled women even more than her societal generation did. He was more enlightened and continually spoke of women as being superior to men. He respected, loved, and adored women.

Sex with them, however, was another story.

It was close to two years after reading several of Marlton's books that she met him at a fund-raising event for the San Francisco Opera Company. Ralph said he couldn't go because he had to work that night. So Julia went with her good friend Suzie, who was very social and always fun to be with. Suzie didn't take any crap from anyone, and was an inspiration to Julia. She wouldn't tolerate playing psychological "games", and, if and when she was ever in that kind of situation she called the shots. Men were very attracted to beautiful Suzie, but her relationships often collapsed quickly. She never married.

Suzie told Julia she refused to be any man's "prisoner". Julia really looked up to her and wished she had the strength Suzie had being so comfortable in her own skin.

At the opera function, Suzie the social butterfly that she was, spotted Otto Marlton. She pointed in his direction and said to Julia, "Let's go meet him."

Julia's heart began to beat rapidly. "Oh, Suzie ..." she said, "we can't just go over to him, not without a formal introduction ... "

"Why not?", Suzie demanded.

"What would we say? We're not important people."

"I can't believe you, Julia! First of all, we'll just introduce ourselves and go from there. And, may I ask, who is important? Besides, this is the moment you've been waiting for ... to meet Otto Marlton in person. So let's just do it!"

"Well, OK ... " Julia relented," but you do the talking."

Julia never expected Otto's warmth and interest in her. She expected him to be a bit pompous given his status as a celebrity. Instead, he seemed humble and kind, as if he wanted to impress her. He was even a little flirtatious. The formality of introductions faded and it didn't take long before they were conversing like old friends. When Otto asked Julia what she did, she blurted out she was a painter. Perhaps, accidentally on purpose, she omitted she was married. They talked for over an hour about art, while Suzie flitted about, "working the room".

Otto was smitten with Julia. She was warm, sweet, gorgeous, and an easy conversationalist. So different than most women who only seemed interested in him because of his fame. He asked if he could see her again, and she gave him her phone number.

Ralph was so busy with his own life, he never knew Julia was seeing

Otto. He was just glad Julia seemed to come out of her "funk" and be in a better mood, which he attributed to "letting her spend his money". By this time sex with her was non-existent, which helped him justify his on-going affairs.

A year passed and Julia and Otto became closer. It didn't take long for them to fall in love. They often kissed passionately, but never made love. Otto knew Julia was married, but in spite of what he wrote, he was old-fashioned and a gentleman. He was also fearful he might not perform well sexually, and Julia would stop loving him. He wanted to be with her for the rest of his life, so he had to play his cards right. He was aware Julia's marriage was a farce, and he didn't want to stress her anymore than she already was with the possibility of an inadequate sexual performance. His prostate problems over the years frequently left him impotent.

Julia never seemed to mind. She had her own reasons for not wanting to have sex with Otto. She thought because he wrote about sex so implicitly, he must be a sexual athlete, and an authority on love-making. Her fear of being frigid was in the back of her mind. What if he lost interest in her because she wasn't up to par?

In spite of the more than 30-year difference in their ages, Otto felt Julia was as mature and as wise as anyone his age. He decided to propose to her.

Julia was aghast. She had loved Otto, the writer, for years, and now loved Otto, the man. She was honored when he asked her to be his wife. But, she had a lot to figure out first, and she didn't quite know where to start. She wanted to accept his proposal, but she needed more time to think.

CHAPTER THREE: Wedding at Big Sur

There was no question Julia loved Otto and wanted to marry him. She felt alive and invigorated when she was with him. While with Ralph she had felt dead for a long time. She and Ralph were simply existing as strangers living in the same house. Ralph was judgmental and close-minded. They barely talked to each other. By comparison, Otto was warm, open, and compassionate.

She was well aware Ralph was in the midst of another affair, and his secret lover was expecting his child! It was time for her to finally end their relationship. She asked him for a divorce.

Their sons, Brad and Charlie were living at a military academy boarding school. That was Ralph's decision. Julia was never fond of the idea, but Ralph always had the last word. His decisions were final. He thought military school would teach Brad and Charlie how to be real men. The boys rarely came home, except during the summer months, or occasionally to pay their respects out of obligation. After all, Ralph was paying all their expenses.

Sandra was a sophomore in high school. Julia worried how a broken home might affect her. As it was, Sandra was not easy to deal with. In the last few years she had become more and more bratty towards Julia. Basically their relationship was estranged.

Sandra had always been Ralph's favorite. He wanted sons, but never could relate to them except competitively. In comparison, he babied and doted on Sandra since the day she was born. She was a beautiful child and

Ralph constantly praised her good looks.

Sandra grew up thinking she was the center of the universe. Nothing was ever expected of her from her father, except to be beautiful. Julia was more of a disciplinarian and Sandra didn't like having boundaries, so they were at odds frequently. Ralph always took Sandra's side and chided Julia saying she was "too hard on the girl".

Julia never thought she was strict, but since she didn't trust her instincts, she began to read books on child-rearing.

Hiam Ginott, who wrote, "Between Parent and Child", and later "Between Parent and Teenager", gave Julia some insights and confirmed her belief of the need for discipline. She read that discipline was not a bad word. What was important was how it was enforced.

Julia never spanked her children, nor did she punish them. She believed in respecting them and talking things out. The boys basically respected her in return, but Sandra often called her mother names and refused to listen to her.

Ralph dealt with their sons more harshly by pushing them to succeed, "to make something of themselves". Brad and Charlie were under constant pressure during most of their childhood, and seeing that, Julia tried to compensate and balance what she considered to be Ralph's unjust scorn. Many times she felt sorry for the boys when Ralph was yelling at them, but felt helpless to do anything. Then later she'd feel guilty. That was when she thought of her own father, and how she had hated him for not standing up to her mother. It wasn't until this similar scenario took place in her own household that she was able to understand her father and how important it was for him to keep the peace, as she also felt compelled to do, repeating the same unhealthy cycle.

Julia quoted Hiam Ginott to Ralph, but he wouldn't listen. He just laughed, dismissing her, saying she was reading too many psychology books. What did Ginott know about Brad and Charlie? They were his sons! Ralph knew exactly how they should be raised and treated.

Paradoxically, Ralph spoiled Sandra, frequently giving her large sums of money to "spend foolishly". It didn't take long for Sandra to learn she could get anything she wanted. She had her father wrapped around her little finger.

Julia knew her home was a dysfunctional one, but she felt trapped. Confused, not knowing how to change. Ralph was of no help or support.

By the early 70s, Julia began to take her art more seriously and painted every day to escape and avoid confrontations. In essence, she became an absent mother. The children learned to make the best of their home situation by watching a lot of television – "The Brady Bunch", "Batman" and "Hogan's Heroes" were their escapes from reality. Once they got their driver's licenses they stayed away from home as much as possible.

Reflecting on the past twenty years, Julia realized a divorce wouldn't be any more harmful for her children than their everyday life. And, for her, it would definitely be better living with Otto, who was loving, tender, and caring. With Otto, she no longer felt worthless. Instead she felt validated.

When Julia asked Ralph for a divorce, he seemed surprised. When she confronted him with his extra-curricular activities, especially, that she knew his girlfriend was pregnant, he owned up to his behavior. In a way he was relieved to finally not have to hide or lie anymore, although he was a little embarrassed. Julia was surprised by his show of weakness. It was his ego, not her, she realized. Ralph put a lot of energy into presenting a "proper" image to the world. His biggest concern was being exposed to the public. In his way of "covering", he asked Julia for an amicable divorce, stating "irreconcilable differences", and promised to give her a substantial financial settlement if she kept quiet about his current affair.

Ralph wanted to keep living in the house, so he offered to pay her a million dollars in cash. Julia knew this was less than half of what their house was worth, as real estate values had increased. Anxious to leave, she agreed, and moved in with her friend Suzie until the divorce was final. She needed time before marrying Otto, especially, because she wasn't sure she could trust Ralph. If he thought that she, too, had been having an affair, he might not give her the money. Julia never considered her relationship with Otto as "an affair" because after all, they never slept together.

Julia called Otto and said, "yes". He was elated. She told him she loved him very much, and wanted to be his wife. But, she was not quite ready to get married, and wanted him to wait a couple of months, explaining her divorce settlement with Ralph. Otto assured her she didn't need Ralph's money, he had enough to take care of her.

Feeling somewhat annoyed when Otto said, "Ralph's money", Julia snapped back at him. "That is money owed to me, and I do not want you to feel you have to take care of me. Otto, this is my decision, so you will just have to wait."

She couldn't believe those words actually came out of her mouth. Ordinarily she would have conceded to a man. But, something had changed in her and had given her a new sense of self-confidence.

Otto backed down, respecting her wishes, saying, "Darling, I love you so much, I'd wait more than a couple of months if that's what will make you happy."

Julia sighed in relief. Then to reassure Otto that she definitely intended to marry him, she suggested, "Well, let's set a date. I'm looking at my calendar now – how about an early summer wedding? Let's go to Big Sur ... and just invite a few special friends. I don't want our wedding to turn into a carnival, and I'd like it if we were able to avoid the paparazzi. I'd love to get married on a cliff overlooking the ocean." Otto agreed thinking Julia's plan sounded wonderful. He had lived at Big Sur for several years when he was a young, aspiring writer, but had not been back there in quite some time. He had once mentioned to Julia how much he loved Big Sur, and it impressed him that she remembered.

During the next two months Julia spent many hours dreaming about her future life with Otto Marlton. She fantasized about what it would be like to be married to him. To live with him. At other times she felt scared, although those moments were less frequent. Had she made the right decision to marry again? He was so much older, and she sensed he might be set in his ways. How would she handle being in the limelight as this famous author's wife? She had always been very reticent to deal with the media whenever the two of them were together in public.

Nevertheless, Julia felt marrying Otto had more positives than negatives. She truly loved him and could not imagine her life without him. The more she weighed the pros and cons, the more she convinced herself she was doing the right thing. Still, there was a nagging insecurity that gnawed at her.

Suzie became Julia's anchor. She never told her not to get married, and was very supportive of Julia's decision. The way Suzie saw it, it was simple, "If it doesn't work out, leave, and move on. It will just be another life lesson." Suzie was not the marrying type. She had broken up many times right before she was about to walk down the aisle. She confessed to Julia, "I must have been crazy to ever consider marriage. It was probably in the heat of passion I accepted any proposals."

Two months seemed to go by very quickly. Julia spent the time shopping for her trousseau, making plans, and reservations at Big Sur. She selected a soft peach silk dress, satin strapped heels of the same color to match, and a lovely white lace negligee for her wedding night. A new bathing suit, and a casual outfit of slacks and a print blouse were also on her list to be worn the day after the wedding.

Her divorce settlement went as expected, and Ralph promptly wrote out a check for one million dollars. Julia was impressed that Ralph kept his end of the bargain, and for a split second she felt nostalgic and sad their marriage hadn't worked out.

Ralph was basically a decent person. Just different. The road they traveled had reached a fork where they each went in different directions. The older Ralph got, the more conservative he became, while Julia had taken the route of becoming more liberal. He often accused her of being a Communist because of her socialist outlook. Like the country, their home turned into a Cold War that was tense with suspicion and fear.

Even rock and roll music, which Julia loved, annoyed Ralph. He called it "the devil's music", and was positive all those musicians were on LSD, which he deemed why they were "crazy and immoral". To keep the peace when Ralph was home, Julia refrained from listening to her favorite radio station that played many of the current musicians she loved – The Rolling Stones, Grateful Dead, The Doors, Jimi Hendrix, Jefferson Starship, and the many other artists of the time.

She blamed herself for not seeing who Ralph really was when she married him. But then, looking back over that time, what did she know at the age of twenty?

Julia married Otto Marlton almost two months to the day after accepting his proposal. There was a colorfully spectacular sunset of orange, purple, and turquoise blazed across the sky, heightening the romantic mood. Only two other people were in attendance. Suzie was Julia's maid of honor, and Otto's good friend, Mark Spencer, was his best man.

Julia was ravishing in her peach ensemble with gardenias in her hair. She carried a small bouquet of orchids and lilies – Otto's favorite flowers.

He wore a casual, dusty blue suit with a ruby red rose boutonniere pinned to his lapel. Under the jacket a crisp white shirt, unbuttoned to the bottom of his neck. No tie.

It was a short ceremony conducted by a Justice of the Peace. Both bride and groom recited vows that reflected their love, respect, and equal treatment of each other, rather than the traditional promises that expected a wife to honor and obey her husband.

After their "I dos", Otto reached in his pocket and pulled out a small box tied with a bright gold ribbon. Opening the box with shaking hands, he took out the most beautiful ring Julia had ever seen. It was a white gold band adorned with sapphire baguettes each surrounded by small diamonds that he placed on her finger. The ring was special. He told her it had belonged to his mother. Looking into Julia's eyes, he said, "My sweet, dear Julia

... I love you so so much. In fact, I loved you from the first time we met ... and I dreamt of this precious moment for so long ... I will cherish you forever ... you are the love of my life."

She looked up at him with tears in her eyes and responded, "Otto ... I love you, too ... so very, very much ... even more than you'll ever know." Especially, she thought, but didn't say it, for rescuing me from Ralph. "I am so happy to be your wife."

The judge pronounced them husband and wife. Otto immediately took Julia in his arms and kissed her passionately.

Being married to Otto Marlton was almost surreal. Her life had taken a remarkably different turn in less than two years. She felt unburdened and free compared to the past twenty years spent living according to the needs and demands of Ralph and her children.

After the ceremony the wedding entourage enjoyed a delicious candlelight dinner at Nepenthe, one of the most notable restaurants at Big Sur. A pianist serenaded the newly married couple with melodic love songs while they dined.

When Otto lived at Big Sur he frequented the bar at Nepenthe, spending hours discussing world events and various philosophies of life with other artists and writers. Some of the bartenders were still there. Of course, like Otto, now old men. But, unlike them, he vainly assured himself he looked much younger than they did. Deep down he was self-conscious that people might think he was Julia's father.

That night Julia and Otto spent their honeymoon at the four-star Ventana Inn, which featured glorious, unparalleled views of the Pacific coastline. She had researched Big Sur and learned the Ventana Inn had been built in the early seventies. It was created by Larry Spector, a current Hollywood producer then. The popular movie of the time, "Easy Rider" provided Spector with money he earned from the proceeds to build a quiet, tranquil getaway, having in mind his friends in the film industry. The interior, as well as the exterior was built with redwood, complementing the tall redwood trees surrounding it. Though rustic, it had a unique allure for people who were used to the finest accommodations. Perfect, she thought.

Julia and Otto were ecstatic when they entered their suite. It was warm and inviting, decorated in exquisite taste with splashes of their favorite primary colors. Adjoining the suite was the bathroom with an extra-large jacuzzi tub. Julia was thrilled that Otto approved of her selection.

That night was the first time they made love, and in spite of both of their fears, sex was more than either had expected.

By the time Julia became Otto's wife, she felt so secure in his arms that even though she still had some fears about being frigid, she looked forward to consummating their marriage.

Otto had fantasized about making love to Julia for such a long time that his desire overcame his fear of impotence. He couldn't wait to have sex with her, especially when she walked out of the bathroom wearing her sexy lace negligee. She turned him on immensely. As she leaned over and French kissed him, he felt an erection beginning. He beckoned her to get in bed with him, and reciprocating he hugged and kissed her over her whole body ever so tenderly. Julia gasped with delight and excitement, as Otto also grew more stimulated. When she complied, he penetrated her moist welcoming vagina with his fully erect penis. "Ah ... Ah ... " he moaned as he slowly moved in and out. When Julia squeezed to his motion, his thrusts rapidly increased. They were both so aroused that within minutes they orgasmed together. Spent and exhausted from their emotionally tiring day they stayed glued to each other, still fondling and kissing passionately.

Making love with Otto seemed so natural, Julia realized having sex could be … well, complex, and feeling safe and trusting ones partner was a necessary component.

She sighed with relief, realizing she wasn't frigid after all. She truly felt secure in Otto's arms. She finally felt loved.

CHAPTER FOUR: Sad Memories

After Otto's death, home didn't seem the same without him. Everything felt lifeless without his effervescent spirit, and the sounds of voices and laughter. Otto always had a house full of people. Now, it was eerily quiet. Almost spooky.

Julia walked into the dark living room and switched on a blue ceramic lamp. Then turned on the stereo. John Lennon was singing, "Imagine", which made her nostalgic for the sixties and The Beatles' music. She felt sad that John Lennon was no longer alive. Such a wonderful talent wasted.

She was exhausted from her trying day at Otto's funeral. Her limp body collapsed onto the beige leather couch next to the lamp. She wanted to fall asleep and forget about the nightmare she had recently gone through. Beat as she was, it was too difficult to sleep. Many thoughts bombarded her. Her mind was in a maze trying to figure its way out and escape.

Julia didn't like some of the feelings she had that were associated with her memories. She felt angry that at this point in her life, she was all alone and aimless. She felt frightened, not knowing what she wanted to do with her life. She was also despondent that Otto was no longer there.

She fondly reminisced about her short marriage as she studied the paintings on the wall. Her thoughts were suddenly taken over by Otto's wonderful art collection. He had known many famous artists who had given him gifts of their work.

There was an early Picasso of two peasants, a man and a woman entwined around each other in a haystack. No one ever guessed it was painted by Picasso because it was so realistic and the colors were soft. Julia, herself, in spite of her vast knowledge of art, had at first thought it was done by Diego Rivera, the famous mural artist from Mexico City.

Next to the Picasso was a Dubuffet. It almost looked out of place. Julia laughed. She loved Dubuffet's comical rendition of the two archetypal figures dancing. His style was raw and bold. It had a primitive quality and seemed as if he had never learned how to draw because his figures were sketched in such a childlike way.

Julia thought Dubuffet's sculptures looked like assembled puzzles. She had seen one of them at the Guggenheim Museum in New York City. She liked it so much that she remembered wishing she could own it. It was a monumental piece, however, standing so high, that only a museum could house it!

Vlaminck's scene of a stormy night hung over on the far wall. Julia wondered if Van Gogh had inspired him. The colors were rich and vivid, his brush strokes powerful and emotional. Though unlike Van Gogh, Vlaminck was not depressed. His bike riding probably provided him with an outlet, a needed break from the emotional strain of painting from his heart. Otto loved Maurice Vlaminck. When they were younger Otto and he had gone on bike trips together. Vlaminck always wore out Otto because he was so much stronger, even though older. Besides, Vlaminck had also been a bike racer.

Julia loved to listen to Vlaminck stories. Her eyes watered as she reminisced about those tender moments with Otto. She began to sob when she pictured herself and Otto sitting on that couch holding hands. He often mesmerized her with his wonderful tales.

In fact, Julia always loved sitting in this room among these paintings. They had a way of speaking to her, of calming her. Soon a warm feeling of tranquility came over her.

Not far from the Vlaminck was a painting she had given to Otto when they first met. It was one of her Fauvist landscapes she had done in acrylics. Julia recalled the pointillist technique she had used. Her eyes traveled over each little dot as she redid the painting in her mind. The sky was several tones of cadmium yellow and orange. It was fun for her to use unusual colors in her paintings. She glanced at the trees, which looked as if a wild person had painted them. They were put on the canvas with thick, heavy strokes of pure magenta, red, and purple. The various hues of turquoise and pastel blue in the grass balanced the brightness of the rest of her painting. Julia wondered why she had chosen those particular colors. It was difficult for her to relate to now. It was as if someone else had done that painting. Her style had changed so much over the years. She still loved to use brilliant colors, but she had not painted for quite a long time. The last few paintings she had done were Surrealistic, solely from her imagination. Otto had inspired her to paint that way, without photos or models.

Otto loved to paint also. He dabbled in water colors and had a wonderful sense of freedom Julia envied. Perhaps it was because he painted for fun, while she once painted to sell her work.

Julia thought about getting back into painting when things settled down. She had not stepped into her studio in months. Her life had centered around Otto so much she never seemed to have any time for herself.

She also began to think about whether she would stay in that big house alone. Perhaps she should rent the wing that was her studio. It had a separate entrance and she could close off the door to the rest of the house. It would be private. That wing was just collecting dust anyhow.

During the three years Julia was married to Otto she had paid the mortgage more times than he had. Since she had money from her divorce settlement and had saved money she earned from selling her paintings over the years, she never had to ask Otto for a cent. In fact, she practically supported him.

Money had never come easily to Otto even though he was a world renowned author. Sometimes publishers were months behind in sending their checks. Also, Otto didn't know how to manage money. Before Julia came into his life his finances were a mess. Fortunately, she had taken some accounting classes that enabled her to feel secure enough to do the bookkeeping and taxes. Most of Otto's money had gone to Uncle Sam before she took over. He owed the government back taxes. Julia paid his debts which helped her feel more entitled and deserving of Otto.

She thought about the funeral again, and about how angry she'd been with Otto for dying so suddenly. Now, she no longer felt that way. On the contrary, she felt deep remorse. She had loved him very much, and now he was gone, she knew she would grieve for him the rest of her life. She subconsciously twisted her sapphire ring, which gave her comfort and a feeling of being connected to Otto.

Otto had provided tremendous support for Julia. It was always soothing to be with him, and she felt strong when he was nearby. All her vulnerabilities seemed to vanish the instant he walked into the room. It was a feeling she had never experienced before with anyone else. He had a magical effect on her, and now, she wondered how would she ever be able to survive without him. She wasn't sure of anything. How could she meet the conflicts and challenges of everyday living? She thought of Otto's infectious sense of humor, how it balanced things and always put things in a different perspective.

Yes, Otto had left her with many great gifts, especially an ability to laugh at the preposterous. Julia had been so serious about everything before she met him. She had taken things too much to heart.

At first Otto's sarcasm stung. As each day with him went by, however, she loosened up and felt less defensive. She began to realize he meant no harm, he saw the satires of life. Julia knew the truth was not easy to hear. But, little by little, she also began to see the ironies, the stupidity of adhering to status quo, and the much ado about nothing many people made over trivial matters.

Julia was jolted out of her thoughts with the ring of the telephone. It was Stephanie's cold voice.

"Julia … Stuart and I want you to know now that our father is gone, the house belongs to us … with everything in it! So, you'll have to find another place to live. We want you to move within three months. If you have anything to say about this you can talk to our attorney. His name is Robert Fredricks, and his phone number is 454-9900, extension 16." Stephanie slammed down the phone before Julia could say a word.

With her mouth still open in shock in response to Stephanie's verbal assault, Julia stood holding the buzzing telephone. She never got to tell Stephanie the house had been in her name for two years. Otto had decided it was the only decent thing to do since she had made most of the mortgage payments, had paid off so many of his debts, and had used her money to refurbish the house.

"What about your children?", Julia remembered asking Otto.

"Don't worry about them. They get enough from their trust fund, and I did leave them some money in my will. So, they'll be alright financially. Besides, those two have to learn how to work. I've realized how dependent they are on me. It's because I was always soft on them, always gave in to what they demanded. They never learned how to manage money. And, Julia, I love you!" Otto hugged and kissed her tenderly. "Marrying you was the best thing that ever happened to me. The best decision I ever made. You're my wife and you deserve to get this house even if you hadn't done all the work redecorating, or put one red cent into it!"

Julia had spent at least a year and a half remodeling and redecorating the house. Everything, including all the furnishings was bought with her money. It was a mess when she moved in. Unkempt and unattractive. Otto lived like a destitute artist in a garrett. He had the same old furniture for at least thirty years. It certainly looked that way. There wasn't a flower or a plant, or anything for that matter, to give the house life. That was until she took over and made it into an attractive, warm, cozy home. The house meant a lot to Julia. All her memories were in it. All her creations.

Shit! As if she hadn't had enough emotional upheavals. Now she was going to have to fight Stephanie and Stuart for the house, fight for what was rightfully hers. Julia felt terribly lonely and terribly frightened.

Do the twins have a case, she worried. What if they win and I have to move? Move where?

She sighed and laid back on the couch. It was too much to deal with at the moment. "Maybe this is all a bad dream ... maybe if I go to sleep ... I'll wake up and all my problems will have disappeared. Julia turned off the light. She had barely closed her eyes before she fell into a deep sleep.

Sleeping was her way of dealing with adversity.

CHAPTER FIVE: Stephanie & Stuart

Across San Francisco Bay in Sausalito, a small houseboat bobbed up and down. It was parked in a slip that looked like a well filled with black India ink. The lavender sky was turning crimson as the sun was beginning to set over the horizon. The landscape looked bejeweled as the city lights twinkled far off in the distance. Off to the east one could catch a glimpse of the Bay Bridge. Its vanishing point ended into what seemed like a soft blue cloud as the night fog rolled in.

Stephanie took off her jacket and adjusted her bathing suit straps. It was a balmy evening. Unusual for this time of the year. Summer nights in the Bay Area were often colder. She put her feet up over the railing of the house-boat, which slowly rocked to and fro as the water lapped up against the sides. It was a tranquilizing sound. She lit up a joint and took a long, deep drag, then leaned over and turned on the radio. Janis Joplin belted out, "Me and Bobby McGee".

Stephanie thought of the time she met Janis Joplin. It was two weeks before Janis had OD'd. They were hardly introduced when Janis boasted, "I have a new boyfriend and he's the best fuck I ever had." Nothing shocked Stephanie. She just thought Janis was crass.

Strange woman, that Janis. She looked like a bag lady, carrying an old dirty carpet handbag. Stephanie couldn't help but laugh at the ridiculous way Janis had dressed, and wondered which character, and from which era she was trying to portray.

She could still picture Janis wearing a ruffled white blouse and a dark blue gauze skirt with a fringed shawl around her shoulders. On her head she sported a large velvet hat with purple plumes that could be seen for miles away. Kooky hats were Janis' trademark. Stephanie got a kick out of the hats, but couldn't figure out why she didn't buy better looking clothes. With all the money she was making, she thought Janis could have afforded to dress with more class.

Stuart was below deck preparing dinner. The wonderful aromas coming from the kitchen were making Stephanie hungry. Being high from the marijuana also had that effect on her. Her stomach was growling.

Stuart wouldn't tell his sister what he was making. Said he wanted to surprise her. Stephanie was hoping it was poached salmon with Hollandaise, which was her favorite. He liked to cook and she didn't, so he often came by to make dinner for her.

That made Stephanie happy. It also made her feel closer to her brother, especially now with their father gone. Of course, she'd never let Stuart know that she needed him. If she did, she feared she'd lose her power over him.

Stephanie and Stuart had not always had much in common. As children they fought a lot and it often made their mother angry. Estelle tried to keep the household quiet and peaceful to allow Otto to concentrate on his writing. Most of the time, she made things worse. The more she yelled at the twins, the more they misbehaved.

Stephanie knew she was purposely naughty just to get her father's attention. And, her mother's wrath. She hated her mother because she thought Estelle favored Stuart. He was a frail child and Estelle always pampered him. Stephanie detested Stuart's baby-like ways. She also hated it when he acted like a silly girl instead of a boy. She decided at an early age, perhaps around seven years old, to take charge of the situation. She became the boy in the family, so to speak.

Most of the time Stephanie had Stuart whining and yelping from her teasing. She did whatever she could to keep him begging for her mercy. At least this accomplished her mission – to make him dependent on her. Stuart was too weak and insecure to fight her. He relented and did as she told him.

When Otto and Estelle divorced, the twins were fifteen years old. It was a difficult time for them. They were confused and frightened. For months before, the entire household was strained. Many nights while lying in bed, Stephanie and Stuart heard their parents shouting at each other. Sometimes the children heard things being thrown. Then, the muffled sounds of sobbing were heard coming from their mother.

Stephanie never felt sorry for Estelle. She felt her mother got what she deserved. Estelle, in Stephanie's opinion was a nincompoop. She saw through her mother's demands on her father. She could never understand her mother's values. Why did her mother complain so much, or why did she put so much emphasis on being "a proper lady"? She thought her mother was shallow and stupid. Nevertheless, Stephanie often felt scared when her parents argued.

The divorce was an ugly one. Estelle carried on in court like a mad woman, accusing Otto of every transgression imaginable. The twins were brought into court only once, at the end of the hearing. That was one of their most horrible memories. Otto fought for custody of the children, claiming Estelle was an inadequate mother because she had no backbone.

Estelle defended herself and said Otto had robbed her of all authority, and that was why she was weak. That she had no say or power in the household. Estelle felt Otto would not raise the children with "good Christian values", claiming he spoiled them and they would grow up without any boundaries. The judge decided to ask the twins which parent they wanted to live with.

Stephanie knew without a doubt she wanted to live with her father. She respected Otto and liked that he respected her. She felt comfortable with him, and she didn't hesitate to tell the judge. Stephanie didn't feel an ounce of remorse or guilt for making that decision.

True to character, Stuart cried like a baby in the courtroom. He stood there shaking, with tears streaming down his face. When he was finally able to speak, he said, "I want to be with Stephanie … so, I guess I'll choose Daddy, too."

Stephanie glowed inside. She had Stuart just where she wanted him. She knew he was helpless without her. Estelle was shocked and let out a loud scream that could be heard throughout the courthouse. She ran over to Stuart and threw her arms around him, screaming, "My baby, my baby … Don't leave me!"

Estelle knew Stephanie would never choose to be with her and she was glad. She never could stand her daughter. It made her jealous when Otto hugged Stephanie, when he did anything with Stephanie.

After the divorce, Stuart and Stephanie saw very little of their father, which they had not expected. Otto was just rising to the peak of his fame. His books were being published in other languages and it seemed he was always on tour to promote his work, or invited to speak somewhere around the world. The twins were usually left at home with a nanny.

Then, there were the ladies. Oh, how the women loved Otto. Every day he received hundreds of fan letters, mostly from female admirers. Some even sent photos of themselves in the nude. Otto never lacked a female companion, and the twins resented every woman he introduced to them. Stephanie, especially, was positive no woman could love her father as much as she did. She was positive they were only after his money.

The twins never knew Otto was living on a shoe string. Whatever they asked for they always got. Since he couldn't give himself to his children, he used money as a substitute and gave them large sums freely. Stephanie and Stuart assumed their father was a wealthy man. They thought because he was a famous writer and had sold many books, he also had a lot of money. What they never knew was often Otto was in arrears and the money they lived on was borrowed from friends. Their home in Saint Francis Wood was very large and old and frequently needed repairs. Taxes and mortgage payments were also burdening Otto.

After his death, Stephanie and Stuart clung to each other more. Even before Otto died, they had formed a special bond with each other. Especially, when Otto informed them he was going to marry Julia Forrester. They were furious. He had been courting Julia for almost a year, but the twins never thought it would amount to much. They were sure Julia was only one more passing fancy for their father. Besides, didn't Julia already have a husband.

Or, so they thought.

Everything happened very quickly when Julia went to Reno and got a divorce from her husband. Two months later she married their father.

Stephanie and Stuart weren't told until "the damage was done"! That was the day Stephanie convinced Stuart they had to make a pact with each other "to get rid of Julia". They would do everything to make her life miserable, they were sure she wouldn't be able to take it, and would leave their father. They never dreamt Julia would stay married to him until he died.

Down in the galley Stuart hummed an aria from "La Traviata". Then began whistling his favorite piece, "Brindisi", as he chopped some fresh vegetables. Stuart loved opera and never missed any of the local performances. He owned most of the Italian albums, especially all the Puccini's and Verdi's.

Stuart was a creative chef, putting as much attention into his presentation as he did the preparation. He always used a variety of color and different shapes and textures to add interest to his designs. He liked carving the carrots into tulips, and tomatoes into roses. A green vegetable was always included to make the plate look like a painter's palette. Stuart's creations looked like a photograph from Gourmet magazine.

Stephanie's mouth watered more as the cooking aromas intensified. "Hey, Stu ... when's it going to be ready?"

"In about five minutes."

"Great. I'm starved."

"Well, come on down and talk to me while I set the table."

Stuart knew better than to ask Stephanie to do anything. She was not one to offer help. They had argued many times over this. He knew what she'd say, that if he wanted to cook, that was his choice. Why should she have to work too? That was not her choice. Besides, this was her houseboat and he had shown up uninvited.

Stuart could hear Stephanie saying she would have been just as happy eating a sandwich and curling up with a good book. Even though he knew this wasn't true. Stephanie loved it when he cooked for her. Nevertheless, he craved his sister's approval. He knew that one way he'd get it was to cook for her.

As the tiny table rocked slightly and the fat candle flickered, the twins ravished the meal. Stuart had made fresh poached salmon with Hollandaise and Stephanie was thrilled.

"So Steph, you said you called Julia the other day?"

"Yeah, I called 'the bitch'… I told her to move within a month."

"NO … you didn't! Really? What'd she say?"

"I never waited for an answer. I just told her to call Bob Fredricks if she had any questions, gave her his number and hung up."

"What do you think will happen? I mean, do we have a case or not?"

"How can you even ask that question? Of course we have a case. Otto was our father for thirty three years and only her husband for three. No court would ever award her the house!"

"But, Steph, what if the house is in her name or something? Then what'll we do?"

"Well, it isn't! But, even if Dad was stupid enough to do that, we could say she forced him to sign the papers."

"That might be hard to prove."

"Nah, don't worry, Fredricks is smart. He knows how to win."

"Well, Steph, I'm not so sure I'd want to leave Marty and move into Dad's house with you. You see, we've become, well, very serious, you know."

"Look, dummy. I'm not asking you to move out on Marty. And, I certainly don't want to leave this houseboat either – I like it here. It's not the house I want, it's the money, the more the better. You never know when something bad could happen, like my divorce … never thought it would take so long or cost so much. That bastard really cheated me."

"I suppose ...", Stuart mumbled. He didn't agree with Stephanie, but he didn't want an argument. "Marty has a pretty good job, and I think I can manage from the trust fund and the money Dad left me in his will."

"Stuart! That's not the point! The point is, we don't want Julia in that house. We never did, you know that. So, why should she live there now? Once we own the house we can rent it until the real estate market goes up. I hear that's happening down in Los Angeles now, so, it's just a matter of time before real estate prices here go up and take off. And, when that happens, we sell and make a killing – fifty-fifty. Is it a deal?"

"Well, yeah ... I guess so ..."

"Then, it's settled. Just leave it up to your big Sis, like always."

"Big Sis! Ha! By five minutes! Well, OK. Steph, I trust you."

With that they lifted their glasses of Chardonnay and toasted.

CHAPTER SIX: Julia's Nightmare

Julia shrieked, her whole body shaking in fright, her hair was soaked with perspiration. She reached up and felt the sweat on her forehead.

Slowly, regaining consciousness, she realized it was only a bad dream. Yet, it all seemed so real. Like the surrealistic paintings she loved, nothing made sense. She tried to recall what had happened in her nightmare.

All she could remember was wandering in a forest, a maze composed of strange plants and animals having human qualities. Though stationary, they were menacingly reaching out to grab her. She felt like a bug waiting to get squashed. A huge prominent figure was chasing her, but she couldn't tell who or what it was. It had several arms flailing about and was clawing at her.

At first the thing resembled Ralph, then Ralph became her mother, and, as soon as her mother appeared in the dream, the scene changed. The place looked like the moon. The terrain was flat and composed of hard, white clay. There were large pits everywhere filled with writhing, hissing snakes. Julia was alone and wandering aimlessly. The absence of other people was frightening, but her main concern was to not fall into the pits.

Suddenly, a gigantic boulder appeared in the distance, it began rolling down a hill heading right towards her. She tried to run, but her legs wouldn't move. She tried to scream, but her voice cracked. She crouched down cowering. Then, when she had the nerve to look up, the boulder was within inches of her. She was certain she was going to be squashed any second. She took a closer look and saw Otto sitting on top of the boulder. In spite of being a frail man, his weight and strength were slowing the boulder's velocity. Then, just as the boulder was about to plunge into one of the pits Otto jumped off and disappeared into thin air. It was as if Otto was just an apparition.

Julia was alone again. She had to rescue herself, but she didn't know how to get out of her predicament. She tried running again, but this time her legs charged like a locomotive. Then, when she tried to scream, her voice shrieked out. She woke up trembling.

What did this all mean? She had had similar dreams most of her life, though the scenario and cast were different, the overall theme was clearly the same.

It was no accident the first scene took place in a forest. She, Julia "Forrest"er, never felt worthy when she was married to Ralph "Worth"ington. She often felt inferior to him and he played that card to the hilt. Early in their marriage she didn't trust what was happening, but looking back she realized Ralph had tried to control her "squashing" any initiative, which often confused her. Once she started reading avidly, she began to feel empowered, little-by-little. Especially, by the female authors and "shrinks" she read, and then by Otto Marlton. When Julia started standing up for herself, Ralph bitterly defended his controlling ways. Then, falling in love with Otto was the catalyst which helped her make the decision to divorce Ralph. Other than their children, she had nothing more in common with him.

Her mother was another story. Julia never really dealt with her feelings about her. She was still carrying around a lot of "unfinished business", a lot of unresolved issues regarding Katherine. It always puzzled Julia that Katherine and Ralph became the same person in her dreams, yet she thought they were such different people in real life, and could never understand the connection.

Katherine and Ralph had nothing in common, nor were their personalities remotely similar, Julia thought. She was still angry with her mother, while with Ralph, she only felt indifference. Ralph had been controlling while Katherine had been neglectful. Ralph had never physically abused her, while Katherine often slapped her and at times actually beat her. However, like her mother, Ralph had tortured her psychologically. He never respected her opinions, never considered her his equal and discouraged her from seeking therapy. Julia never felt she had the right to spend her "husband's money", though she sold her paintings, earning a substantial income. Besides feeling guilty about even spending her own money, she felt ashamed. Ralph's take on people who went to "shrinks'" was they were all a "bunch of kooks". He made fun of "California cults", as he called them, and thought seeing a therapist was just "another hippy-dippy fruitless pursuit". A definite waste of money. Ralph adhered to what he termed "old-fashioned" beliefs and values.

There were times when Julia wondered if she had been destined to marry someone who treated her as her mother had. She remembered the sadistic way her mother taunted, criticized and laughed at her. Her mother's seemingly deliberate lack of encouragement of anything she wanted to do made Julia grow up feeling unworthy. Katherine was always wrapped up in herself to give Julia any of her time or a crumb of love. Katherine's weakness also incensed Julia. She was a spineless jellyfish constantly needing the approval of everyone she came in contact with. It baffled Julia that her mother could be such a bully with her.

Illiterate and emotionally immature, Katherine was like a constant thorn in Julia's side she couldn't remove. For as long as she could remember, Julia felt ashamed of her mother. She hated to take her friends home to meet her because Katherine was so uncouth. She was also an alcoholic and Julia could never predict when she'd find her mother inebriated. As it was, Katherine barely had a vocabulary of fifty words, and when she was drunk, she garbled cuss words.

Otto provided rescue from Julia's haunting feelings. Even before she met him, she found strength and inner solace from him through his books. His writing taught her to question authority, to trust her own feelings and learn from experiences. Then, after being married to the "giant" himself, she found herself changing more.

Otto often discussed Julia's feelings of rejection with her. It was always a painful experience that conjured up old anger and still unresolved Katherine issues. Julia felt her mother never gave her the love she deserved, leaving a big hole in her heart. Her feelings of bitterness towards her mother seemed insurmountable. Otto pointed out that no child ever gets unconditional love, which helped her realize she wasn't the only one in the world with these problems. Otto, too, even in his seventies, still had unresolved issues with his mother, who never encouraged him to write or to be the person that he was. He commented often that when he began writing seriously, his mother would say "write a story like Gone With the Wind". She was totally ignorant of his writing style and for some unknown reason measured and compared his work against Margaret Mitchell. That infuriated Otto every time he talked about it.

It was difficult for Julia to be objective about Katherine. So much was still uncertain in her mind. As a teenager, she blocked out many hurtful times when her mother disappointed or abused her. Blocking these memories seemed to ease a lot of the pain. Julia reasoned if she didn't talk about them, she'd forget what happened. And, if she could forget long enough, perhaps she could believe those painful times never existed. Perhaps, her pain would go away forever.

Of course, that could never happen. Otto helped her to be able to see that. Even when she didn't speak of her mother or her unhappy childhood, her behavior reflected those old bottled up feelings. Her reactions to other people's comments, feelings of rejection, and low self-worth constantly plagued Julia.

Otto gave her an empathetic ear. Unfortunately, she had never come to any understanding of how to resolve her negative, bitter feelings before he died. Now, with Otto gone she had to fend for herself. There were many "pits" to avoid and many "snakes" to encounter and overcome along the way. Julia now knew intellectually, the time had come for her to take charge of her own life, work out her own problems. No one would or could do it for her.

But, how? Everything was so overwhelmingly frightening.

CHAPTER SEVEN: Andre

Andre Kramer splashed in the shower, singing at the top of his lungs. It felt good to let the water rush over his muscles. It soothed and revived him, it felt great. He needed that.

It had been a rough couple of months. Losing his dear friend Otto had jolted him. Even though Otto was up there in years, his death was still an unexpected shock. Especially, since Andre had worked on him the day before and Otto seemed in such good spirits – his sense of humor was at its peak. Andre laughed so much that day that his sides hurt. Otto's descriptions of the publishers he had to work with was hilarious. He had a salty tongue and an uncanny way of characterizing people, and once he got started, he spared no one.

"You know that asshole with Rogers Press? Pierre Dubois? I introduced him to you about a month ago ... makes me want to puke just looking at him ... remember? ... the one with the craters on his face! He probably has them on his ass too! And, that schnoz, it goes on forever ... twists and bends like it's trying to reach into his tight little pinched mouth! You know, that guy would make a great Cyrano de Bergerac! Well, yesterday he calls me and says, "Meester Marlton ..." He's French, you know, and doesn't speak English clearly. Jesus Christ! is he hard to decipher sometimes! Anyhow, he tells me he's been very busy lately and which is why he hasn't called ... as if I care! He got a case of the clap ... can you believe that? That little twerp! What kind of woman would want to shack up with that bed bug? He said his pecker was so sore he could barely pee. Then, while he was recuperating, what does the dumb bastard do but snores so loudly he falls out of bed and breaks his right foot! Now he can't drive his car. What a jerk!"

Otto talked non-stop as Andre massaged his tired, arthritic body. He remembered thinking how sad it was for such an alive, youthful mind like Otto's to be imprisoned in an aging, deteriorating body. Andre thought it didn't seem fair. Otto still had so much to give, but so little energy left.

Then, only a week after Otto's funeral, Andre's best friend Henry was killed in an automobile accident. Some car smashed head-on into Henry's. Right in his own neighborhood. Henry wasn't going more than 35 mph, the other guy was doing at least 65 and survived without any serious injuries most likely because he was drunk. He wasn't even wearing a seat belt. The alcohol probably helped facilitate his agility when he was thrown from his car. Poor Henry was killed instantly, however. The steering wheel rammed into his chest, the impact severing his aorta.

The news was a real blow to Andre. He was devastated. He sat by his desk for over an hour trying to absorb the reality of what had happened. Andre and Henry had grown up together. As children they played marbles in the streets of New York, shared their baseball cards, went to camp together, and had their Bar Mitzvahs only two weeks apart. Andre was best man at Henry's wedding. He was at the hospital the day Henry's son Alex was born. Was there at Alex's bris. Now, Alex was studying for his Bar Mitzvah, which was scheduled to take place in six months. Henry wouldn't be there to share in the joy the day his son would become a man.

Andre shivered at the realization of his own mortality. It scared him to think in a split second one could be snuffed out. All the hard work people go through to become educated, to grow into adulthood, to cope with problems, and then eradicated just like that! He felt angry with whoever played this cruel trick on humanity. He didn't believe in an afterlife and the thought of being dead for all eternity overwhelmed him. It made him feel insignificant, small and powerless. It depressed him when he thought about death.

Andre arrived at Henry's house, his widow Natalie was a mess. She had never been a strong person, to Natalie, everything was always a catastrophe. She was a real drama queen. Ever since Andre first met her, she was neurotically dependent on Henry. Even into adulthood, she had been babied by her parents. And, then, after she and Henry married, Henry carried on the tradition. Andre suspected Henry needed someone like Natalie. He needed to feel superior to a woman because of his own feelings of inferiority. Henry was short and was always nervous around the opposite sex. It bothered Henry when they were teen-agers and the other boys grew tall while he remained only five foot five.

When Natalie heard Henry had been killed, she collapsed and remained in a catatonic state for hours. She laid on the bed staring at the ceiling. Alex was frightened and helpless. He was sitting by his mother's side holding her hand when Andre arrived. Alex looked pallid, his cheeks were tear stained. Andre hugged him for one long minute.

"Alex, I've made arrangements with Dr. Casey to cover for me ... to take care of my patients this week. I'm here for you, to do anything I can to help."

"Thanks, Andre", Alex barely whispered. His voice cracked as he continued, "Oh Andre it's so awful. I'm scared. I'm really confused ... what will mother and I do now?"

"Well, first we'll have to make funeral arrangements, and then, it's really one day at a time. Somehow life will continue. It'll be difficult at first, but it will get easier. Death is part of the cycle of life. I know it's hard to comprehend, right now, but it happens to all of us eventually. Right now, we must concentrate on the living, especially your mother. She needs all the support we can give her."

For the first month after Henry's funeral Andre visited Natalie and Alex every day. Natalie navigated through the house like a zombie, but with each passing day she improved a little. Alex remained stoic, regarding himself now as "the man of the family". He had to keep things together. Circumstances forced Alex to mature way before his time. He was only six months from turning thirteen, but he behaved as if he was thirty.

Andre grieved terribly for his two friends. It was difficult to function, and to work on his patients in his usually cheery manner. But, as time passed, he was feeling more in control of his feelings and knew he had to let go and live in the present. In spite of his pain, he made the best of the days that followed these two tragedies.

Just as he was feeling a little better he received a letter from his daughter Allison, who was sixteen ... and pregnant. She sounded desperate. She had not told her mother yet, and In fact, she preferred not saying anything to Lauren, Andre's ex-wife, who was moralistic and self-righteous. Those were two of her characteristics that drove Andre away. Lauren was impossible to talk to or reason with. Regardless of the situation, or other people's feelings, Lauren was always right. After ten years of marriage, Andre couldn't take living with her anymore and asked for a divorce. It was a difficult decision, but he saw it as a matter of his emotional survival.

After the divorce, Lauren barely spoke to him. And, whenever he visited the children she treated him like a leper. He had always gotten along well with Allison and his son Jamie, but now, with him out of the house, there was a strain between the three of them. Andre suspected Lauren was responsible. He knew the children were caught in the middle and most likely felt guilty for wanting to spend time with him.

It was a crucial time for them all and many adjustments had to be made. Andre decided he needed a new start. He left Los Angeles and moved to San Francisco. Eventually, Lauren started working as a hospital volunteer and began dating. When she became involved with a social worker her focus on Andre lessened and she was not as venomous. The pressure on Allison and Jamie was also minimized, though living five hundred miles away made visits less convenient. Andre missed his children very much.

As soon as he read Allison's letter he immediately telephoned her. Luckily it was Tuesday. He knew Lauren worked at the hospital Tuesday afternoons and Allison got out of school at noon that day.

Allison answered the phone on the first ring. She sounded anxious.

"Allison, baby, it's Dad. How are you?"

"Oh, OK, I guess ... well, not really ... I ... uh ... had ... an abortion yesterday. I still feel pretty weak."

"Does your mother know?"

"Oh, god, no! Are you kidding? Tell her? Never! She'd kill me and never shut up about it. I'd rather die than talk to her!"

"Well, I suppose the worst is over. I just hope you went to a good doctor ... that you won't get an infection. Are you bleeding heavily?"

"No, I'm fine. It wasn't that bad. The bleeding is only a little worse than my periods. But, Dad ... I wish you were here. I feel so alone."

"Who was the father? Does he know?"

"It was Brett. Yeah, well, kinda ... you know we've been going together for six months, and, well, you see, I mentioned I might be pregnant and he turned white. I could tell he wouldn't have been much help. So, I just went by myself to a local doctor my friend Trish recommended. At first the doctor hesitated, saying I should get my parent's consent, but I insisted I didn't want that! Good thing Roe v. Wade made it legal. I reminded him of that. Still, I was scared and began to cry, so he backed off realizing I knew what I was talking about. You know, California has a confidentiality law that says a girl is not required to get her parents' consent. I checked that out before I went to see him. Anyhow, he did the abortion. Dr. McHugh is his name. But, I don't have all the money. It cost $1,000 and all I had was $300 ... my savings. But, I gave him my word that I'd pay the balance this week. The receptionist wasn't very sympathetic. She was real business-like and threatened if I didn't pay by next week, she'd call my mother. That would be awful. Mom would go crazy! You know her. So ... could you lend me the money? I have a job and I could pay you back ... maybe fifty dollars a week?"

"Allison, I do wish you had called me before you had the abortion. I would have checked into this Dr. McHugh's record. Now that it's all over and it seems you're alright, well, I'll call his office and say I'll be sending the balance of the money. You know I love you very much and would do anything for you, but I do think Brett should own up to some of the responsibility, too. I think you should talk to him about it. I hope that from now on you'll practice birth control. Talk to Dr. McHugh ... maybe you should get fitted for a diaphragm ... you don't want this to happen again. I'll send the check today. And, Allison ... please be careful. I love you."

"Oh, Dad, you're awesome! Thank you sooo much ... I love you, too."

"When can you come to San Francisco so we can spend some time together? I think we have a lot to talk about."

"Well, I have to work all next weekend. I took this weekend off because of the ah ... abortion, you know ... so I asked another girl to work for me. Maybe I can arrange for a weekend next month? I'll call you, OK?"

"OK, Sweets ... now you take care of yourself ... I expect to hear from you soon ... and tell Jamie I love him, too. Bye."

"Bye, Dad."

Andre felt a chill remembering Allison's nervous voice. Yes, the last two months were quite eventful. As he reflected, he hoped he would never have to go through a time like that again. For days after the two funerals he had been on edge. His nerves felt as though they were being pulled like taffy. Now, this with Allison.

Andre stepped out of the shower and grabbed a large blue-gray terry cloth towel. While drying off, the door bell rang.

Who could that be? He wasn't expecting anyone. It was a Saturday and he didn't usually see patients on weekends. He wrapped the towel around his waist Polynesian-style and ran down the stairs to the brown-tiled entry of his Victorian house. He lived alone. Since there were several extra rooms, he chose to live upstairs and made the downstairs rooms into his office.

"Who is it?," he yelled, looking through the peep hole.

"It's me, Julia Forrester."

"Julia? Oh, Julia! Yes, of course." Andre opened the door. "Please, come in."

"Thanks." Julia stepped inside and Andre guided her to the waiting room, motioning for her to sit down.

Julia looked embarrassed when she saw the towel wrapped around Andre's waist. "I ... I'm sorry," she stammered. "I should've called first, but I wanted to talk to you in person and I was in the neighborhood so I decided to see if you were in your office. I thought you saw patients on Saturdays?"

Julia had taken Otto to Andre's office on occasion. Usually after one of their jaunts to the Museum of Modern Art. Walking stiffened Otto's joints.

"It's OK. I just got out of the shower ... so excuse me for a minute while I go upstairs and put on some clothes. Make yourself comfortable."

"Sure ... go ahead ... I'll look at your photos ... "

Before she finished talking, Andre disappeared. Julia walked over to his desk. There a large photo of a young girl and a younger boy was positioned predominately. She assumed they were his children. He had mentioned once he had been married, but was divorced. Julia wondered where the children lived and if Andre saw them often. She wondered what kind of relationship he had with them.

It was only a few minutes later when Andre returned. He was barefoot and had on a pair of sweats. He was pulling a polo shirt over his head as he walked in the room.

"So how are you, Julia?"

"I'm fine. I mean, I'm better since Otto's funeral. It took me a while to get back into my routine ... I'm still really grieving for Otto ... I miss him so much. But, now I have another problem. I came to talk to you because I couldn't think of anyone else who could help me. You see, Stephanie and Stuart are taking me to court for the house. It's in my name because Otto couldn't make the mortgage payments. They're probably saying I forced him to change his will ... he wasn't in his right mind, or was senile the last year. You were at the house at least once a week for the last six months of his life and you know Otto was perfectly alert and aware. Will you help me?"

Andre looked into Julia's pleading eyes. She was hard to resist. He had always liked her. But, while she was married to Otto, Andre remained a gentleman. Never once did he make a pass at her, though there were many times he wanted to.

"Of course Julia ... I'd be glad to help you. But, first you'd better hire an attorney ... sounds like those two mean business."

## CHAPTER EIGHT: Phone Call to Valenti

"Yes, this is Valenti", said a gruff male voice. Then, in a pompous tone he continued, "What can I do for you?"

Julia swallowed hard. "My name is Julia Forrester ... and, I ... well ... Andre Kramer said I should call you."

The gruff voice softened slightly. "Andre Kramer? Oh, yes, Andre." Then, nostalgically, "My buddy from high school ... haven't seen him in ages. How is he? What's he been up to these days?"

"Andre is a chiropractor. He lives here in San Francisco. He moved here about five years ago. He says to give you his regards ... he'd like to see you one of these days, but, he's been very busy. He works in the South Bay sometimes, once or twice a month."

"Ah, yes, for sure. Yes, I can picture Andre as a doctor. He always had a way with people. And, your name again?"

"Julia. Julia Forrester." Julia hated small talk. She wanted to get straight to the point. "You see, Mr. Valenti, I need an attorney right away, and Andre said you were the best."

"Of course, I am. I certainly am." Then, suspiciously he questioned, "how did you get my home phone number?"

"Andre had it from an old holiday card you sent him. We took a gamble that the number was still the same. He hoped you wouldn't mind. He wouldn't give your phone number to just anyone. And, I'm very discreet. I promise I won't give it to anyone else."

Julia lied. Actually, she had Valenti's phone number for several years, but she didn't want to tell him. She didn't want to tell him her former husband, also a lawyer, had a special file on the top attorneys in the Bay Area. Ralph and Isadore Valenti were arch enemies.

When Julia was packing to leave Ralph, she thought it was a good idea to make her own copy of that file just in case. She had a feeling she might need legal help some day. As it was, she had felt uncomfortable with Otto's children from the beginning and anticipated problems with them.

"So, what do you want?" Valenti was anxious to get down to business.

"Well, my husband recently died a couple of months ago and his twin children, Stephanie and Stuart, from his first marriage, are suing me for the house. It's in my name and they're claiming he was senile the last couple of years and that I forced him to sign the papers. But, that's patently untrue because ..."

"Look, Mrs. ah, ah, Foster?"

"Forrester."

"Excuse me, Forrester ... I don't really work with cases like yours. You see, I'm very important, a very busy man. I only take big cases, not like this. But, I could refer you to someone else ..."

This is not a small case, my husband was Otto Marlton."

"Otto Marlton? The famous Otto Marlton?"

"Yes, the author."

"Well, why didn't you say so?" Valenti rudely interrupted. "So you're the honey who married that old geezer. Yeah, now I remember you. I saw your picture in the paper once or twice. Yeah, a blonde, right? A real cutie pie. Ah, now I get it, you and Andre want to live happily ever after in Marlton's place."

She was intimidated and didn't quite know how to respond. She bit her lip holding back what she felt like saying "what a self-righteous egomaniac".

Instead, she politely, but firmly replied, "No, that's not true! Andre and I are just friends. And, Andre was also my husband's friend. Otto thought very highly of him."

At that moment she regretted calling Valenti and wanted to hang up on him. Inwardly she was seething. She resented hearing Otto being called an "old geezer". It hurt her to think anyone would say that about a man, who, in his seventy-plus years, was more youthful than most thirty year olds. She also hated Valenti for referring to her as "a cutie pie". It made her feel as if she was merchandise advertised in a sex magazine.

Julia wished she could be with Valenti in person. She wanted to spit in his face. Would she be able to tolerate working with such a creep, she wondered? Yet, she knew Valenti was the type of attorney she needed. She knew Stephanie and Stuart would play dirty and she needed someone tough and insensitive – just like Valenti.

Mustering up all her courage and self-discipline, Julia continued, "I would like you to represent me. I am able to pay you handsomely."

"Look ... money's not the issue. But, we should talk about this privately. Why not meet me somewhere for a drink so we can talk more ... how about in room 410 at the Mark Hopkins? I hold a lot of my business meetings there. It wouldn't be good for us to be seen together in public, 'cause I'm a very important figure in this town, you know. And, you know how the paparazzi are ... always tryin' to get some dirt on celebrities. What do you say?"

"Mr. Valenti! I am still grieving for my deceased husband. I loved him very, very much, and well, I'm really not up to going out just yet. I would prefer to see you in your office."

"Now, don't get me wrong Mrs, uh, is it Forrester, or Marlton?"

"It's Ms. Forrester, like I said. I didn't take Otto's name when we got married."

"OK, Mrs. Forrester, or, how 'bout if I just call you Julia? How's that? As I was saying, now don't misunderstand me. I'm a religious man and devoted to my family, but my wife, she has diabetes and is sick a lot. She's kind of, let's say, out of commission, if you know what I mean. Now, don't get me wrong, I'm a good paisano, I swear on my dead father's grave, I'd never do anything to hurt my wife, never leave or divorce her, or anything like that, but ..."

Valenti's crass presumptuousness shocked Julia. She sat down. Was she hearing him correctly? She wasn't quite sure how to respond. Isadore Valenti was the right guy she needed if she was going to successfully fight Stephanie and Stuart for the house. But, she certainly wasn't going to sleep with him in order to get his help.

Regaining her composure, and in her most assertive toneΔ131
j149
Julia coldly declared, "Mr. Valenti, I called to hire you as my attorney!"

Being so uncharacteristically assertive, Julia surprised herself. She hid her true feelings well – weak, scared and intimidated. Her heart was pounding. She was shaking all over. Then, she thought to herself, this jerk is supposed to be the top attorney in San Francisco? Maybe. But, far from the top gentleman.

It made her nauseous just thinking about a man like Valenti touching her. She had seen him several times and as far as she was concerned he rated minus ten on her scale. Fat, balding, ugly – those were the words she had once used to describe him to her friend Suzie. He had acne scars and lesions on his face that made her squirm just to look at him. She shivered as she momentarily imagined Valenti dressed as the Marquis de Sade.

Shortly before she left Ralph they went to a huge banquet for attorneys at the Fairmont Hotel. Valenti was the guest speaker. Julia could still picture him adjusting his crotch as people were congratulating him for his fine speech.

Julia thought then that Valenti was a total egomaniac. An articulate showman, he entertained the audience talking for over an hour about nothing of any significance. The banquet was an arena for him to toot his own horn. Still, everyone applauded giving him a standing ovation. People respected Isadore Valenti because he was the District Attorney and the prosecutor on the Don Whitehall case. For almost a year Valenti received so much publicity he became a household name throughout the city.

Valenti succeeded in getting Whitehall convicted and sentenced for killing the mayor, George Sandone, and Harry Melt, who was one of the City Supervisors and gay. Hardly a day went by that Valenti's picture wasn't in the newspapers or on television news. Whitehall pleaded not guilty because he had too much sugar in his system. He said chocolate made him crazy and lose control.

When Whitehall said he had eaten four chocolate Ding-Dongs the morning he shot Sandone and Melt, Valenti made mincemeat out of him on the witness stand. Valenti had a wonderful way of twisting words and confusing a witness. Whitehall stammered on his own words and finally broke down admitting he had always been angry with Sandone and was even more angry with Melt because he was gay.

After the trial, the name Isadore Valenti was spoken with reverence by everyone in the city – as though he was Jesus Christ! Except by Julia.

From the first time she saw him Julia disliked everything about him, especially his characteristic misogynist style. There were rumors he might have political ambitions. Heaven forbid, a man like Valenti could ever have that kind of power. Julia shuddered at the possibility of Valenti becoming Mayor of San Francisco, or worse, Governor of California. Usually her trust in people bordered on naivete, but not with Valenti. Intuitively, she readily saw him as the Machiavellian ass he was.

Fortunately, soon after the Whitehall trial Valenti's popularity faded. He had a heart attack a month after the case was closed and couldn't work for almost six months.

When he finally was able to work again he joined a small law firm on Sutter Street. His doctor advised him to avoid stress so he never went back to the D.A.'s office.

As soon as Julia's timidness turned to assertiveness, Valenti shrunk. The change in his voice was astonishing. Like a disobedient child, he meekly answered, "I'm s-s-sorry ..." then added, "please ... will you accept my apology?"

Julia was perplexed. Was she hearing correctly? Is this guy for real? First he's a pompous ass, now he's Caspar Milquetoast.

In her typical fashion, instead of verbalizing her thoughts, she cooly replied, "Yes, yes ... of course."

Changing the subject, Valenti asked in a more confident tone, "Well, ah, let's see, didn't Otto have an attorney draw up his will?"

"Yes, he did. I went with him to Harrold Bowles who was his estate planner, but Bowles is out of town on a safari or something in Africa for three months. I can't wait until he gets back and his partner is too busy. I decided if I had to work with a complete stranger I might as well work with the best. So, will you represent me, or not? It's possible Stuart and Stephanie will settle out of court, especially when they find out you're handling this case for me." Julia knew flattery would get her everywhere with Valenti. "I expect it won't take very long, and probably won't take up much of your time if you have other more demanding clients ... "

Valenti pondered Julia's words for a few seconds anticipating the rise of his popularity again. He liked being in the newspapers and on television, loved the spotlight. It made him feel important. It made him feel potent. It had been a while since the Whitehall case ended and he hadn't had anything newsworthy happen in his career since then. Valenti was a glutton for fame and attention, never getting enough of either.

"OK, call my office in the morning and ask Miss Simpson to make an appointment for you on Wednesday, the 10th. Valenti took out his appointment book and scribbled the name, 'Julia' in big block letters with a heart around it in the Wednesday, September 10th space. "Meanwhile, write down as much as you can ... as much as you know about those Marlton brats ... Stephanie and Stuart, did you say their names were? Especially, any, say ... bad habits they might have like alcohol or drugs, and how often they visited their father. And, what kind of relationship they had with him. Oh, do you keep a calendar?"

"Yes, yes I do."

"Good. Go back over the past year, or better yet, as many years as you were married to Marlton ... if you have any old calendars lying around. Make a list of all of Otto's acquaintances and visitors. Hopefully, we can settle out of court, but if not, we'll need several key witnesses to prove Otto wasn't senile."

As Valenti spoke these words he knew in his heart he'd never settle out of court. He wanted a big stink made out of the Marlton clan, he wanted a big trial. Valenti decided he would do everything in his power to make this suit, and his name, reach every newspaper in the world. Otherwise, why take on such an insignificant case?

"Thanks! I'll see you on Wednesday, then. Good evening Mr. Valenti."

"Good-evening Mrs., ah, Forrester."

Valenti adjusted his balls and smiled.

CHAPTER NINE: Romantic Dinner

"Oh, Andre, I don't know about Isadore Valenti", Julia said as she lifted her glass of champagne. She took a sip, then glanced out the window down at the Bay. It was a magnificent sight from Aliotos restaurant at Fisherman's Wharf. Boats moored to slips looked like toys floating in a bathtub. The light of the full moon cast a shimmery white path on the indigo water that spanned an area of several miles. Julia looked out across the Bay at Alcatraz in the distance. Nostalgically, she thought of the tour she took with her three children through the rocky island after it was closed down as a prison. It made her wonder what Brad, Charlie, and Sandra were doing now. She hadn't seen them in months and felt guilty. It was painful to think about them.

Quickly erasing the thoughts of her children from her mind, she continued her conversation.

"Valenti makes me nervous. He seems so, so ... sleezy."

Andre was studying the menu, then looked up at Julia. "Oh, Valenti's all talk. He was that way as a kid, too. Always tried to act like a big shot – a classic case of a Napoleon complex."

"Well, he's not acting now. He is a big shot. I mean, in the law world, anyway. Ever since he prosecuted Don Whitehall. Now everyone wants to hire him."

"That's what he'd like you to think. Truth is, Julia, he's lost a lot of popularity since his heart attack. Don't let him intimidate you, he needs your business."

The waiter hovered with his pencil and pad, "Have you decided yet,

Madam?"

Julia's trend of thought was broken. "Oh, ah, yes ... " She pointed to a spot on the menu. "I'll have the chicken piccata and a salad with vinaigrette dressing."

"And you, sir?"

"The fish, the swordfish – broiled, and salad too, but with blue cheese." Andre poured more champagne into Julia's glass and continued talking. "Don't get me wrong, Valenti is good, there's no doubt about that. He's tough. He has to be. Otherwise, no one would respect a little guy."

Julia smiled graciously as if to thank Andre for filling her glass, then asked, "But, Andre, why does he have to be such a chauvinist? So 'macho'? I hated the way he talked to me. It made me feel so uncomfortable."

"Look, Julia, I know this is a difficult time for you, but I swear, Valenti will serve you well. I'm positive of it." Andre knew Isadore would love to take a case like Julia's, being the showman he was. It was the kind of PR he needed."

"I hope you're right, because I dread having to meet with him next week. But, at least it's in his office."

"Trust me, Valenti won't try to take advantage of you. He's really a jelly-fish behind that tough facade."

"What was he like as a kid?"

"Pimply."

"Pimply?"

"Yeah, I met him in high school. Actually at the Jewish Center."

"The Jewish Center? I thought he was Italian?"

"He is. He's also Jewish. His mother's Jewish, a survivor of the Holocaust. She fled to Italy after the war where she met Marco Valenti, Izzie's father."

That's interesting! So, she raised Isadore as a Jew?"

"Well, yes and no. Actually, Izzie was raised Catholic. His father passed away when Izzie was in high school, and then his mother got religious. She had never converted to Catholicism, but went along with her husband's religion for her son. Then, the father was diagnosed with cancer. It was an awful ordeal for the family. He died a year later. Izzie's mother became very distraught. She had had such a hard time in the concentration camp, you know, so this was the last straw for her. She embraced Judaism again, and became very religious. Went to synagogue every week. And, Izzie joined her a few times."

"So, did he decided to give up Catholicism and follow Judaism?"

"Not exactly. It wasn't because he was such a devout Catholic either, he hardly ever went to church. He just liked the Jewish Center. That's where all us kids hung out. We had dances and a lot of fun events."

"Sounds like it was great."

"It was. We all had a feeling of belonging there, and Izzie really liked that. In high school he was just a little fat nobody, but at the Center he was accepted."

"Was he liked?"

"Yeah, he was. He had a wacky sense of humor and the more laughs he got the funnier he became. The other kids always looked forward to him being there."

"Sounds like that was the beginning of his courtroom training."

"That's true. He was really damn funny during that Whitehall case, wasn't he?"

"Thanks to the Jewish Center. Who knows, perhaps if he never went there he might have stayed a nobody."

"Maybe."

"What about you, Andre? Are you religious?"

Andre melted as he looked into Julia's warm blue eyes. Momentarily, he fantasized grabbing her and passionately kissing her. His gaze moved down to her chest, his eyes slowly traveling over the folds of her light mauve chiffon blouse. The exposed skin looked so tender and juicy. Imagining how creamy her bosoms might taste as he sucked on them, Andre could feel a swelling in his groin. Thankfully, the table concealed his desire. It was difficult to concentrate on a conversation about religion. Instead, he wanted to take Julia home and make love to her. But, he knew he had to play it cool, and he had to patiently work up to seducing her. Taking a breath he politely answered her question.

"No, not really. Actually, I'm an atheist."

"You don't believe in God? Or, a higher power?"

"Well, that's a matter of interpretation. You see, I think I'm God." Julia interrupted, "That sounds pretty egotistic! And, here I thought you were a fairly humble person."

The words just blurted out. Julia shifted back and forth in her seat. She felt uncomfortable because she wasn't accustomed to confronting men. She also felt disappointed in Andre, worrying if she was a good judge of character.

Prior to his statement about being God, Julia had felt immensely attracted to Andre. While he spoke she had been studying his features and found them quite appealing. She imagined painting his portrait. What color would she mix for his rugged complexion? Would she use tones of red, yellow, and blue and pointillistically create his curly brown hair? How could she portray that seductive look in his dark, bedroom eyes? Perhaps, instead of painting she would sculpt a bust of him. His long, crooked Semitic nose was extremely conducive for clay, as was his thick, strong neck. It was also a temptingly huggable neck. Andre's lips, however, were the most captivating. Julia couldn't take her eyes off them. She wanted to touch them, to feel what they were made of. They seemed elastic because of the way they stretched in unusually expressive ways. She had an impulsive desire to lean over the table and kiss this handsome Adonis. She also wondered what he would be like in bed. What would a relationship with him be like? Her fantasy was interrupted by Andre's voice.

"I know it sounds egotistical, but I don't mean it that way. You see, I think you're God, too."

"I am?"

"Yes, God, a higher power, nature, life, whatever you want to call it, him, or her. It's just semantics, anyhow. To me it's all the same."

"But, don't you believe someone, or something is controlling you and your destiny?"

"Absolutely not! I control my own life and destiny."

"So, what is your destiny Andre? Do you believe in an afterlife?"

"No, I wish I did. But, as a scientist it's difficult to buy that stuff. I think Man is just an accident. And, when we die, well, that's it."

"What about reincarnation? Do you think it's possible we come back in another life form?"

"You know, Julia, I really wish I could believe that, but I don't."

"So, what about the Bible and all the people who swear by it?"

"I'm convinced the Bible is just a lot of stories, written by men who wanted to keep people in line. What do you believe?"

"I was raised Catholic, and I really believed it all as a kid. I even thought of becoming a nun. I didn't have a great home life. My parents fought a lot, and my mother was abusive. In looking back, I think the church and the nuns were my surrogate home and family."

"Then, I married Ralph in a Lutheran church. He was raised Protestant, so, according to the Catholic church, because I didn't get married by a priest, I was excommunicated. Actually, in the eyes of the church I was not even married. I was living in sin. Then, a Justice of the Peace married me and Otto, so I guess I'm still damned." Julia laughed slightly, as Andre gave her a queer look.

"Well, what do you believe now?"

"Oh, I'm confused, I guess."

"Well, do you still feel a connection to Catholicism?"

"Very little. Very, very little. I haven't gone to church in years, except for weddings. The last time was right before Otto died."

The waiter interrupted again as he was clearing the plates from the table, he asked, "May I get you some dessert?"

Julia smiled, "No, thank you. Just coffee, please."

"And, you sir?"

"What do you have?"

"Let's see, there's chocolate mousse, cheesecake, fresh berries, and apple pie."

"Nothing else chocolate?"

"We did have a chocolate decadence cake, but I think it's all gone. I'll run back to the kitchen and see if there's a piece left. Madam, do you take cream with your coffee?"

"Yes, thanks." Coquettishly, looking at Andre, "... where were we?"

"You were talking about church ... the last time you went to church."

Andre really wanted to talk about sex, not about church. He wanted to take Julia in his arms, smother her with kisses, and carry her away. He wanted to take her home with him and make love to her all night long. Behave yourself, he ordered himself under his breath.

Julia giggled, "Yes, I guess I'm a bad girl. I stopped counting my mortal sins a long time ago." She laughed, "I'm never going to make it to heaven's pearly gates."

"Do you really think there is a heaven?"

"Gosh, Andre, I really don't, yet there is a teensy part of me that does. It's hard to go through all those years of Catholic school and catechism lessons and just forget it all. Intellectually, none of it makes sense. But, emotionally I still feel dependent."

"On whom? On what?"

"I don't know. I mean, I wish I knew. It's just so hard being all alone."

"But, you are alone. No matter how many people you have around you, you are alone. You live alone, and you die alone."

"That sounds so cold ... even kind of gruesome."

"It's not. It's just the way it is."

"I suppose so. But, I'd rather not think about it, or dwell on it. It's too frightening."

"Actually, to me it isn't frightening at all. In fact, it's rather exciting, in the sense that I'm in total control of myself. I take complete responsibility for me and no one else."

"Intellectually that sounds good, but what about in your personal relationships?"

"Well, I've been divorced for over five years, and presently I'm not involved with anyone."

Julia felt a tinge of excitement and glowed inside. She wasn't sure what to say next. Secretly, she wanted to tell Andre she would love to get involved with him. Instead, she asked, "Did your wife believe that, too?"

"No. She resented I was so autonomous. She wanted me to be more dependent on her, because she was so dependent on me."

"In what way?"

"Well, in many ways. She was very jealous for one thing."

"Did she have reason to be? Did you cheat on her?"

"No, I didn't. I'm a monogamous person. I believe in commitment and honesty. But, my wife was so insecure she never believed me."

Julia felt better about Andre, no longer doubting his integrity. She saw him as a man with the strength of his convictions. She also saw a very sexy hunk.

"So ... " Julia smiled, "Are you interested in getting involved again?"

Andre smiled back, "Of course."

Self-consciously Julia looked down into her coffee cup and blushed. She forgot everything she had read in her women's lib books.

CHAPTER TEN: The Affair

Julia lay awake wondering why sex with Andre was so much better than she had ever expected. Why had she had so few orgasms previously? Did the passion that had built up from her fantasies about him over the last year contribute to climaxing so readily? Was it because sex had happened spontaneously without any preconceived conscious plan? Was it Andre's rugged, handsome looks that were so appealing and hard to resist? Julia watched his body vibrate steadily as he breathed deeply. He was sleeping as soundly as a baby. No wonder. They had made love for close to an hour. After climaxing together, they wrapped themselves in each other's arms for several minutes, until Andre passed out. As spent and as exhausted as she was, Julia, however, couldn't sleep. She was too excited. Many thoughts were racing through her mind.

Julia couldn't tell Andre that she rarely had orgasms while having sex. Nor could she tell him he was only the third man she ever had sex with. Ralph and Otto were the only men she had previously slept with. Because Ralph was a "wham, bam, thank you ma'am" kind of guy, she rarely had orgasms with him. Many times Otto was impotent, and when they did have sex, he often climaxed prematurely. And, other times he was in too much pain to make love. Most of their sex life was based on kissing and hugging, and sometimes he fondled her to orgasm. But, the more infirm Otto got, the less that happened. Julia resorted to masturbation for relief, her Catholic upbringing often making her feel tantalizingly like "a bad girl".

Sexual frustration was familiar to Julia. Ralph treated making love like one of his courtroom cases, very business-like. Foreplay was a waste of time, he wanted to get it over with. Just put it in and come. No warmth, no tenderness. Ralph needed his almighty orgasm regularly, it didn't matter to him if she was satisfied or not. She felt used. She wondered if her infrequent orgasms drove Ralph to other women.

Being a virgin when they married, Julia had no one to compare Ralph to. Not knowing any better, she had few expectations of him during their twenty years together. She simply figured this was the way sex was supposed to be. Until ... she read those articles by Masters and Johnson and discovered that she, too, was entitled to actually enjoy sex.

This marked the beginning her marital dissatisfaction. When she confronted Ralph about their sex life, he seemed surprised. True to character, he denied having any problems with it, saying he felt perfectly satisfied, questioning why Julia was complaining.

Ralph apparently measured good sex by frequency, not quality. He'd often brag, "Our sex life is so much better than most other people's". He based this concept on reports he had read, and said, "According to this or that survey, the average couple married more than seven years has intercourse once or twice a month." Ralph backed his beliefs by quoting "authorities", who said, "most women never experience an orgasm. It's probably in the female genes", he concluded.

When Ralph wanted sex, Julia began resorting to feigning physical ailments, headaches or backaches, or saying she was too tired. Each time she refused his advances, Ralph lost patience, then tried intimidating or coercing her.

"So, what if you have a headache? Headaches are psychosomatic anyway.

But, don't worry, I'll make it quick."

"A backache? Ha! Well, sex is good for backaches. I'll cure you."

"Tired? I can't believe you. You sleep nine hours every night. You must be tired from too much shopping."

"It's your duty as my wife to please me. I've got it coming."

"It's my right."

"I'll take you away next weekend if you're good to me."

"Here's a credit card, but you know what I expect in return?"

"Sure, you can visit your friend Jane in LA, but I expect to get laid every night before you leave."

As each day passed with Ralph, Julia grew more and more angry not only with him, but with herself. She felt raped by him and began to loathe it whenever he touched her. It scared her to feel so much anger towards the man she was married to, the man she once loved.

Julia felt trapped.

Fortunately, she discovered Otto Marlton's books which saved her sanity for a couple of years. Otto wrote in graphic detail about sex and it titillated her and awakened her sexuality. She began masturbating for the first time in her life at the age of thirty-six! Or, at least the first time she could remember. Perhaps she had masturbated as a child, but if she did, she was sure she had blocked it out because of guilt. Catholicism considered masturbation sinful.

When she experienced her first orgasm through masturbation while she was married to Ralph, she felt cheated. She realized he never gave her enough time to become stimulated. She also realized too much damage had been done to their relationship. Her anger festered, she began to totally resist his advances. She knew in her heart she would never be able to resolve her differences with him. She also knew it was because of fear and insecurity that she stayed married to him. It wasn't until her relationship with Otto began to blossom that she had enough courage to leave Ralph. His affairs were an added catalyst, the ultimate insult that helped her make the decision to divorce him.

With Otto, Julia never felt cheated. Otto gave her so much more than sex. He had told her he loved her more than life itself, and she believed him. She felt strengthened by his tenderness and respect for her, by his encouragement for her to respect and trust in herself. Since she felt emotionally fulfilled in this relationship, she rationalized the unimportance of sex.

Thoughts of Otto and her marriage to him evoked sad and lonely feelings. Ah, if only he had been a younger man when they met. She was sure that in his day he was a sexual athlete. Time had not been on their side. Julia's eyes got misty, a tear trickled down her cheek.

Julia looked over at Andre again. The moon shone through the window casting interesting shadows on his muscular body. The light and dark abstract forms created from the rays of light fascinated her. Julia liked to study and memorize body shapes. It helped her when she painted from memory, when she didn't have a model. Her eyes traveled slowly over the ringlets of Andre's dark curly hair and finely chiseled profile, then down his thick neck and bare, strong back. The blanket covered him from the waist down so her gaze continued up his side, then traced the bulging deltoid muscles of his upper arms. It was tempting to reach over and run her hand over his nude frame. Sex with Andre was so good. Julia realized that she had waited a long time for this precious night. Fearing repercussions, she avoided waking him. It was already two in the morning and he had to get up at six. He mentioned he was going to have "a very busy day tomorrow".

Julia rolled over and closed her eyes. Her heart was still beating rapidly. She couldn't fall asleep. She reached down under the covers and put her hand over her pubic area, the hairs still moist. The moistness aroused and stimulated her. Slowly her fingers crept up into her vagina, her body rocking to the rhythm of her pulsating hand. She gasped. Within seconds she had several successive orgasms. Andre stirred and turned over, but stayed asleep.

Thankfully, she had learned to have orgasms through masturbation. But, what had been a fear for years, was whether or not she was capable of having an orgasm with a partner. The sexual failure of her marriage to Ralph had plagued her, and she worried she might be sexually deficient with a man. Her wedding night with Otto, so filled with love and passion, disproved those fears. Tonight, with Andre, totally erased any lingering doubts. There was no question now, Julia loved sex.

Tonight everything happened so naturally with Andre. When he took her home, he leaned over and gave her a little kiss good-bye. That little kiss turned into a big one, and Julia invited him in for "a cup of tea". She didn't realize how love-starved she had been until Andre's arms embraced her. Melting to his touch, she immediately responded. She put her arms around him and held him tightly. As she opened her mouth, Andre's tongue charged in. Her whole body tingled, and she felt her panties becoming wet.

They barely made it to the bedroom. Panting with passion they tore each other's clothes off. Julia looked up at Andre's strong, naked body, and instinctively took his huge, throbbing penis in her hand. Her subconscious reflections of the movie, Deep Throat (Thank you Suzie for dragging me to see that film, she thought), shamelessly guided her next movements. She put her mouth over his penis, as if eating a delicious morsel. She nibbled at the circumcised tip, and with her free hand she massaged his scrotum. Then with her tongue, she started at the shaft, and in a slow fluttering motion she licked up, then around and down. Andre's body writhed with ecstasy as one hand stroked Julia's long silky hair, while the other grabbed her firm, small buttocks.

"Ah, Julia, that feels wonderful," he moaned breathlessly. "But, stop, I want to please you, too ... and you're driving me crazy! I feel so weak. Stop now before I come."

Startled, Julia looked up at him. Andre was concerned with her pleasure, too?

"Oh, Andre," she sighed as she leaned up. Their mouths met again. He bit and blew softly into her ear, then pecked and sucked her neck. Julia's whole body was full of goose bumps. They hugged each other tightly. They kissed for what seemed an eternity. Then, with a gentle push Andre instructed her to lie back and relax.

"It's my turn now. I want you to enjoy yourself too," he said. He bent over and sucked on the nipples of her large, creamy breasts. "You taste so sweet, so so sweet," he whispered. His hand reached down and spread her legs apart. With his fingers he gently separated her labia. Very slowly his tongue licked her throat, chest, abdomen, then gently moved to her clitoris. The tickling sensation caused her to squirm and giggle. When Julia felt Andre's tongue enter her in a twirling motion she let out a scream. Her body reacted as she bounced to the rhythm of his licking.

"Andre, oh, Andre ... I can't stand it anymore. It feels soooo good. Let's make love now," she pleaded.

Andre didn't need coaxing. He, too, was extremely aroused. He couldn't wait to get inside Julia, but he didn't want to take the chance of getting her pregnant.

"I have some condoms in my wallet."

"No, no, that's not necessary. I had my tubes tied after my third child."

Andre didn't need coaxing and got on top of Julia. His saliva and her secretions helped his penis glide into her without any difficulty. Julia let out another scream as Andre began to thrust forward. Slowly and gently he pumped and rode her, nice and easy. "Oh, my god! Oh ... my ... god!" Julia could barely stand the feeling of Andre's huge penis penetrating her. It felt like it was going to reach up to her throat and choke her because it was so hard and long.

They tried several positions. First ,the missionary. Then, on their sides. Julia had never had sex other than in the missionary position, so she was eager to experience something new. Andre instructed her to get on her knees.

"No, Andre, I don't want that."

"Not anal, Julia, I just want to enter you from behind."

Reluctantly, Julia got on her knees. Andre mounted her doggie-style, put his arms around her waist and straddled her. When she felt his first thrust, her body quivered with excitement. The thrill was indescribable. She couldn't believe how different it felt from the missionary position. On her knees she was not passive and felt she was able to be more of a participant. She squeezed her vaginal muscles as Andre moved in and out. Then, with all her might she clamped down with such force, he couldn't budge. Trapped inside her he felt deliriously hot with passion. He felt as if he was going out of his mind as she repeatedly contracted her muscles around his penis.

The thought flickered through Julia's mind as she remembered her gynecologist's Kegel exercise instruction, and a small chuckle escaped her lips between gasps of delight.

It was too much for both of them. Neither one of them ever experienced such satisfying sex. As Andre ejaculated, the spasm and warm sensation of his sperm shooting into her was more than Julia could handle. She exploded with him.

Sweating and spent, their bodies lay locked together.

Andre gave her a tender hug and kiss and said, "Thank you, you were absolutely wonderful." With a satisfied expression on his face, he immediately fell into a deep sleep.

Julia couldn't believe how free she had felt during sex, not for one moment during their love making was she distracted by her "Catholic guilt". Anyway, how could something so wonderful ever be considered bad, she asked herself.

Dismissing those thoughts, she wanted to stay in Andre's arms forever. She longed to make love to him morning, noon, and night. She didn't want to do or to think of anything else. She wished the clock had stopped while they were making love. She wished it could have lasted for several more hours. She was amazed at Andre's staying power and endurance, though not surprised. Intuitively, she had suspected he would be great in bed. She saw it in his hands, the way he massaged and adjusted Otto.

Julia remembered the first time she met Andre, and how she had blushed when they were introduced. When Otto asked her to call Dr. Kramer and make an appointment for him, she expected an older man to show up, and was quite taken back by Andre's youthful good looks and charm.

Though Andre was always very professional when taking care of Otto, Julia felt he liked her. But, there was also an unspoken cautiousness they both seemed to sense. Perhaps it was because they feared that their attraction to each other was too risky. Their loyalty and respect for Otto kept their relationship a purely platonic one.

After tonight Julia wondered what the future would hold. What would the outcome be for her and Andre? Would they be as compatible in other areas of their lives as they had been in bed? Confidently, she reassured herself they would be. Closing her eyes once again, and with a warm feeling of contentment, she hoped for a sexy dream.

## CHAPTER ELEVEN: Golden Gate Park

"What the hell is Kaposi's Sarcoma?", Stephanie asked as she and Stuart strolled past the planetarium in Golden Gate Park.

It was a brisk autumn day and overhead black clouds were rolling in from the west threatening a downpour. A rainstorm would be no surprise. On the news the night before, the weatherman predicted a cold front moving in. Stuart clasped his umbrella as he looked upward, expecting to get rained on any minute, then looked back at Stephanie.

"Beats me ... all I know is that's what the doctor at the clinic told Marty he had," he answered with a bewildered expression.

Stephanie tightened the scarf around her neck, buttoned up her camel-colored jacket and commented, "Burr ... it's getting chilly. I hope it doesn't rain until later, like after midnight. So, what're Marty's symptoms?"

"He feels run down and he's had a rash for over a month and it's not going away."

"Well, what's the doctor doing for it? Did he put Marty on antibiotics, or something? Did he give him any kind of ointment for the rash?"

"No, he wants Marty back tomorrow for more tests."

"More tests! Jesus Christ! Those damn doctors, always trying to run up the bill. What kind of tests?"

"How should I know!"

"Did Marty go to a dermatologist?"

"Uh, I don't know, but, yeah, I think so. He went to a clinic over in the Haight. They say the doctors are really good there. They're all specialists. I think the one Marty saw was a skin doctor. Oh my god, Steph, I'm really worried. The doctor said that Marty may have an immune system problem or something like that. Marty's so nervous. They have blood tests to do and he's deathly afraid of needles."

"So, why doesn't he get another opinion?"

"Who could he go to?

"Doesn't he have a family doctor?"

"Yeah, but the family doctor is a friend of Marty's parents."

"So?"

"Well, Marty's afraid the doctor might tell his parents he's gay."

"They don't know? How can he hide something like that?"

"Easy. He acts differently around them."

"How? How can a person be one way one minute and a different person the next?"

"Marty's good at it. He pretends that he's straight at work, too. Nobody at his office suspects. The guys he works with are really macho. They always make jokes about "fags". Marty would die if he thought they knew he was gay, so he laughs with them. But, he cringes inside."

"So besides me, who knows about the lie you two are living?"

Why did Stephanie have to be so blunt? Stuart didn't like to think that he was living a lie. It was an important secret that he and Marty made a pact to keep. It was necessary for Marty's job, and his parents' mental health, he thought. They're so traditional it would kill them if they knew their son was homosexual.

"Two guys who live around the corner on Castro Street, Mike and Jim, they know. We play cards with them once a week."

"Do you ever, ah, double date with them?"

Stephanie was merciless. Stuart felt the blood rush to his head. He wanted to choke her for being insensitive. Instead, he suppressed his anger, no need to start a fight, and answered, "No, Mike and Jim flaunt it too much. It's embarrassing to be with them in public. They hold hands walking down the street and sometimes they even kiss each other out in the open. Marty and I like their company 'cause they're funny. But, no, we never go anywhere with them."

"How does Marty hide it from his folks? I mean, don't they ever come over to your place to visit?"

"Not often. They moved south about two years ago. The cold was more than they could take ... up in their eighties, you know."

"Did they ever meet you?"

"Once, when I helped Marty move from their house. They just think we're friends who share a townhouse. We have two bedrooms, so, they wouldn't think of anything like that. They're really naive, simple people."

Stephanie mumbled something about "coming out of the closet" then pointed to a bench, "Hey, let's sit down, my dogs are barkin'", she said as she flopped on the bench. It was a lovely spot overlooking the Japanese Tea Garden. Asian tourists were milling about, posing and taking pictures.

Stephanie loved the Tea Garden. She liked the challenge of trying to walk over the rounded bridges. She also loved studying the rare plants and shrubs. Most of all she enjoyed the exotic flowers. Their brilliant colors provided a sharp contrast to the greenery surrounding them.

Stephanie missed not having a garden of her own. She thought of her father's house and the gardens sprinkled over the several acres. Most of the property was flat and easy to stroll around. She had planted many different types of flowers and plants on that property over the years. She loved living with her father … until he married Julia. That bitch! She and Stuart had wagered that Julia wouldn't last a month after marrying their father, but she lasted until Otto died, three years later. Stephanie was deeply hurt that her father had chosen Julia over her.

Stuart's mood changed and he laughed at Stephanie's remark about "her dog's barkin". "I haven't heard that expression in ages", he said. As if reading her mind he brought up their father, asking, "Didn't Dad used to say that?"

"Yeah, that's an old expression." Stephanie's train of thought was broken. "Sounds silly doesn't it?" Then, more seriously, she asked, "Do you suppose that Marty has that new disease? What do they call it? … AIDS?"

"Aze? What's that?"

"No, AIDS – it's spelled A. I. D. S. I'm not sure what the letters stand for. It has something to do with the immune system. It's a disease that only affects gay guys."

"Why just gays?"

"I think it's some kind of venereal disease."

"Well, then Marty can't have that. Neither of us ever even had crabs. We've been together for three years and are faithful to each other … at least I've been faithful to Marty. Stuart paused, "And, I'm positive he's never fooled around on me either."

"But, Stuart, I think it's more than just a venereal disease … I think, I heard it has something to do with butt fucking."

Stuart squirmed with embarrassment. Even though he had told Stephanie he was gay, it was uncomfortable going into detail about his sex life. He tried to change the subject. "Marty and I are the most fastidious guys I know. We're very clean. We shower twice a day. We take vitamins and eat fresh, nourishing food. We don't drink much ... a little wine now and then, but that's all. No hard stuff. We don't smoke ... not even weed anymore. And, we get plenty of sleep and exercise."

"Look Stu, don't jump to any conclusions. AIDS is supposed to be a rare disease. It's from Africa, or someplace like that. I only heard about it recently. They say it originated from screwin' monkeys."

Stuart let out a relieved laugh. "Monkeys! That's hilarious! Who would want to screw a monkey? Only a pervert could be that hard up."

Stephanie put her hand on Stuart's shoulder. "Chances are Stu, Marty's fine. He's probably just got the flu, and maybe a bad case of poison ivy. Weren't you guys camping up in Yosemite right after Dad died? And, even if it is that AIDS sickness ... well, I'm sure it's treatable. Don't worry, Marty'll be fine in a few weeks."

"I hope so, Steph. It really hurts me to see Marty out of sorts. He's usually in such a good mood, always positive and laughing. But, lately he's just not himself."

"I said don't worry. He'll be OK."

"Yeah, you're right. You always are. Marty's too young and has led too healthy a lifestyle to be seriously ill."

"Stephanie looked at her watch. "I have to be home by six. Going out with a new guy tonight, but there's still time for a drink over at the Cliff House. What do you say?"

"Sure, sounds good."

They walked quickly back to the parking lot and jumped into

Stephanie's old BMW. As Stuart strapped himself in with the seat belt, he stretched his neck and looked out the window.

"We made it just in time. Look over there. It's starting to really come down."

"Shit! I was hoping it wouldn't rain … that the clouds would just pass. I hate going out in the rain. Especially, on a blind date. My hair gets so frizzy when it's wet."

"A blind date? I thought you never go out on blind dates?"

Stephanie ignored Stuart's remark. Her attention was concentrated on driving. The traffic through the parkway was pretty heavy. "God damn Chinese drivers! They're all bad! They make me crazy!"

"Aw, come on Steph, you sound prejudiced."

"Well, I am when it comes to driving. Every accident I've ever read about was caused by a Chinese driver."

Stuart rolled his eyes. He knew arguing with his sister was a complete waste of time, so he conceded, "Yeah, I suppose so."

It felt warm and cozy at the Cliff House. Stephanie led Stuart to a table by the window overlooking the ocean. "How's this?", she asked. Without waiting for a reply, she sat down and began loosening the belt on her jacket.

Stuart looked out the rain-soaked window. Directly below giant waves crashed against the huge boulders that surrounded the restaurant. "Oh! Ah, this is fine," he said.

Did he have a choice? He wondered what Stephanie would say, or do, if he ever disagreed with her.

The waitress walked over and placed a basket of pretzels on their table, "May I get you something from the bar?"

Stephanie didn't wait for Stuart to answer, and replied, "Yes, I'll have a banana daiquiri and he'll have a glass of white wine."

"Chablis or Chardonnay? We also have a lovely white Zinfandel." Without giving Stuart a chance to speak up, Stephanie started to answer for him saying, "Char ..."

Stuart interrupted her, "No, I think I'll try the Zin ..."

Stephanie was taken a back. "You always drink Chardonnay!"

"I know, but, this time I feel like trying something different," he answered defiantly.

"Thank you," the waitress said, and strutted away.

"So, a blind date, eh? You never said who fixed you up?"

"Carol, you know, my friend Carol Chen. She works at the Museum of Modern Art."

"Carol Chen? That Chinese girl!" Then poking fun at Stephanie, Stuart chided, "You were just putting Chinese people down."

Showing some discomfort Stephanie shifted positions and looked away. Stuart knew that when she didn't make eye contact it was because she wasn't speaking the truth. Regaining her composure, she said strongly, "That's different. Carol is an American. So are her parents. She's smart and bright ... and a good driver."

"Well, then that discounts all Chinese as being lousy drivers." For once Stuart felt in a position of power, he had his sister squirming.
Stephanie was not one to be beat, however. In retaliation she accused Stuart of being stupid, of not being capable of understanding her logic. Stuart weakened and conceded.

"OK, OK, I'm sorry I brought it up. So, who's the guy?"

"Forget the guy! I want to tell you something about Julia."

"Julia? What about Julia?"

"Carol saw her at the museum a few days ago ... "

"Well, that's not so unusual. Julia and Dad always went to art museums. You know, Julia is an artist ...".

"I know, but, guess who she was with? And, holding hands?"

"I can't imagine ... who?"

That Kramer guy, the chiropractor who used to work on Dad."

"Andrew Kramer?"

"No, Andre! His mother was French. Dad told me."

"Well, so what? Julia's young, you can't expect her to mourn for Dad forever."

"Stuart! Dad's only been dead three months! Don't you think she should at least have the decency to wait ... until Dad's body is cold?"

Stuart hated hearing those words. It bothered him to picture his father in a grave, cold and lifeless. He tried not to think of things like that. It made him feel sick to his stomach. He wanted to change the subject, but Stephanie was relentless.

"Stuart! Listen to me! I say Julia is screwin' that doctor!"

"You can't be sure of that. I mean, holding hands is one thing. You can't be sure she's sleeping with him."

"Boy, are you stupid Stuart! Or, maybe ignorant, because you don't know women. Maybe because you never fucked a woman."

That stung. Stuart felt ashamed enough for being gay. He had to defend himself, "That's not fair, Steph. I did take a few girls out. Once."

"But, did you ever fuck any of them?" Stephanie showed no mercy.

"Well, kind of ... "

"Ha! What do you mean, kind of? Either you did, or you didn't!" Stuart lowered his eyes. "No, I guess I didn't. I was too scared of girls. I always felt more comfortable with guys," Stuart admitted sheepishly.

"Anyhow, getting back to Julia ... "

"Yeah, getting back to the bitch!"

"Boy, you must really hate her! But I don't. Actually, I thought she was good for Dad. I think she probably added a few years to his life. He adored her. I saw it in his eyes when she walked into a room."

Stephanie was steaming. She resented Stuart's defense of Julia. She didn't want to hear that her father loved Julia. "Julia just had Dad snowed. And, I wouldn't be surprised if she and that Kramer guy were hanky-pankying on the side while Dad was still alive."

"Oh, I don't think so, Steph. Julia was very devoted to Dad."

"Shut up Stuart! You'll ruin our case! If we can prove that she and Kramer were sleeping together before Dad died, then, maybe we can even say that they collaborated on his death."

"Now, wait a minute! That's going a bit too far. What you're saying is ... murder! That they killed Dad. No, Stephanie, I don't believe that. I know Julia isn't that evil."

"Stuart! Do you want the house or not?"

"Yes ,I did. But, I won't lie."

"You don't have to lie. Bob Fredericks will word things in a way that you won't have to say anything but the truth. He's a sharp guy."

"What have you heard from him?"

"That's the one thing I hate about Fredericks. He's so god-damn slow. I called him a few days ago, and he told me that he's on the case, but, has been very busy. The usual crap excuse."

"Steph, wouldn't it be easier to just leave well enough alone? I mean, we got a lot of money from Dad's will. The house isn't necessary."

"Look, Stu, you don't have to do anything. Just leave it up to me."

## CHAPTER TWELVE: Allison

Allison Kramer walked down the ramp of a 727. She looked up at a sign that read: SAN FRANCISCO INTERNATIONAL AIRPORT PSA TERMINAL. Thank God, we made it, she thought to herself. She was tempted to bend down and kiss the ground.

She looked at her watch. It was 7pm. Her flight from LA was only supposed to take an hour. But, what an hour! Actually, her total time aboard the plane had been two hours. They were due at six.

Takeoff was late because of heavy traffic. The plane sat on the runway for more than a half hour. And then, about fifteen minutes before they approached the Bay Area they flew into a storm. Thunder and lightning caused the plane to rock from side to side. It felt as if it was turning upside down. The seat belt sign came on a lot.

An old lady in the seat next to Allison grabbed the plastic bag sticking out of the pocket in the seat in front of her, put it up to her face, and heaved a few times. Allison heard the bag filling up, and gagged. She had to turn her head away, toward the aisle. She couldn't watch the lady, nor did she want to look out the window. Looking down from so high was too scary, especially when she couldn't even see the ground below. Shortly after they took off, the pilot announced they would be cruising at an altitude of thirty-three thousand feet! Very high up!

Allison's white knuckles clenched the arms of her seat. She could feel her stomach churning. She frequently got diarrhea when she was nervous. She broke out in a cold sweat thinking about what she would do if she suddenly had to go to the bathroom and couldn't make it? Would anyone be able to tell? Maybe everyone would think it was the old lady who had pooped in her pants. She entertained herself with the thought.

Suddenly, the plane plunged as if it was falling out of the sky. Several passengers screamed. Allison reached for the other barf bag. She wondered how it would feel if the plane crashed, dropping down thirty-three thousand feet. Would she suffer, or would she die quickly? Would dying hurt?

She wondered how her father would feel if she died. Would he cry a lot for her? Would he ever get over losing her? Would he ever forget her? Allison pictured him crying at her funeral.

Then, she pictured his expression when he saw her strutting down the plane-way, looking beautiful, like a woman of the world. She was determined to live so she could see him again.

Andre and Allison hadn't seen each other in over six months. She crossed her fingers hoping he would like how she looked now. She wanted more than anything for her father to be dazzled by the woman she was becoming.

She had turned seventeen only a week before, and felt very grown up. She had to be. She had no other choice. Circumstances had forced maturity on her, particularly the abortion that she recently had. She felt as if she had aged three years in three weeks.

The turbulence finally ceased and the plane stabilized. The seat belt sign went off. Everyone on the plane breathed a sigh of relief. Allison reached into her purse and pulled out a small mirror. Studying her face, she rubbed her fingers across her cheeks to smooth the oil into her skin. Then, she applied her favorite brand of lipstick, Revlon. Lastly, she readjusted and fluffed her matted hair.

The pilot's voice came on the loud speaker again. Several people moaned. "Ladies and gentlemen ... the San Francisco Airport is covered with heavy fog, and so is Oakland. I've radioed San Jose, but it doesn't look clear there either. But, please folks, relax, sit back and have a drink on PSA. Please, tell the stewardesses what your destination is so we can call ahead to inform your connecting flight that we'll be a little late. But, before I head east towards Sacramento, I'm going to circle the airport for a while longer and stay in touch with the tower. They say there's a possibility the fog will lift soon. Maybe, if we wait a bit, we'll be able to land in San Francisco after all."

Allison shuddered. She always hated to fly. Shit! Now this. She thought, Great! I fly once in a blue moon and look what happens? And, I can't even have a drink! She was tempted to tell the stewardess that she was twenty-one so she could get drunk. Maybe, if she was drunk she wouldn't know it, or feel it if the plane crashed.

It was only about ten minutes later, but seemed like an eternity, when the pilot's reassuring voice came on the loud speaker once again, "Ladies and gentlemen, it seems the fog is steadily moving out to sea, so it looks like we'll be able to land in San Francisco in about five minutes. We're only an hour behind schedule! Sorry for the delay."

Every passenger yelled "Hurray!" and then applauded when the plane safely touched the ground. Who cared if it was an hour late? At least it landed. Allison vowed to take a train or bus back to LA.

When she saw her father standing by the gate, she quickly forgot the ordeal she had just gone through. Andre looked so handsome in his tan corduroy jacket, navy blue turtleneck sweater, and jeans. From a distance he could've passed for a college kid. A big smile came over his face when he saw his daughter in the crowd. She was so nervous she could feel her pulse increasing.

Allison took a second look and studied Andre for a few seconds. Something was different. What was it? Ah, he shaved his beard! That's why he looked so much younger than she remembered.

They hugged each other and kissed European-style, on both cheeks.

"Sweetheart, how are you? I was getting worried. How was your flight?"

"Awful! I don't ever want to fly again. I want to go home by Amtrak. I'll even go by bus if I have to."

"Oh, honey, I'm sorry. But, don't worry about it now. You've got four days. We'll decide later."

We'll decide! Allison couldn't believe her father. He still wanted to treat her like a baby. And, she was feeling disappointment that he didn't mention what a grown up woman she had become ... and he didn't notice how beautiful she was.

Andre, however, had noticed. He noticed that she was bigger-breasted and had fuller hips. He noticed that she was wearing mascara and lipstick, even though most of her mascara was smudged. She also skillfully covered her freckles with make-up, but he wasn't aware of the special tricks women use to hide their perceived flaws. He scanned her face wondering what had made her freckles disappear. He always loved them and was saddened to see they were gone. Allison hardly resembled the little girl he had last seen.

He fleetingly thought of the various stages of his daughter's short life. He remembered her as a newborn. How tiny and fragile she was. How protective he had felt the first time he held her. He thought of her childhood. How he had marveled as he watched her change literally from day-to-day. By the time she was seven she began to look more and more like her mother, even with her missing front teeth.

It shocked him to see how much she resembled her mother, now. In fact, standing there, she looked just like Lauren did when he first met her. Allison had the same strawberry blonde hair, green eyes, small pugged nose, and rose-tinged complexion. She looked like a typical Irish lass – no surprise.

Lauren's mother was of Irish descent. However, she had been adopted as an infant and was raised Jewish. Her adoptive parents were good to her. Yet, something always gnawed at her. Something always seemed missing.

From her first date with Andre, Lauren talked about feeling rejected. He never quite understood why she felt that way. As far as he could tell, Lauren's parents doted on her and loved her very much. They treated her well and provided a comfortable, affluent life style. She never wanted for anything. Nor could she deny that her parents cared for her very much. Nevertheless, she would often say, "It's not the same. I feel like a misfit, misplaced, like there's a missing link."

It wasn't until years after their divorce that he was able to understand Lauren's feelings. Through conversations with friends who had also been adopted, he learned that they, too, had similar deep-seeded feelings of rejection and abandonment. Of not ever feeling good enough.

In retrospect, Andre also understood Lauren's need to please. He realized that she was compensating for her deep feelings of inadequacy. Perhaps, being a "pleaser" made her feel more acceptable. He felt himself recoil with guilt.

For the first few years of their marriage, Lauren had waited on Andre hand and foot, catered to his every need, all of which he had taken for granted. Over their ten years together he rarely showed any appreciation of her giving nature. In fact, at times he found Lauren's behavior contemptuous. Andre wanted a woman he could respect, and felt that Lauren's obsequiousness was a sign of weakness.

Unfortunately, by the time he understood Lauren's pain, it was too late. Too much damage had been done in their relationship, and he blamed Lauren's insecurity and possessiveness. She was always fearful that he would leave her, as her birth mother had. It made her cling to him in a smothering way. Her dependency and jealousy eventually drove him away.

Momentarily, Andre felt an ache in his heart. He realized, that in spite of her shortcomings, he had loved Lauren very much. He felt disgusted with himself for not being more sensitive and understanding of her needs. It hurt him that he never understood her feelings of despair until long after they divorced. He regretted that he wasn't more mature, or a more reassuring and comforting husband.

His thoughts were interrupted by Allison's voice demanding recognition. "Daddy! I'm a big girl now! Look at me!" Smiling, she posed like a model standing on a runway.

"Uh, oh! Ah, yes. Honey, my gosh, you are quite a young woman, aren't you?" Andre looked Allison over from head to toe. "I can't believe how much you look like your mother."

Allison's smile turned in to a pout. A frown formed on her forehead. As if suddenly attacked, she looked wounded. Lashing out at her father, she shouted, "No I don't! She's old! And, ugly!"

Andre was jolted. He wished he had bitten his tongue before he said what he did. He hadn't given his words much thought and quickly realized it was inappropriate for him to voice those observations.

From the time Allison was a baby, she and Lauren had intensely competed for his attention. Andre never knew where their rivalry came from, or who started it. Since Allison was the younger of the two, he usually felt a need to side with her. It never dawned on him that Lauren, in a way, needed his love more than Allison. Defending and championing Allison only added to Lauren's jealousy.

Andre put his arm around Allison, "Oh, Honey, I'm sorry. I never meant to hurt your feelings."

"Forget it!" Allison said with a sulky expression. She reached into her purse and pulled out something that resembled wire on a handle. When she ran it through her hair, Andre guessed it must be some kind of new model hairbrush.

"Are you hungry, Alli?"

"Alli" was the endearing nickname her father always used when he wanted her to know how much he loved her. She knew it was his way of apologizing for comparing her to her mother. She decided to forgive him. Smiling seductively, she answered, "A little. Yeah, I s'pose I could eat. For a while I couldn't even think of food, I was so scared on that plane. But, yeah, now I'm starving. How 'bout Mexican? Know a good place?"

"Yeah. There's a great little authentic Mexican place not far from here, owned by some people from Guadalajara. They make the best tamales and enchiladas. It's about ten minutes away. Tell you what ... you go to baggage claim and I'll get the car and meet you right outside, OK? That is, ah, unless you have a lot of luggage or a heavy suitcase."

"Oh, no, I just brought a small bag and it's on wheels. I can manage. So it's a deal. I'll meet you outside." Allison was elated.

She hated sharing her father with her mother, or her brother. Now she had him all to herself.

CHAPTER THIRTEEN: Meeting Valenti

The cars on Sutter Street were crawling at a snail's pace. Julia couldn't believe there was so much traffic at that time in the morning, rush hour was usually between eight and nine. She looked at her watch, it was ten minutes to ten. Then at an address on a building. Her appointment with Isadore Valenti was at ten, and she still had four blocks to go.

What would Valenti do if she was late? Would he be upset with her? Would he yield his ugly face of power and reprimand her? Old, uncomfortable feelings of being "a bad girl" stirred inside her. She hated it when people scolded her for not being on time, particularly the nuns at school. They had a way of making kids always feel guilty. Julia felt her stomach churn.

"Hurry up, damn it," she cried impatiently as she honked the horn. The guy in the car ahead of her gave her the finger, and Julia yelled, "Shut up you ass!" It didn't matter that he couldn't hear her. Expressing her feelings made her feel better.

It seemed forever before the light finally changed. Julia wanted to drive straight ahead, but the only cars in front of her that weren't at a standstill were ones turning right. A parking lot caught her eye. She decided to follow the moving traffic and walk the four blocks to Valenti's office. It was a warm day and she wanted the exercise anyway. She liked smelling the clean, fresh air after the rain.

She drove her brown Mercedes into the underground garage. The attendant started to direct her to a level where there were vacant spaces. Paying no attention, Julia jumped out of her car.

"I'm in a big hurry ... I have to be somewhere in five minutes! Will you please park my car?" She handed the attendant a crisp ten dollar bill.

"Muchas gracias Senora. I do for you," the young man said as his grease-stained hand grabbed the money. His beaming smile indicated his appreciation.

Julia could see that the poor boy wasn't much older than twenty and already some of his front teeth were full of cavities. She wondered what he would do with the ten dollar bill. Would he spend it wisely, like at the dentist? She wondered about his future. Would he have other opportunities? Was he illegal? Would he grow old and weary working at this job?

Leaving the garage she ran towards Sutter Street and looked up at a large clock in an antique store window. It was ten o'clock on the nose. Shit! She hated to be late. Especially, for Valenti. She still felt intimidated by him from their phone conversation.

Out of breath from running, she finally arrived at a tall, white, modern building. The address was correct. Yes, this was the place. Thank God, her feet were killing her. High heels were not comfortable for walking in San Francisco, but she wanted to present herself as chic and business-like. Her toast-colored heels were the only pair of shoes that coordinated with her burgundy suit and beige blouse. She had to wear them even if they weren't ideal walking shoes.

Inside she read the registry. Valenti's office was at the top, on the 10th floor, suite four.

She looked at her watch again, ten after ten. She hoped Valenti was running late, too. Catching a glimpse of herself in the shiny silver mirror-like door of the elevator she readjusted her collar and ran her fingers through her hair. Anxiously, she watched the numbers above the door as they lit up, counting down. Six, five, four, three, two, first floor! Finally.

The door opened. Then out of nowhere, a tiny elderly lady appeared pushing a wheelchair with a white-haired old man sitting in it. His hands were shaking. Julia suspected he had Parkinson's. She held the elevator door so the old couple could enter. The old lady smiled, "Dearie … will you please press the bottom floor."

"Oh, this elevator is going up."

"Oh my. I didn't know that. Would you mind letting the mister and me go down to the bottom floor first? He has to go to the bathroom very badly and we were told that the restrooms in the basement are the only ones with doors wide enough for a wheelchair. Would you mind terribly?"

Julia did mind. But, she didn't have the heart to say no. Screw Valenti, she thought. He'll just have to wait.

"No, it's alright. I'll take you down." Julia wondered how long an elevator operator could remain sane. A job like that would drive her crazy.
It was twenty minutes after ten by the time Julia walked into Valenti's office. A pretty redhead receptionist looked up from the paper she was typing. "You must be Julia Forrester?" Well, at least Valenti remembered to tell his secretary that she went by Forrester, not Marlton.

"Yes, I am."

"Please be seated. Mr. Valenti will be with you shortly."

"Thank you." Julia sat down on a soft navy blue velour arm chair and picked up a copy of MS magazine. Leave it to Isadore Valenti to take out a subscription to MS, Julia thought. N.O.W. (the National organization for Women) was making a lot of news these days and Valenti was not stupid. He was just the type to capitalize on every situation and opportunity that he could. Always thinking ahead about his political ambitions. A sly fox.

Julia leafed through the pages and stopped when she saw an article by Germaine Greer. She remembered reading Greer's, The Female Eunuch, years before. It had influenced her immensely. She wondered if her unhappiness with Ralph began from that book. It certainly made her take a long hard look at herself and her marriage. She remembered how uncomfortable it felt when she didn't like what she saw in herself, particularly the "eunuch" Greer had described. Julia was like a castrated man, rendered impotent. That's how Ralph had her, under his thumb. She had no power, nor was she given any respect. She was, well, just there, part of the decor, and it didn't feel good. She felt like a worthless zombie, going through the motions of everyday living without any passion for life.

She had little sense of herself in those days. It still bothered her that she believed "a good wife" was submissive and servile. It reminded her she was still not strong enough to go against her upbringing. She was a product of the 1950s – the "happy days" when boy meets girl, they fall in love, get married, and "live happily ever after". What went wrong?

She recalled Betty Friedan's, "Feminine Mystique", which was actually the first book she read that planted seeds of discontent. It was probably the first book promoting women's rights that made the best seller list. Poor Betty Friedan. What a bad rap she got when her book was published. Julia remembered some of the comments made about Friedan – how she encouraged women to take over and rule men. Sexists said she had a "sour grapes" attitude, because no man would ever want her because she was fat and ugly. And, because of her perceived retaliation against men, she started her "dumb campaign". Dumb campaign alright! Friedan started a movement that fashioned a whole new era for women. Thank Goodness!

Julia glanced at the clock on the receptionist's desk. It was almost eleven! She had been waiting for close to forty minutes. After all that rushing and running. The balls of her feet were still stinging. That S.O.B. Valenti! Another one of his power trips. How timely it seemed for her to be thinking of Greer and Friedan and the liberation of women. Julia felt tense with anger.

The receptionist was chewing gum and seemed to be on a personal phone call, giggling. She thought Julia looked agitated because she was shifting from side to side in her seat, and sighing, she commented, "I'm very sorry Ms. Forrester, but Mr. Valenti had an unexpected call before you arrived. I'm sure he won't be much longer."

Ms. Forrester, hmmm ... Valenti has her well-trained. She doesn't look or talk like she has a brain in her head. But then, who knows? Maybe she actually reads MS. If she did, then why on earth would she work for someone like Valenti? Maybe she needs the money. Bet she's divorced and has several kids to support. Poor thing.

Julia faked a smile, "Oh, that's fine. I'm enjoying this magazine anyhow." God-damn-it! Why am I such a mealy mouth? Why can't I say what I really feel? I'm pissed off for having to wait so long – even if I was late. Then, Julia heard a buzzing sound.

"Oh, that's Mr. Valenti. That's to let me know he's ready for you. You may go in now."

"Thank you." Julia got up, straightened her skirt and walked towards Valenti's office door.

He was sitting in a reclining chair with his feet up on his huge mahogany desk, chomping on a cigar. When he saw Julia he laid his cigar in a ceramic ash tray and gave her a broad smile.

Julia hesitated by the door. She didn't notice Valenti's smile. She was too taken a back by the many wonderful modern paintings on the walls. They were large and brightly painted. Many were mixed media reliefs and the textures were astounding. Obviously, original works. Each one was more exciting and spectacular than the other. A true surprise to see in someone like Isadore Valenti's office. Julia never expected an uncouth guy like him to have such splendid and sophisticated taste in art. She would have predicted he'd be the kind who would buy "schlock art" – mass produced, stiff, and unemotional paintings bought to match his emerald green leather couch.

Seeing that Julia was studying his art collection, Valenti spoke up. "So, you like my paintings, eh?"

"Yes, I do, very much. I'm very impressed. You have excellent taste."

He looked pleased and lapped up the compliment. "Yes, I do have excellent taste. I know art. I visited some of my relatives in Italy and learned a great deal about The Masters. The Italians take pride in their history, in their immortal geniuses. Even the average peasant is passionate about art. Of course, most of the older generation prefer the Renaissance style, especially the works of Michelangelo, da Vinci, Botticelli, Rafael ... all those guys from way back. Some even before the Renaissance. Did you ever see the Sistine Chapel?"

"No, only pictures of it. I've never been to Italy, but I'd really love to be able to go someday."

"Just let me know ... " Julia gave Valenti a perturbed look and he seemed embarrassed. Wanting Julia to think of him as a gentleman, he quickly clarified his statement. "I mean, if you ever plan a trip to Italy, let me know and I'll tell you about all the important places to go. I know the best hotels and restaurants that are not tourist traps. I've been to Rome so many times I could be an official tour guide. I know that city like the back of my hand. And, believe me, it's not easy finding your way around all those piazzas."

Though Julia heard the word before, she wasn't exactly sure what it meant. "What are piazzas?"

"They're neighborhood town squares. The streets and alleys all end up in them. They're open courtyards and there's usually a church or a monument and outdoor cafes and restaurants. People congregate in the piazzas. They sing and dance and sell their wares there. You see, that's where all the action is in Italian cities and villages. Anyhow, as I started to tell you, it was my art education in Italy that turned me on to modern art, strange as that may seem. You see, going through the churches and galleries taught me to appreciate form and color, the purity and honesty of creativity."

"That's not strange at all. I totally understand. I'm an artist, too."

"You are?"

"Yes. I ... I've even had several solo exhibits."

"I'm very impressed Ms. Forrester, very impressed! Not only are you a beautiful woman, but talented, too. Marlton was a lucky man, to be married to you."

Julia lowered her eyes. She was uncomfortable handling this flattery, she mumbled, "Thank you".

"By the way, I apologize that I'm running late. When you didn't arrive at ten, I thought you had forgotten our appointment, so I returned my mother's call. She had called earlier and was frantic ... hasn't been well. She's in a home for the aging. Did you know they now call them "homes for the aging", not the aged? My mother fractured her hip a month ago and needed surgery. The doctors didn't think she'd make it. Old people like that die from broken hips because they can't move in bed and often get pneumonia. But, she has great fortitude. Guess it's from a lot of practice. She's a Holocaust survivor, you know. Spent two years in Auschwitz."

Julia ignored Valenti's comment about Auschwitz and wanted to get down to business. Not to seem uncaring, she commented, "I'm sorry. I hope your mother will be better soon."

She didn't feel angry with Valenti anymore. Nor intimidated by him. She was beginning to see that he wasn't such a bad person after all, and not lecherous like he was on the phone. In fact, he actually showed human qualities when he talked about his mother and the people of Italy. He seemed to actually have a sensitive side. Julia wondered if she had been too quick to judge him. Or was it possible she might be feeling warmer towards him because of his knowledge and love of art? She was always a sucker for anything related to art.

"Well, enough of my problems. You came here for my services, not vice versa. So, let's get to work. Here, come and sit down." Valenti pointed to one of the black enamel chairs opposite his desk, motioning for Julia to be seated.

"Yes, I'm sure you have a busy schedule ahead of you, and I'm curious to see what you've found out regarding my case."

"What I've found out Ms. Forrester ... look, may I call you Julia? I don't like formalities, and you may call me Izzie. OK?"

Julia hated formalities, too. But, she didn't want Valenti to get the wrong idea. She didn't want him to become too familiar. Nevertheless, she decided to take a chance. After all, if he was going to be her attorney and represent her, she had to trust him.

"Sure, you may call me Julia."

"Well, as I was saying, Julia ... I talked to Bob Fredericks and he said that the twins – Stephanie and Stuart? Am I correct ... told him you and Andre Kramer collaborated on their father's death."

"What! That's preposterous!"

"Fredericks says the twins told him you've been having an affair with Kramer. That you two probably planned this whole thing."

"That's insane! I loved Otto, and Andre Kramer also cared deeply for him. We are both still grieving for him."

"But, you are having an affair with Kramer?"

Julia turned red. "Well, ah, well, yes, I am, but ..." She put her head down. "But, I swear, it was not going on when Otto was alive. Andre and I only began seeing each other about a few weeks ago. Right after Stephanie called and said she and Stuart were going to sue me for Otto's house. I turned to Andre for help. It was right after I talked with you on the phone that Andre and I had dinner together to discuss this. And, well, things just happened."

"Yes, I know how that is sometimes." Valenti seemed almost fatherly. "But, how do we prove it?"

"Well, they aren't accusing us of murder, are they?"

"I don't know yet. They'll have to come up with some pretty damn good evidence to make an allegation like that. And, to prove it. It depends on how desperate they are ... how far they'll go. Or, what they'll stoop to. But, I have a feeling that Fredericks is trying to scare us, since they haven't served you papers yet. He implied that they might forget the whole thing and not press charges, if you turned the house over to them."

"Well, Mr. Valenti, ah, I mean, Izzie, I think Stephanie and Stuart are playing dirty. They want to make me sweat with a ridiculous accusation like that, but there's no way that I'll give in to them." Julia was furious. "It's not just that I want the house. Otto would be upset if I turned it over to them. He told me many times how he regretted spoiling them as kids. He loved them, but he felt they never learned the meaning of work or responsibility. He frequently had to rescue them by giving them money when they were in trouble. So, I couldn't let Otto down. I will fight them, and I'm not worried. I'm perfectly innocent, and so is Andre."

"Whose name is the house in?"

"Mine."

"Do you have documents?"

"Yes, I do."

"Bring them to me to look over, and any receipts that show how much money you spent on the house."

"Well, I made all the mortgage payments during the last three years, and I used my money to remodel the house."

"Good. That will all help. Hopefully, I can talk to Fredericks and get him to drop the case. But, if those twins claim that you and Kramer did their father in, you're going to have to come up with some good evidence to disprove that allegation. Though, I think, they too, will have a hard time proving foul play even if you and Kramer were having an affair on the side. But, don't worry, Julia, I'm confident that things will work out in your favor."

"Thank you." Julia wanted to hug Valenti but she was afraid he'd get the wrong idea.

"Will you please sign this contract stating that you have hired me to represent you?"

"Yes, of course. Julia hastily read the piece of paper stating Isadore Valenti had the authority and power of attorney to represent and defend Julia Forrester. In smaller print it read at a fee of $200 per hour. In beautiful cursive she wrote: JULIA FORRESTER on the dotted line, then stood up to leave. "I'll call you, say, in a day or so?"

"Wait a week. Let's see how serious they are. Maybe, I can convince Fredericks they're barking up the wrong tree. Better yet, let me call you after I talk to him."

Julia felt tremendously relieved when she left Valenti's office. He wasn't as bad as she had anticipated. In fact, her meeting with him was encouraging and she left feeling positive she had nothing to worry about.

As soon as she walked out of the room, Valenti picked up the telephone and dialed.

"Bob Fredericks? Isadore Valenti here."

## CHAPTER FOURTEEN: Meeting Julia

"Oh, Daddy! Do I really have to meet her? Do we have to go?"

"Allison, I told you Julia is a very nice lady. I'm sure you'll like her and that she'll like you."

"But Daddy, I was counting on us being alone," Allison exclaimed, indignantly.

Andre was aware of his daughter's need to monopolize his time during her short, four-day visit. He was also aware of her manipulative tactics. Kindly, but firmly, he reiterated what he had told her when she arrived from Los Angeles. "I know, baby, but I planned this evening with Julia weeks ago, before I knew you were coming. It's her birthday and I want to celebrate it with her."

With a sour expression on her face "How old is she anyway?"

"Forty four, I think."

"That's old!" Then realizing that her father was in his mid forties, she emphasized, "for a woman… she's probably full of wrinkles."

"Actually, Julia's in great shape. In fact, most people think she's a lot younger," he responded.

That was just what Allison didn't want to hear. Disregarding Andre's reply, she demanded further, "Is she pretty? Is she prettier than me?"
Andre knew his daughter was jealous and competitive. He also knew he had to tread lightly, so, he ignored her questions.

"Allison, I have always thought you were beautiful from the day you were born – from the moment I laid eyes on you. And, I'm still taken by your beauty."

Andre wasn't lying. He did think his daughter was a lovely young woman. He just wished she had a lovely personality to match her appearance. He wished she was more mature and not so self-centered. It took away from her looks. But, how could he tell her that without hurting her feelings? He breathed a sigh of relief when he thought about her abortion. Allison was far from ready to be a parent. She still had so much more to learn, and bringing a child into the world would have been disastrous for both her and the baby.

"Daddy, I asked if ... what's her name ... Julie? Is she pretty?"

"Her name is Julia, with an A, and yes, yes she is. She is a very attractive woman. And, she has the charm and warmth to go with her good looks. She's a very lovely person."

"Do you love her?"

"I, ah, I'm not sure yet. But, I like her very, very much."

"Are you going to marry her?"

"Possibly."

"Possibly! Daddy! I thought you'd never get married again. You said that after you and Mom got divorced!"

"Well, time changes things."

"Yeah, that leaves me out of your life, again!"

"That's not so, Allison. You will always be a part of my life, whether I'm married or not. And, if I do get married again, it doesn't mean I will care for you any less, or see you any less." Andre put his arms around his daughter and hugged her tightly.

She smiled slightly, momentarily reassured of her father's love. But, inwardly she wasn't as confident. She put on her London Fog trench, tied the belt impetuously, and grabbed an umbrella from the rack by the door.

"Well then, let's get on with it. But, I know I'm not going to have a good time and I won't like her." Secretly, Allison couldn't wait to scrutinize this new woman in her father's life. She was extremely curious to see what his taste was like. She wondered if Julia was going to be anything like her mother.

Andre knew he would be wasting his time trying to convince Allison that Julia was a wonderful person. He knew Allison would resent her more if he tried to build Julia up too much. He smiled at his daughter as he opened the front door for her to walk out first.

"We'll see," he said.

Andre hated driving in the rain, so he had called ahead for a taxi, which had just arrived. Like a gentleman, he held the back door of the cab open so Allison could get in before her hair or clothes got wet. He was sure she wanted to make a good impression. Allison was very vain. "Saint Francis Wood, please," he directed the driver.

The cabbie drove through all the puddles like a madman. Allison loved the ride. "Wow! What a fun ride this is," she exclaimed, as they seemed to fly up and over the steep hills.

Andre preferred a slower ride, and couldn't wait until they arrived safely at Julia's home. Nevertheless, he agreed with Allison. "Yeah, this is a lot of fun, isn't it?" He reasoned that if Allison enjoyed the ride, she might not be so negative towards Julia when they met.

They pulled into the circular driveway and Allison was star-struck.

"Ooh ... this is a cool place!" She wiped the steam from the window and poked her nose up against it. "Wow! What a fancy house. It looks like Beverly Hills ... like a movie star lives here."

The white colonial house looked important, and the grounds added to its impressiveness. Cypress trees lined the driveway and brilliant flowers framed the front entrance. A large marble statue of a female figure had been made into a fountain. Water was spouting out from a porpoise-like fish that the figure was holding.

While Andre paid the cab driver, Allison opened her umbrella. She didn't want her hair to get wet, or her make-up to get smeared. She was too self-conscious. Heaven forbid she not look her best when she met her new rival.

They rang the bell, and Julia opened the door Allison was totally shocked. She never expected Julia to be so beautiful, or as young looking. Allison studied her intently, wondering if she worked out to Jane Fonda tapes. The tight black wool jumpsuit she was wearing revealed Julia's firm hourglass figure. A red, yellow and blue scarf was tied loosely around her neck. The modern design on it made Allison realize Julia was no fuddy-duddy. Julia's blonde hair was pulled back tightly into a pony tail which helped accentuate her large, gold-loop earrings. Her face didn't look like it had a line or wrinkle and her light make-up was applied impeccably.

Allison looked down at the outfit she had on and worried if she looked alright. Did Julia think she was dressed properly? Was she wearing too much make-up? Allison had a habit of packing it on thickly.

Julia's softness and warm smile took Allison completely off guard. "Please come in. I am very happy to meet you, Allison." Julia extended her arm, then gave Allison a tender hug. "Your father has talked so much about you that I feel as though I know you. And, you are as beautiful as he said you were. Here, let me take your coat and umbrella."

Julia guided them into the adjacent living room, saying, "Let's visit for a bit before we go to the restaurant. I made some hors d'oeuvres and chilled this bottle of champagne to be ready when you got here." Julia popped the cork and poured a moderate amount in three glasses, not making any point of Allison's age. Until they "clinked" their glasses, Julia focused all her attention on Allison barely acknowledging Andre.

He was thrilled. Very impressed with Julia's graciousness and poise, and her attentiveness to Allison, Andre winked his approval.

Allison wasn't sure how to act in front of Julia, who seemed so natural and so at ease that it made Allison fidget. Trying to appear worldly and sophisticated, Allison groped for something to say. She looked around the living room and noticed the paintings. "I, uh, like your art work," she stammered. "Dad said you were an artist … did they take you a long time to do?"

"Julia smiled. "No, not exactly. I bought them. But, thank you for the compliment."

Julia chose not to embarrass Allison by informing her that most of the work was done by famous artists and most people with any knowledge of art would recognize who had painted each piece. She was already aware of Allison's awkwardness.

To break the ice, Julia deftly changed the subject, "I love the colors you're wearing. But of course, turquoise and lavender always look great on redheads."

"Oh, thank you." Allison blushed.

"You know, I always envied redheads. So, I've decided that when my hair gets too mousy, or too gray, I'm going to color it red. What do you think Allison? Do you think red hair will look good on me?"

"Oh, sure. You're so pretty, any color would look good on you."

Andre could not believe what he was hearing. Allison had become a lamb. Julia had her eating right out of her hand. At that moment he had the urge to take Julia into his arms and smother her with kisses. He was so pleased with how well they were getting along. Smartly, he decided to remain quiet.

"Allison, your father said that you work and go to school. I'm impressed. It must be difficult for you. I was never able to do that when I was your age."

"Well, uh, yeah, it is. I mean, nah, it's nothin'. I mean, it's a cinch 'cause school is pretty easy."

"You must be very intelligent."

"Well, yeah, I guess so. I make the honor roll most of the time."

"Perhaps, if you didn't have a job, you would make the honor roll all the time," Julia countered.

"Yes, I would." Allison lied. Work didn't take that much away from her studies. Brett, her boyfriend did. If she didn't goof off so much with him maybe her grades would be better. But, she didn't want to bring up Brett. That asshole. He got her pregnant and then, like a coward, ran off and left her to take care of everything all by herself. With that awful abortion done and over with, well, now she was going to play hard to get. She was going to get him jealous by flirting with Tommy Hartford, his best friend. That'll show Brett! That'll teach him a lesson!

When school was mentioned Andre had a hunch that the conversation might be getting sticky for Allison. He knew she was bored with school talk, so he intervened, "Well, Alli, what would you like to eat tonight?"

Even though it was Julia's birthday, Andre wanted to make the evening a special treat for Allison as well. It was their last night together because she was leaving late the next afternoon. He knew Julia understood. Her agreeable, easy-going nature was what had attracted him to her from the first time they met.

"Dad! It's Julia's birthday! She should decide!"

Andre nearly fell off the chair.

"Why thank you, Allison," Julia said graciously. "But, it isn't that important to me, and since you are our out-of-town guest we would like you to choose. What is your favorite kind of food?"

Allison had never been treated with such respect and equality in her life! By her Dad, yeah, a lot of the time. But, most adults treated kids in a put-down way, like because they were older and knew better. She hated that about her mother and her mother's boyfriends.

Julia seemed different. Allison decided Julia was OK in her book.

"I love Chinese food," she declared.

"Well, I do too! So, it's settled." Julia looked over at Andre and pointing to the phone asked, "Andre, why don't you call the Imperial Palace and see if they can take us in an hour? They shouldn't be too crowded on a week night."

"Right on," Andre said as he lifted his thumb of approval.

Julia took Allison's arm, directing her out of the living room. "How would you like to take a tour of the house before we go?"

"Oh, Julia, I'd love it!" Allison beamed, a wide smile came over her face. Her father told her that Julia had been married to the famous author, Otto

Marlton. A few of Allison's friends had read some of Marlton's "dirty books", and she couldn't wait to go back to school and brag that she had been in Otto Marlton's house.

CHAPTER FIFTEEN: Marty

The only parking space Stephanie could find was on Castro Street. Stuart lived just a few blocks away on Diamond. It was a nice day so she didn't mind the walk. She wanted to lose some weight anyway.

As she headed towards Stuart's, she began to feel repulsed and uncomfortable. She hadn't been in "the Castro" in months and had forgotten how blatant some of the men were. It wasn't that she was prejudiced or anything. After all, her brother was gay and she loved him. She didn't have anything against gays. But, the guys on Castro were so flagrant – ostentatious freaks – so flamboyant in their behavior and dress.

Stephanie thought she'd been around and seen a lot. She even considered herself worldly and sophisticated. Very little really shocked her. Even the guys who were standing on the corner  French kissing and feeling each other's crotch were no big deal. But, the one guy, who was dressed in black leather and chains walking his lover down the street like a dog on a leash was too much for her to look at. She was vicariously embarrassed for them.

Stuart opened the door. Stephanie could tell by the frown on his forehead he was worried, and could tell by the way the house looked that something was wrong. Stuart was usually a fastidious housekeeper and the place was a wreck.

"I came as soon as I could, Stu. How's Marty?"

"Terrible! He's got pneumonia now, still running high fevers and coughing even though he's on antibiotics. He's awfully depressed too, won't eat or drink anything. He's been sleeping a lot, but when he's awake he just sits and stares into space. Says he has nothing to live for." Stuart began to sob. "He says he wants to kill himself, Steph."

"When did he first talk about suicide?"

"Yesterday. Four days ago I took him to the doctor and they took an X-ray. That's when they diagnosed the pneumonia and they told him he has that AIDS disease. His immune system is shot and there's no cure."

"So, what does that mean?

"It means, Steph," Stuart lowered his head and whispered, "that Marty's going to die."

Stephanie never expected this. She had heard a little about AIDS being a serious illness, but she had no idea it was that serious.

"How long does he have?"

"The doc says it's already in the advanced stage. He's not giving Marty more than six months."

"Six months! Jesus Christ! That's depressing. Oh, Stuart, I'm so sorry."

"Yeah, me too. It really hurts. I love Marty so much, and there's nothing I can do. I feel so helpless." Stuart's lips quivered as he spoke, his face was pale.

"Where is Marty?"

"Up in his bedroom. He refuses to leave. I take food up to him, but he won't eat anything."

"Maybe I can put some sense into his head." Stephanie said as she hurried up the winding staircase toward Marty's bedroom. She'd been to their house many times and was familiar with the layout.

She knocked on the door and a few seconds later heard a faint response, "Come in."

When she saw Marty lying in bed she couldn't believe how much he had changed in the two months since she had last seen him. His skin was ashen gray and she could see many pussy lesions on the parts of his body not covered by his pajamas. She could tell he'd lost a tremendous amount of weight. His face was drawn and his bones were more prominent.

Stephanie faked a smile. In her most cheerful tone she said, "Hi Marty, how're ya doin'?"

He looked up at her, his eyes were glassy and his voice was strained. He whispered, "Not so good, Steph. It's pretty bad, you know. I have a hard time breathing."

"I know Marty. I know how badly you must feel. But, you have to try … you have to have hope. You … "

Marty interrupted, "Steph, it's all over for me - there is no hope. I'm a goner." He turned over, put his face into the pillow and began to cry.

"Now, Marty … that's nonsense! There's always hope. You never know when a miracle might happen. Researchers are always coming up with new drugs and new treatments. You have to hang in there."

Marty sat up. His face was tear-stained and he looked angry. "It's easy for you to say. You don't have an incurable disease. You're not dying!"

"That's not so, Marty. I am dying too. Everyone is. Every person has an incurable disease called life. Death is what eventually happens to every living being."

"It's not the same. You don't know when you're going to die. But, I do. And, it's only a few months away."

"You're right, I don't know when I'm going to die. And, neither do you. I could die before you do. I could walk out of this house and get hit by a car.

No one ever really knows when the jig's up."

"That's true, Steph, but at least you feel good. Me ... I feel like shit!"

"Maybe part of that feeling is your attitude. Maybe if you ate something or did something besides vegetate in bed you might feel better."

Stephanie knew she was being harsh, but it was the only way she knew how to help poor Marty. "You know, it's the quality of life that's important and what's ironic is that you're depressed about not having long to live. Yet, you've given up living. What you want most ... life, is what you're denying yourself."

Stuart had just walked into the room carrying a tray of food. "She's right you know, Marty. Didn't I tell you Steph's a tough one ... she wouldn't give you any sympathy, right? And, she'd give you a kick in the ass instead. Here, try to eat some of this salad I made and drink this chicken broth. It might make you feel better. Didn't your Jewish mother always say that chicken soup was the cure for what ailed you? So, drink it. You've got to have nourishment to get your strength back."

Stephanie smiled. Leave it to Stuart, she thought. He was always a Jewish-mother type. Always caring, always wanting to please. She could see how he was trying to be the "good wife".

Obediently, Marty sat up allowing Stuart to place the tray of food on his lap. Marty's energy seemed slightly restored. His voice was a tiny bit more energetic. Stephanie's philosophical words had released some adrenalin in him.

"I can see what you're saying Steph, and you're right, I have been wallowing in self-pity." He perked up slightly as he drank the warm broth. Still, he looked defeated and distressed. "But ... ," a tear ran down his cheek, and he began to sob, "I'm scared, oh God, I'm so scared. I mean, fuck ... I'm only thirty-one for Christ's sake. I wasn't counting on dying this young. It's hard, you know ... damned hard to face."

"I know," Stephanie softened. She put her hand on Marty's shoulder. "Marty, I know how hard it must be, but what're your alternatives? You can give up and just lie there wasting away, or you can try to lick it, get as much out of life as you can."

She looked over at Stuart who was also crying. "Stuart and I will help you. We'll do anything and everything we can."

Stuart's voice was barely audible. "She's right, Marty. We'll stand by you. We'll be your support system ... because ... " Stuart bent over and hugged him tightly, "I love you Marty. Oh, I love you so much."

Stephanie couldn't watch these two lovers. Their pain stirred up so many uncomfortable emotions in her. Tears welled up in her eyes and she left the room. She wasn't one to cry openly, or publicly. She didn't like revealing her feelings, which to her was a sign of weakness. She needed to keep her "tough-girl" image intact, even if it was a facade.

She sat down on the brown couch in the living room and lit up a joint. Taking a deep drag she wondered how she would really feel if she was in Marty's shoes. Stephanie knew in her heart she would never be able to deal with a deteriorating disease like that. She'd kill herself first. She hated to lose control, or be dependent on anyone. There was no way she'd allow herself to be at the mercy of anyone.

So, why am I encouraging Marty to fight for his life? Why not just let him kill himself? She pondered the issues of euthanasia, an individual's right to take his own life. Wouldn't Marty be better off dying, instead of suffering for the next six months? Or, going through the torture of this mental anguish?

Stephanie knew she was being a phony when she said all those things to Marty. But, she didn't know what else to do or say, especially in front of Stuart who was so fragile. She hated seeing him falling apart. She had been protective of him ever since they were kids, and always intervened to rescue him by trying to solve his problems.

Stuart came down the stairs a few minutes later. "Marty's asleep now. Thanks, Steph. He ate more than he's eaten in a week. So, you think he has a chance, huh?"

She couldn't face Stuart and lie. She laid out a small piece of rolling paper and sprinkled some marijuana onto it. She knew she already had a rolled joint in her purse, but this was an excuse to distract her from having to look at Stuart. "Hell, sure, he'll make it," she said as she licked the paper and sealed the joint. "Marty's always been a strong guy. I'm … I'm sure this is just a phase, an acute attack. I've read that if you can survive the first couple of weeks, you can beat AIDS."

Stephanie was outright lying. She had never read a damn thing about AIDS, and hardly knew any of the current statistics. In fact, she never realized how serious an illness it was.

Stuart brightened. "Really Steph? You really think Marty will make it? Even though that doctor said he only had six months?"

"Look, Stuart," Stephanie said slightly defensive. "I'm no doctor, nor am I God, but neither is the doctor God. He doesn't know everything, even though most doctors act like they do. It really pisses me off when doctors predict when someone is going to die. Even if Marty does only have six months to live, his doctor should never have told him that."

"Yeah. Marty went downhill fast right after that doctor gave him the bad news. Marty wasn't that sick until then. Then he got pneumonia and the sores got worse because he was bed-ridden, and, well ... you saw how weak he is."

Stephanie could see that Stuart was hanging onto her every word of encouragement, and her deceitfulness bothered her. "Stuart, you must also prepare yourself for the worst."

Stuart blanched. "But, Steph, you said ... "

"I know what I said, and, well, I meant everything I said. We must encourage Marty to have hope, and we also have to have hope. Then there might be a chance he'll go into remission. And, if he does, well, maybe he could live a few more years."

"A few more years! Jesus Christ, Stephanie ... I thought you were saying he could be cured?"

"I never said that. If I implied it, I'm sorry. I don't know what the future holds for Marty, or for you, or for myself for that matter. But, we all have to go on living until we die."

Stuart wasn't listening. His head was buried in his hands. "What am I going to do if Marty dies?"

"You'll just have to deal with it, Stuart. Get on with your life."

"No, I won't want to live anymore either. I'll kill myself if I don't have my Marty."

Stephanie's heart sank. If Stuart committed suicide she'd never forgive herself. Even though he was her twin, she felt like he was her baby brother and she loved and needed him. She slapped him across the face. "Don't you ever say that again!", she reprimanded.

The sting of Stephanie's hand jolted Stuart, "I, I'm sorry. I'm getting too emotional."

"So ... ," Stephanie continued, "let's change the subject, OK? Besides, I wanted to tell you about the bitch ... "

"Julia?"

"Yes. Bob Fredericks says he spoke with her attorney. I think he said it's Isadore Valenti, and ... "

"Isadore Valenti! Fuck, Steph! He's supposed to be one of the best. Didn't he prosecute Don Whitehall?"

"Yes, he did, but that was a couple of years ago. Then he had a heart attack and didn't work for a while. Then he joined some group and he'll take any case he can get. He used to be a prosecutor, but now, sometimes he's a defense attorney. He's gotten less popular since that Whitehall case and supposedly he's not that sharp anymore. I heard he had a stroke too, which affected his memory. Fredericks says we don't have to worry, that Valenti is on his way out."

"So, do we have a case or not?"

"Of course we do! We're charging Julia and that chiropractor boyfriend of hers with conspiring to do away with Dad."

"Do you really think they did?"

She ignored his question. "Well, it seems pretty suspicious to me that right after Dad's death she got so lovey-dovey with that doctor."

Suddenly, a loud bang came from upstairs. Jumping out of his seat, Stuart frantically ran up to Marty's room. Stephanie was right behind him.

Marty was still in the upright position that Stuart left him in, except he was slumped over. Blood was gushing from his head. Stephanie noticed a small revolver lying next to his right hand.

Stuart dropped to the floor on his knees and bellowed out a wail, "Oh my God!  Oh my God!"

## CHAPTER SIXTEEN: Lake Tahoe

Julia paced around the living room like a wild animal in a cage. She took a long drag from her More cigarette, then crushed it into an ash tray she had sculpted that was shaped like a cupped hand. She flopped on the sofa, looked up at the tall oak grandfather clock. Shit! Where is he? He was supposed to be here an hour ago.

Andre had awakened her at seven in the morning. Julia was in a deep sleep when the phone rang. Still groggy, she recognized Andre's voice, "I just wanted to remind you that it's a four hour drive to Tahoe, and I made dinner reservations for seven thirty. So please be ready when I get there at one."

When Julia was fully awake, she wondered if Andre had really called her, or if she had been dreaming. It seemed odd that he would call her at 7am, six hours before he was due to arrive.

The grandfather clock chimed twice. Julia got up from the sofa and walked over to the window. It was drizzling. The steam on the window made everything look foggy. She went to the front door, impatiently opened it and looked out hoping Andre's car would suddenly appear. Nothing. She decided to pass the time by calling Suzie.

Julia hadn't seen Suzie since that stormy night they spent in Inverness together. The night Otto died. Suzie had gone on a four-month trip to Europe right before Otto's funeral. Apparently, she had just returned because she had left a message on Julia's answering machine the day before.

The phone rang six times. Julia was about to hang up when she heard Suzie's out-of-breath voice, "Hel ... Hello."

"Suzie, it's me, Julia. I hope I didn't catch you at a bad time."

"Julia! Oh no, I was just exercising on my bike." Panting, she continued, "Julia, it's so good to hear from you, I'm really sorry I wasn't there for Otto's funeral, but, you know, I had my airline ticket and had to leave two days before."

"Suzie. Don't worry about it. Everything worked out alright, like it does. Like you always told me it would."

"So, how are you?  How are you feeling ... after that ordeal?"

"I'm fine. Well, actually I'm not fine. Right now I'm really kind of perturbed."

"With me?"

"Good gosh, no. It's Andre. Andre Kramer ..."

"Andre? Andre Kramer? That chiropractor dude?"

"Did he cancel your appointment or something? Are you sick?"

"No, nothing like that. Andre and I have, a, well … we've been having an affair, and … "

"Really? God, I guess I have been away a long time. So, tell me. I'm all ears. When did this all start? Why are you angry with him?"

"It's kind of a long story. I don't have time to talk about it now. See ... Andre and I are going up to Lake Tahoe for a few days. He's due here any minute. Actually, he was due here an hour ago."

"An hour ago? Why is he so late? Did he call?"

"No, he didn't call. And, I don't know, but I'm really furious ... and, also getting worried. Maybe he had an accident."

"Is he usually prompt?"

"Uh, yes, I guess so – come to think of it I never really paid that much attention to that."

Suzie laughed. "Yes, I know … that's why this is humorous. Forgive me for laughing, but of all the people I know you're the least concerned with time."

Julia laughed slightly with Suzie. "Yes, I suppose you're right, I'm usually not bothered by tardiness, but Andre woke me up at seven this morning to remind me."

"Why did he have to remind you? I'd kill the son-of-a-bitch! Calling at seven in the morning! Especially, you! I know how you love to sleep in. What does he think you are a child or something?"

"No, no Suzie, don't misunderstand, Andre doesn't treat me that way. He respects me and he's usually very considerate. Which is why I'm starting to get worried."

"Julia, I know Andre very well, after all, I was the one who recommended him to Otto, and well, apparently you and Otto really liked him. But, waking you up at seven in the morning sounds controlling to me. What an ungodly hour!"

Suzie was used to sleeping until ten, so Julia wasn't sure how objective she was being. "You think so? You think that's controlling?"

Before Suzie could reply, the door bell rang. Julia glanced at the clock, it was a quarter after two. It looked like Andre's shadow through the glass in the front door. "I think it's Andre, Suz, look, I'll call you when I get back. We have a lot to catch up on, OK.?"

"OK, but don't let him try to run your life, or you'll be sorry."

"Don't worry, I won't."

Andre acted as though nothing had happened. "Hi, ya ready?" he asked with a big grin.

Ignoring his question, Julia hesitated, then coldly asked, "Where have you been? I was really getting worried about you. You're over an hour late!"

"Oh, you know how it is, I had a lot of last minute stuff to do and the traffic driving over here was really heavy. What time is it anyway?"

Andre! It's two fifteen! You were supposed to be here at one!"

"Was I? Uh, yeah ... but ... I said I'm sorry."

"You did NOT say you were sorry. And, look, I really don't care what time we leave for Tahoe. But, why on earth did you have to call me at seven o'clock this morning to remind me to be ready at one?"

"Well ... 'cause we hadn't talked in a few days and I wanted to make sure you hadn't forgotten."

"But, why at seven? Why didn't you call last night, or at least wait until nine or ten this morning?"

"I was afraid you might not be at home last night and maybe you had some errands to do today."

Andre grabbed Julia, hugged her tightly and said, "Hey, relax already, don't be so uptight. I said I was sorry." He kissed her passionately. Melting to his warmth and touch, Julia's anger faded. She decided it was stupid to argue over something as trivial as the time.

The drive across the Bay Bridge was bumper-to-bumper. It was a quarter to three. Julia stretched her neck to see if anything was delaying the traffic. She looked up at the Berkeley hills, a thin brown layer of smog was settling over them.

"Do you see anything ahead, Andre?"

"No, guess it's just that time of day. A lot of people get off work between two-thirty and three."

"Damn it! Now, by the time we get to Sacramento it'll be rush hour!"

"Will you relax, Julia. We have a four hour drive ahead of us." Andre smiled. "But, at least I have good company." He reached over and patted her hand. Julia forced a smile back.

"So, what's happening with that law suit?"

"I was served papers the other day. I have another appointment with Valenti in a few days, the day after we get back from Tahoe. I had to dig up old receipts from the house. He needs them to prove I paid for most of the remodeling and furnishings, besides a lot of the mortgage payments during the last couple of years."

"Allison was quite impressed with your house. You're very creative. She also liked you very much which surprised me because she is so critical and competitive with her mother."

"Thanks, I liked Allison too. Yes, the house needed a lot of work. Re-modeling it was quite a challenge and shopping for the furnishings took years."

"It didn't seem like it was that difficult for you. Creativity seems to come naturally to you."

"Actually, it doesn't come that naturally."

"Still, I couldn't do what you do. I don't think I have a creative bone in my body."

Julia laughed. A chiropractor would refer to his bones. "That's not so", she disagreed, "I think everybody is creative in their own way. I think creativity is inborn."

"Maybe, but it takes talent too."

"It's not talent. People who are more creative are just more right-brained."

"What does that mean?"

"Right-brained people are more intuitive and imaginative, while left-brained people are more intellectual and analytical. Actually, everyone is a combination of both. But, some people have a tendency to lean more one way or the other."

"How scientific is all this stuff anyway?"

Julia resented that Andre didn't take her word without a scientific explanation. Nevertheless, she bit the bait trying to prove her point.

"I read about a study done at UCLA, about people who've had brain surgery. The ones who had the right hemisphere removed were almost emotionless, whereas, those who had the left part removed sat and cried all day. Artists and teachers have talked and written about the right brain personality for years, and now it's being proven scientifically."

Julia lost her enthusiasm for the conversation and stopped talking. She realized that she was still feeling annoyed with Andre for being late.

Then she looked over at his profile. He was so damn appealing. It was difficult for her to stay angry with him, especially after he had kissed her so passionately when he picked her up. Just looking at him made her horny. She couldn't wait to be in bed with him. It had been too long.

Allison had taken up a lot of Andre's time during her visit. It had been over a week since she and Andre made love. From the first time they had sex, they slept together a few times a week. And, every time making love was as spectacular as the time before. Julia felt a throbbing between her legs as she remembered the multiple orgasms she always had with him.

"Julia, why did you stop talking? Is something wrong?"

"No, I was just thinking."

"About what?"

"Oh, nothing much. Just tripping out," she answered abruptly. Her annoyance with Andre was returning. Why did he have to invade her thoughts? Why couldn't she have some privacy?

But, she said nothing, remembering that every time she argued with Ralph she lost. She hated confrontations. It just wasn't worth the time and energy. Instead she stewed, wondering if she had a right to be angry? Was she still in a bad mood from the morning? Was she looking to nit-pick? Ralph had frequently accused her of that.

Andre sensed Julia's anger. He was sure he hadn't done anything wrong, so he concluded that she was probably having pre-menstrual symptoms. Otherwise, it wasn't like her to be snippy. Damn! Maybe she was menstruating. That would make sex messy. He decided it was best to be quiet and say nothing.

For almost an hour they sat in silence. When Andre finally spoke he remarked, "Hey! We're almost empty. We've got to stop for gas. Are you hungry? Wanna get a snack?"

"Well, yes, I could have a bite. Seven-thirty is a long time away."

"Oh shit! That's right. I made reservations tonight at Le Cheminee. We'd better not eat now. We'll spoil our appetites." Andre looked at the dashboard clock, it was almost five. "Besides, we don't have time to eat. Sacramento is supposed to be a two hour drive to Tahoe."

Julia liked to take in her surroundings in new places. She looked forward to perhaps relaxing in a hot bath after a long drive, taking her time getting dressed for the evening. She had also fantasized about making love before they went out.

"Andre, we'll never make it. We'll barely get there and we'll have to leave immediately for the restaurant. Why don't you call them while the attendant is gassing up the car and change our reservation for tomorrow night?"

"No! We can't do that Julia! Le Cheminee has a waiting list of several weeks. If we don't go tonight, we won't be able to get a reservation on this trip."

"Well, it doesn't matter to me if we go there or not."

"But, Julia, I read rave reviews about Le Cheminee in one of those restaurant guides and my friend Howard said it was the best cuisine in the world. Howard travels a lot, so he's a good authority, and he said the food was superb and the atmosphere's very charming and romantic. We have to go there!"

"Andre, I thought this was supposed to be our special getaway, not a study of restaurants. I came on this trip to be with you, not to go to Le Cheminee. I'm sure Tahoe has other fine restaurants."

"Yeah, sure, but not as renowned. Look Julia, let's see if we can make it, OK?"

"OK." She could see from his enthusiasm that Andre seemed to have his heart set on having dinner at this particular restaurant. It was no big deal to her if they went out to eat first. Perhaps a romantic restaurant would enhance her mood. She reminisced about the first time she and Andre had dinner together. It was so romantic, so titillating. And, afterwards, the sex ... well, the sex was the best she had ever experienced.

When they pulled out of the Chevron station and onto the freeway,

Andre slammed his foot on the gas pedal as if he was taking off in a race. Julia clutched the sides of her seat as her right foot automatically pushed down on an imaginary brake.

"Andre, please don't drive so fast! It's scary." She looked at the speedometer. Andre was barreling down the freeway at ninety miles an hour.

"Relax, I'm a good driver. I used to race motorcycles. Besides, it's a wide open road."

Again, Julia suppressed her feelings. She closed her eyes and said a little prayer hoping they would arrive at their destination safely. Then she dozed off. Whenever she felt disturbed, she relied on sleep as an escape. It postponed facing uncomfortable feelings.

She slept soundly for over an hour. When she opened her eyes they were climbing over the summit. The scenery was magnificent. The Sierra mountain range was abundantly framed with evergreens. Brilliant autumn hues of rusts and oranges shone through the dense green and further ahead some of the mountains were already snow-capped. She looked through the rear view mirror and saw the sun setting beyond the horizon. The sky was pink and large cumulus clouds were a deep purple. It made her feel romantic again. Dismissing the anger she had felt only an hour ago, she looked at Andre warmly. He was certainly an improvement over Ralph.

She thought about how miserable she was the one and only time she had been to Lake Tahoe, when she was married to Ralph. That was about ten years ago. She and Ralph had taken the children there to ski during Christmas vacation. Some vacation that was!

The crowds were unbearable. So was the noisy hotel where they stayed on the South Shore, at Stateline, Nevada. Ralph and the children were not much better. Julia could still hear their demands ...

"Maah ... buckle my boots."

"Maah ... help me put on my skis."

"Maah ... carry my equipment ... it's too heavy."

"Maah ... I'm hungry."

"Maah ... I'm tired."

"Maah ... maah ... maah!"

The cacophony of "maah-do-this", and "maah-do-that" rang loud in Julia's head. The kids never shut up. There were times that she wanted to scream. Times when she contemplated murder. But, as quickly as that "evil thought" entered her mind, she suppressed it.

Ralph didn't make her life any easier. He expected her to be super-woman, tending to all the children's demands. Yet, he treated her as if she was incapable of doing anything without his direction."

"Julia, make sure you don't get lost when you get off the elevator. Remember, turn right. Our rooms are 450 and 452."

"Julia, don't forget where the car is parked. It's in row F. Say it ten times so you'll remember."

"Julia, be careful who you talk to in the casinos. Tough people hang out at these clubs, especially colored people."

"Julia ... Julia ..."

Ralph had his share of prejudices which Julia never understood. She had grown up with black people and a lot of them were her friends. It bothered her that Ralph was such a bigot, but she never said anything to him. It was easier to keep her opinion to herself than arguing with him. Secretly, she saw him as an "Archie Bunker".

If it hadn't snowed for five straight days, Julia would have left Ralph and the children. Because of the snow storm skiing was not on the agenda during those days. She remembered how relieved she was. The last time she skied her whole body was still sore a few days after they returned to San Francisco.

Andre spoke, "Look Julia, look at Donner Lake, over there. Look how beautiful it is."

"I've never seen Donner Lake. At least, I don't remember. Yes, it is gorgeous, isn't it," Julia sighed. "I read about Donner Lake and the early pioneers who were stranded there. What a tragedy that was."

Distracted by the beauty, she began to paint the landscape in her mind. She did that often. If she memorized things, colors and shapes, it was easy to paint from her imagination. She did that with people too, she was an ardent people watcher. She never minded waiting in a place where there were various faces and body types. It helped her pass the time pretending she was sketching them.

"Wait until you see Lake Tahoe," Andre interrupted Julia's thoughts again. "It's even more beautiful than Donner Lake."

"I know, I came to Tahoe years ago. But, it was snowing so much that I couldn't totally appreciate the Lake's beauty. It was so cold and gray then." Julia wondered if her memories had anything to do with her marriage, which was also cold and gray then.

"Well, this weekend will be a memorable one. The weather is predicted to be mild, no precipitation is expected."

He hoped the next three days with Julia would be memorable. He felt like they hadn't spent much time alone and wondered if he would like Julia as much after they returned home. Would she still like him? He knew he wasn't the easiest person to get along with. Other women told him he was selfish, self-centered and controlling, though he never could understand why. He always thought of himself as a sensitive, considerate person.

They finally drove up to a cozy looking house right on the Lake that Andre had rented from a friend. It was painted white with dark green shutters. The front door had a mountain design carved into it. Large pine trees, bushes and shrubbery framed the panoramic view of the Lake. It was breathtaking. Julia wanted to study the scene so she could paint it later.

"Julia! It's five after seven! We'd better hurry! Le Cheminee is a ten minute drive from here. So, we only have about fifteen minutes to get ready."

"Yes, OK." Julia rushed into the house and threw her suitcase on the bed. She turned on the shower as she hastily got undressed. She longed to soak in a tub after that long drive, but knew it would take too much time. "Julia! You're wasting water! You shouldn't turn on the shower until you're ready to get in!"

"Oh, I didn't mean to ... but ..." It was useless to try to explain herself. Andre was right. It wasn't very ecological for her to use extra water. Feeling guilty, she quickly jumped into the shower. In less than five minutes she soaped and rinsed herself off. She rationalized that a quick shower made up for all the water she had just wasted.

It was exactly seven-thirty when they arrived at Le Cheminee. Julia felt like a wreck, as if she had thrown herself together. She hadn't had time to wash her hair and it felt gummy from old hair spray. Nor did she have time to press her dress, and was embarrassed by the wrinkles in it. Nevertheless, it did please her to see how happy Andre was.

The maitre d' welcomed them warmly, as though they were old friends, then promptly seated them at a candlelit table in the corner. Immediately a waiter came with a plate of interesting appetizers, a basket of warm French bread and two round butter dishes. One, he explained, was salted and the other unsalted. "A nice touch," Julia thought.

But, before she could even decide for herself, Andre picked up a piece of bread, buttered it, and placed it on her bread plate.

No date had ever buttered her bread before and she didn't appreciate it! Andre didn't even ask if she wanted bread, or butter for that matter. Or, if she liked salted or unsalted butter.

Julia felt her anger returning. But, she didn't want to ruin the evening, so she said nothing except, "Thank you, Andre", and faked a smile.

CHAPTER SEVENTEEN: Suzie's Advice

Back in San Francisco Julia felt drained. The weekend at Lake Tahoe hadn't turned out the way she expected it to. Nor did she think Andre was the same person she had fallen in love with. Even sex with him had not been satisfying those past three days.

She couldn't stop thinking about him and was troubled that her feelings were changing. She wasn't sure what to make of it all, or if she could even trust herself anymore. Nor was she sure what she was even feeling, except that most of the weekend she was annoyed with Andre.

Before going up to Lake Tahoe, she was convinced that Andre was the perfect man and he was what she had been searching for her whole life. He was sensitive, intelligent, loving and caring. She felt very comfortable with him. Besides being extremely compatible sexually, they shared many common values. And, laughter. Andre was certainly not deficient in wit or charm and had a wonderful sense of humor. Julia knew she could never be with a man who didn't have a sense of humor.

That was one of the qualities that had attracted her to Otto, especially after living with Ralph, who was so god-damn serious about everything.

He also condescendingly talked about the guys with long hair, saying they look like they stepped out of the bible. Julia never responded to Ralph's put downs. She thought those guys dressed in creative "costumes" instead of the "uniforms" conservative men wore, who looked like they stepped out of the "Godfather". She laughed to herself remembering the comment her mother often made, "uptight people wouldn't smile if they saw Jesus riding a bicycle". She thought that was funny, and now, living in San Francisco, that statement would be a reality. Half the men in San Francisco looked like Jesus with their long hair and beards and many of them rode bicycles. The mainstream public simply took these "freaks" for granted.

Julia thought of Andre again and searched her heart for his good qualities. She was sure he was not interested in her because she was rich. He made a good living and had a steady, substantial income. He took pride in his work. He was not the type to free-load. Julia knew, after Otto's death, that she had to beware of suitors whose only interest in her was her wealth. She was realistic enough to know that most men in her age group wanted younger women and she could fall prey to their monetary desires and ambitions.

Then she thought about Otto and the ironies of age. One of the biggest barriers between them was their age difference. If only he had been a younger man, perhaps they could have shared more physical activities together. And, of course, if Otto had been younger, perhaps she wouldn't be a widow now. Only several months ago she was considered the "young one" in Otto's circle of friends. Now at forty-four, she was considered "over the hill" by people only fifteen years younger. Julia thought she should be thankful that Andre was still fairly young and healthy. Besides being attracted to his mind, she could also enjoy his body.

As these thoughts went through her mind, she wondered had she been too critical of Andre while they were at Tahoe? Perhaps his bothersome habits reflected his insecurity being away from familiar territory. She heard people got weird when they were on foreign soil. Perhaps Andre's system reacted differently. Should she forget what had happened, chalk up the experience, and give him another chance?

They didn't say good-bye on the best note. In fact, Andre sensed Julia's iciness from the first night at Le Cheminee and seemed bewildered by it. He kept asking her if anything was wrong, but as usual, she didn't want to "make waves". She didn't want to be the one to spoil their "good" time.

Upon reflection, Julia realized that not communicating with Andre was exactly what had spoiled their time together. She was afraid if she told him how she felt they might have gotten into an argument. On the other hand, they might also have been able to air out their differences. How could she blame poor Andre for behaving the way he did if he didn't know what he was doing was bothering her? Deep inside she knew he had tried his best. Guilty for being so deceptive, she knew she had always been a coward when it came to any type of confrontation.

Her mother always called her a "bad girl" when she was little. To get her mother's love and approval Julia became "good", a model child and did what she was told, to be seen and not heard. She had learned to avoid saying what she felt even when it hurt. It was a price she was willing to pay because she was terrified of not being loved. When she behaved as she was "supposed to", her mother seemed pleased and affectionate, which gave Julia hope that her mother might really love her after all.

It seemed Ralph took over where Katherine left off. Ralph was really not a bad sort. A bore to talk to yes, but generally a likable guy. There were times when he was kind to her and treated her as if he loved her. But, like her mother, Ralph could be verbally abusive. Fortunately, unlike her mother he never laid a hand on her. Forgiving Ralph's faults, she nostalgically wondered if her marriage to him might have lasted if she had been a different person, if she had felt more sure of herself, and behaved with more confidence. If she was that kind of woman then, she wondered, would she have married Ralph in the first place?

Otto seemed to be everything Ralph wasn't. Initially, that was his most appealing quality. Otto wrote and spoke a good line – he was sincerely in favor of all people's rights, all ages, sexes, and racial and ethnic backgrounds. He was a champion of the underdog, of freedom and equality. However, few people besides her knew he was also a chauvinist.

Julia could still hear Otto's voice as he ordered her around, "Julia, call David Martin, tell him that I won't be able to see him tomorrow. Julia, call Alvin Marks, and set up a date for us to talk over my new manuscript. No, better yet, call my publisher first, ask him when he thinks the book will be out. Julia, don't forget to take my suit to the cleaners. By the way, lay out what you think I should wear today. I never know what to put on and you have such good taste. And Julia, don't make any plans next month. We have to go to Europe. I have several speaking engagements in London, Paris, and Geneva."

At times Otto treated her as if she was his secretary, not his wife. She wouldn't have minded if he had asked her, rather than told her what to do, or said, "please" and "thank you". Nor would she have had any complaints if he had asked her once in a while what SHE wanted to do. He seemed to take her for granted, giving her the feeling that it was her duty to drop everything and serve him and his needs. During their marriage, Julia felt her life was not her own, that she was required to live according to Otto and his schedule. She was usually agreeable and rarely complained. Yet sometimes she couldn't help but feel angry with him, which she never felt entitled to, and would quickly suppress.

Her marriage to Otto, nevertheless, was generally pleasant and a huge improvement over her relationship with Ralph. She still ached terribly when she realized she would never again hear Otto's words of wisdom, his funny ways of saying things so succinctly, and even his "orders" which now made her smile. Now, she understood it was all a part of who Otto was. She longed for his touch, for his love. Julia felt loved by him in spite of some uncomfortable feelings. So, she forgave him for the times she was annoyed with him, believing that he was the way he was because he was a product of an older generation with a different paradigm.

When she thought of Otto she relived her own mortality and it frightened her. Her life was probably half over and she wondered where was she headed. Forget where she was going … Where had she been? Who was she?

Most of her past life seemed a blur. Everything seemed to have happened quickly, too quickly for her to fully grasp its true meaning. Julia had a lot of random feelings which, intellectually, didn't make sense. Sometimes when she was confused she feared she might be losing it and going out of her mind.

Her thoughts of Andre returned, and she toyed with the question: did she really love him? What if he was just filling a gap in her life? She hadn't been alone for more than a few months after Otto died before she and Andre got involved, which made her feel as if she was cheating on Otto.

Even though they had separate residences, she and Andre spent many nights together. Julia hadn't experienced living alone for more than a few days at a time. She questioned whether she was capable of living independently. She had spent most of her life living with other people. First, with her parents, then in a girls' dorm, then with Ralph and their children, and lastly Otto.

Thoughts of her divorce from Ralph and how her children were upset haunted Julia with sad, guilty feelings. At the time of the divorce she thought the children really didn't need her. The boys, Brad and Charlie, she reasoned, needed Ralph's money and approval more than hers. Sandra, being the princess that she was, wanted to live with her father and remain in the "big house" where she could throw parties. It had hurt Julia when the children called her selfish. Selfish? Good god, she had spent close to eighteen years catering to their every need and demand. Many times she canceled her own plans, or postponed what she wanted to do, to be a good wife and the perfect mother.

Three children were a handful. It seemed as if a major portion of her life was driving them everywhere – to doctors, dentists, classes, birthday parties, sporting events, you name it. Seeing to it they received a good education, which meant belonging to stupid committees, listening to dry, boring lectures. Being the referee when they fought. Listening to their silly, spoiled demands. Pajama parties and the screams of pillow fights that kept her awake most of the night. The messes the next day that she cleaned up. The agony she went through when they were sick. The worry when they learned to drive. The rest of the time – what time? – she was taking care of the house, seeing to it they had physical comforts and proper, nourishing meals.

What appreciation did she get? None! Her children were wrapped up in their own lives and were probably still angry with her for breaking up their home. They barely talked to her, or visited. They had a closer relationship with Ralph now, who had previously been the absent parent. Or, at least that's what Julia assumed when Sandra called and said, "Daddy and I are going on a trip together to Cabo San Lucas", or "Dad bought me a new car". That stung. Julia had tried countless times to include her children in her new life with Otto, but it seemed their schedules never coincided with hers. She was often out of town with Otto when the children had time off from school, during holidays, or summers. The few times they did visit her in her new home, the strain was unbearable. It was obvious Otto was jealous of them, and they of him. Otto revealed his feelings by being cold and un-friendly, and the children retreated from him. They seemed afraid of him and Julia sensed they could never understand why she left their father for this "old fart".

Now, Julia was free physically, but mentally she still felt trapped. It was as if she had just been released from prison and didn't know which direction to turn. Her thoughts wandered to Suzie, who could usually make her feel better. Suzie was an inspiration, a source of strength, being the most honest, liberated woman Julia had ever known.

The two women had completely opposite lives and personalities. Suzie never married, nor did she have any children, which seemed odd and chal-lenging for Julia to relate to. As long as she could remember, Julia wanted a husband and longed to be a mother. It never entered her mind to do any-thing else.

Suzie was a career woman for the eighteen years they were friends but was still somewhat of an enigma to Julia. Suzie was very attractive to men and had many suitors. When she was unhappy in a relationship, however, she never groveled or was defensive. She took full responsibility for what she said or did, and when a guy didn't "get it" she had little patience. She'd simply tell him, "Figure it out!" Then she'd bow out of the relationship not wasting any more of her time.

Suzie was very sociable and often the life of the party. People genuinely liked her and gravitated towards her. Yet, she was dependent on no one. Nor, did she ever live with anyone. That was the way she preferred it. She often remarked, "I live in the present, according to how I feel at the moment." Yet, because she was very kind and caring of other people, strangely enough, Suzie was able to pull off her autonomy without alienating anyone. Instead, people respected her and never tried to take advantage of her or tell her what to do.

Julia wondered if she could ever be like Suzie. Could she ever be her own person? Could she ever be that autonomous? Was it possible to live life one day at a time? The thought was scary.

But why not? It could be a challenge, a new, exciting way of experiencing life. She felt a slight adrenalin rush, walked over to the phone and dialed Andre's number.

CHAPTER EIGHTEEN: The Law Suit

"Well, tell that son-of-a-bitch to get his ass in gear!" Valenti screamed and slammed down the phone. He looked over at Julia, momentarily forgetting she was in the room. She sat across from him, studying the paintings on the wall. He calmed down, "Excuse my language, Julia, but sometimes that's the only way people listen. You gotta show them that you mean business!"

"It's OK, you don't have to apologize. I don't shock that easily."

"So, let's get on with your case ... it seems that Bob Fredericks wants to take this suit as far as he can. Those Marlton brats are out 'to kill' you if they could. I hate messy civil trials and would really like to avoid going to court. Now, what I'd like to propose is this: you give me free reign over this case, meaning you give me permission to make all the decisions ... "

"Well, I ... "

"Of course, you'll have to sign this document first."

Julia took what looked like a letter from Valenti. In terms that she didn't completely understand, it stated that he, Isadore Valenti, would take full charge of Julia Forrester's estate, and make all the decisions regarding it. Julia took a pen from the desk, then hesitated ... wondering could he be trusted. She heard Andre's words in her head, "He's OK Julia, Isadore Valenti will serve you well." She signed the paper on the dotted line.

"Mr. Valenti, uh, Isadore, what do you think will happen? I mean, do you think I have a chance of winning this case?"

"Don't worry. I've already got Fredericks shitting in his pants – excuse the expression. See, all he knows is that these two clients of his are the kids of a famous author. And, I've got Fredericks all figured out. He probably only took the case so he'd get some notoriety. He has no idea that he doesn't have a leg to stand on, 'cause he's gonna have to come up with some pretty damn good evidence to prove their father was senile."

"Such as?" Julia laughed inwardly. Was Valenti projecting? Andre said the same thing about Valenti, that he loved notoriety, being in the spotlight.

"First of all, he'll have Marlton's doctor testify. And, of course, the twins, too. And, anyone else who might have known Marlton. Fredericks will word things in his sneaky way to imply that Marlton was not all there upstairs."

"Well, Andre was one of his doctors for the last year of Otto's life. He saw Otto more than any of the others. He came to the house at least three times a week and he knew Otto wasn't senile."

"Good. Kramer is one of our best witnesses, but his word may not hold much weight because of your affair with him. Can you think of anyone else?"

"Well, yes, Alvin Marks and David Martin. Jefferson Allen, too. They were all good friends of Otto's and mine. Otto saw them all regularly, at least every couple of weeks we'd get together and have dinner with them."

"Can you think of anyone else? All those people will help, but we need someone who might seem to be more objective. Someone who isn't your friend."

"How about the housekeeper? Mrs. Miller? Elsie Miller. She took care of Otto and the house before we got married. Then she came to clean twice a week during the past three years."

"Do the twins know this Elsie Miller?"

"Stephanie did. When she lived with her father. She fired Mrs. Miller a few weeks before I married Otto. Then, when I moved in, Otto suggested that I rehire Elsie. He said Stephanie never got along with any woman he brought into the house. He said she was mean to Elsie and treated her with disrespect."

"Do you get along with Mrs. Miller? Is she your housekeeper now?"

"Well, no she isn't. But we got along wonderfully. I liked her, and she seemed to like me, too. She once said I was a lot easier to be around than Stephanie. But, about a week before Otto died, Elsie said she was moving to Daly City. Otto told her to take a month off if she needed to. I haven't heard from her since. In fact, she probably doesn't even know Otto died. She had a lot of problems with her husband for as long as I knew her. He was physically abusive. I told her many times not to stand for it, but she was really afraid of him. I'm actually worried that something could have happened to her, or maybe she ran away and is in hiding."

"Did you ever get her new address in Daly City?"

"No, I never did. When Otto died so suddenly, my mind was preoccupied, you know, with grief and funeral arrangements and all. But, I have Elsie's old phone number in San Francisco. Maybe if we called it, the operator would give us her new number." Julia reached into her red purse and took out a small address book. "Here it is: 654-4126."

"Thanks." Valenti scribbled the number on a piece of paper. "Now, look Julia, it might be a while before you hear from me again, but don't worry. I'll take care of everything. I'm going to call Fredericks and try to intimidate him, and convince him to drop this case. I will remind him that he doesn't have a chance and that we have several key witnesses."

"I hope you're right. I hate this whole thing."

"Trust me." Valenti stood up, then reached over and put his arm on Julia's shoulder. By now Julia knew he was harmless. Nevertheless, she resented his forwardness and attempts at intimacy. She walked towards the door to leave, "Thank you, I'll be in touch."

On the way home Julia wondered if she had done the right thing by signing that document Valenti had given her. Could he really be trusted as Andre promised? If not, what harm could come from a signed paper? After all, Valenti was on her side, wasn't he?

At home Julia leafed through the mail. All junk. Otto had supported every liberal cause there was, and his reward was to be on every mailing list in the world. Julia resented the time it took to sort through the piles, wondering if there might be a better way to change society. She knew she was being idealistic, but it seemed that all these organizations just perpetuated their machines and their own jobs. Usually, they represented worthy causes, but if causes no longer existed, what would happen to the people who worked in these organizations? Was all the donation money just paying their salaries?

A post card from Suzie was a refreshing surprise: "Sorry we didn't have more time to talk last week. I'm dying to hear about your new romance. Guess I'll have to wait 'til Thanksgiving. I'm in Tahiti with "Mr. Right". Will get in touch as soon as I return. Love always, Suzie".

"Mr. Right?!" Julia reread the card, positive Suzie must have missed a word. Suzie had never, in the eighteen years she had known her, ever said that any man was right for her.

Julia's curiosity was getting the best of her. Who was this "Mr. Right"? Was he good-looking? What did he do for a living? Was he after Suzie's money? Was she going to marry him? Suzie, of all people, was never the marrying type.

Julia was feeling protective of her friend and was really worried. She didn't want anyone taking advantage of Suzie. Of course, Suzie was smart, perceptive, and savvy, but "Mr. Right"? Julia hoped Suzie wasn't making a mistake. Well, Julia reasoned, Suzie was in her forties, so maybe she didn't want to grow old alone. And, she certainly had plenty of money.

Suzie was born into wealth. Her family went back several generations in the antique business. She loved antiquities, so she joined the family dynasty right after graduating from UC Berkeley with a Masters in Art History. It was a perfect career. Many of her family members were older and didn't take to traveling for long periods of time. Suzie, on the other hand, adored going to new and exotic places and seeing the world. She became the family's world "rep", buying and selling antiques in foreign countries, particularly in Europe. She was never put on a budget, so she often combined business with pleasure. Suzie had integrity, never spending more money than was necessary and her family respected that and her vast knowledge of art.

Julia loved antiques and met Suzie when she began decorating her home in Pacific Heights. When she stepped into Suzie's family business, Clemmens World of Art and Antiques, they hit it off immediately. Suzie's knowledge of art impressed Julia so she trusted Suzie's opinions about the purchases she made, which were not only wise investments, but pieces that were functional. Julia had a good eye and eclectic taste, loved mixing old and new pieces together.

After her house was fully decorated Julia enjoyed hanging out with Suzie, and vice versa. There were times when Suzie called her just to have lunch. She often asked Julia to accompany her to check out an estate sale or an auction.

Those were happy memories of their friendship. Now, Julia was confused and felt a little disappointed. Suzie had always been her role model. Julia's ideal woman. Suzie spoke "pearls of wisdom" on the merits of staying single. Was she bullshitting? Did she secretly want to get married in spite of saying she didn't?

Julia wondered if she knew her friend as well as she thought she did. She wondered if she knew anybody, or anything for that matter, as well as she thought she did.

She wondered how well she knew herself.

## CHAPTER NINETEEN: Stuart

Stephanie walked down the seemingly endless white corridor and stopped at Room 302. Looking at the card in her hand, it said 305. She turned around and saw the closed door of room 305.

As she reached for the door knob, she heard a man's voice yell, "Please, don't come in now! Please, wait … a few minutes."

Stephanie sat down on the bench across the hallway. She fidgeted with the straps on her purse worrying that the situation was more serious than she had anticipated. A loud scream came from the room. Recognizing Stuart's voice, she jumped up and rushed toward the door. It swung open and a young man with a stethoscope around his neck stormed out. He appeared disturbed.

She ran into the room. Stuart was lying in bed, an intravenous bottle hung by his side. The tube was attached to a needle in his left arm. His head was turned away from the door. He was whimpering.

"Stuart, baby, it's me, Steph … It's gonna be OK." She put her hand on his shoulder and began rubbing his neck. "I'm here now. Don't worry."

"Don't worry! Shit! Are you kidding me Stephanie, this is not kindergarten. I've just been jabbed with ten needles!" The excitement of talking caused Stuart to cough uncontrollably. "And, that bastard says …" cough, cough, "I can't be cured … and I'm dying!" His hacking brought up phlegm and blood. Stephanie handed him a Kleenex from the bedside stand.

Tears were streaming down her cheeks. She quickly turned away and wiped her eyes with the extra Kleenex she had in her hand. She didn't want

Stuart to see how upset she was.

"Hey, listen," she said in the strongest voice she could muster, "it's only one doctor's opinion. All you have is a bad case of pneumonia. And, with some antibiotics it'll clear up in a few days." She knew she was lying to him.

A month ago Stuart began losing weight. He had always been slim, but loosing twelve pounds in two weeks was something to be concerned about. Especially, since he hadn't changed his eating habits. As soon as Stephanie noticed how boney he was looking, she joked, "Hey, watcha' doing, going to Weight Watchers? Or, have you upped your jogging to ten miles a day?" As she spoke the words she felt an inner nervousness. It wasn't like Stuart to go on a diet. He never had to. His metabolism was high due to being so active. He usually ate a lot, but was very careful about what he ate. He didn't like anything that was processed. His diet consisted of whole, fresh foods. Regardless of what he ate, his weight always remained stable.

"Aw, Steph, I don't know, I guess it's not as much fun eating anymore with Marty gone. I mean, I like food and all, but I don't like cooking for just me."

The truth was that Stuart had been eating more than he had ever eaten before. As soon as he lost three pounds in three days he began to make himself thick, rich chocolate smoothies every morning and every evening. He wanted to defy what he suspected ... that he, too, had contracted that horrible illness that killed his beloved Marty.

Stephanie lived in denial. It helped her to be strong. If she didn't allow herself to believe something maybe it wouldn't become a reality. She wanted to think that the sudden weight loss was the result of Stuart being unduly stressed over Marty's death. She knew how Stuart was dependent on company and agreed that it wasn't as much fun eating alone.

"Look silly, anytime you want company ... that is, anytime you want to cook for me, I'll be there. Just call me."

"Steph, I know you're busy and I know you like your privacy. You hate coming to my house. I know you feel uncomfortable in, ah ... my neighborhood. And, I'm usually too tired at night now to drive over to Sausalito."

Too tired? Stuart? Mr. Pep Boy? Stuart never, ever complained of being too tired. He ran five miles every day and was hardly ever tired afterwards. He always seemed to have more energy than anyone else. Stephanie felt the knot in her stomach tighten.

"Maybe you're working too hard lately and probably not getting enough sleep?"

"I can't sleep."

"What's bothering you?" This was also unlike Stuart. He never had trouble sleeping. He was always one to fall asleep in the middle of a movie, or in a group conversation, especially if he was bored enough.

"I get into these coughing fits and can't stop. Nothing seems to help."

"Maybe it's time for you to get a complete physical. When was your last chest X-ray?"

"A couple of years ago."

The rest was history. She knew Stuart wasn't well and feared he was seriously ill. But, she had no idea Stuart was afflicted with AIDS.

Not many people were informed about the devastating character of this new disease. Jokes were whispered about it in relation to homosexuals. Other than that, the average person was not aware of how it was transmitted, or how terminal it was.

When Marty died, Stephanie sensed gloom. She had no information to back up her intuition, but somehow she knew disaster was in the air. She knew it was just a matter of time for Stuart, but she didn't expect it would happen this soon.

"Stuart, the doctors could be wrong. They're not always perfect you know. And, even if the diagnosis is correct, I know you can fight it. You have to have hope. You have to be strong." Stephanie heard herself bullshitting and saying almost the same words she had used when Marty was dying.

"That's easy for you to say. You're not in my shoes. And, it's not easy to be strong when I'm feeling so shitty."

"Look, we'll take it one day at a time, OK?" Her voice became punitive. She had to direct Stuart like she had done when they were children. If she was too soft on him, too sympathetic, he'd crumble. She had always been his rock, the foundation for him to lean on.

"Aw, OK, but today I feel awful." In reality Stuart actually felt stronger when Stephanie was by his side. Somehow her presence always gave him a lift. He recalled whining as a little boy when he had a cut or a bruise, and she was the only one who could ever make it feel better. As soon as she put her arms around him, or put a Band-aid on his wound, the pain seemed to disappear.

"How long do you have to stay here in the hospital?"

"At least a week, until the pneumonia clears up, then, I don't know. The doctor talked a lot. He seemed so nervous while he was telling me about this auto-immune disease. He seemed confused, like he didn't know all the facts either, and I'm confused now, too."

"See! I told you they don't know everything. I told you it's not as bad as you think it is."

"Shut the fuck up! I hate it when you say, I told you ... I told you so."
He mimicked her tone of voice. "You're always fuckin' acting like you're
some god-damn psychic or something. It pisses me off!"

Stephanie was shocked. It was so unlike Stuart to get angry with her.
But, inwardly it made her feel better. His anger was strong and it signified
hope. Perhaps, he really could conquer this disease.

"I'm sorry, I ... " Stephanie was taken off guard. She surprised herself
that she was apologizing to Stuart, and feared he might sense her anxiety.

Regaining her composure, she lashed back. "Well, what do you want to
do? Lie there and wallow in self-pity? Be a wimp? Come on, you're a Marlton! And, we Marltons have what it takes to fight!"

"Except this Marlton. I'm not like you, Steph. I'm not tough. I've always
been emotional and a scaredy-cat. I don't know how to fight."

"Well, you're going to learn. You're not going to accept defeat. We'll fight
this together." Stephanie hoped she'd have the fortitude she needed to give
her brother courage. She hoped she'd be able to conceal her own fear and insecurity. If, not ... NO, there would be no "if". Stuart was going to get well
and she was going to get him the best doctors and the best care possible.

"Speaking of fighting, I wanted to tell you about our suit with Julia."
She had to change the subject. She no longer knew what to say to him.

"What about Julia?"

"Well, Fredericks said he talked with her attorney, that sleeze-ball Isadore
Valenti, remember him? Apparently, Valenti says that he wants to fight us in
court. That he doesn't want to discuss anything more with Fredericks over
the phone. That he has some strong witnesses lined up and he's going to

make a big case out of this."

"Stephanie! I never wanted to take it this far. I wanted to settle out of court. I'd hate to have to be on the witness stand and testify. I'd be too nervous. I'd probably blow it and say all the wrong things."

"Don't worry. I told you before that Fredericks is smart. He has his ways of intimidating the other side and I'm sure he'll work it out with Valenti. I'm also sure we'll get the house. When you get out of the hospital, we'll list your duplex and I bet that within three months we'll be able to move back into Dad's house and stay there until you get well. We'll have the beautiful grounds and gardens to walk through every day as you get your health and strength back. Remember, we used to play hide-and-seek in those lovely gardens when we were kids? And, hide in the bushes when our nanny called us in to do our homework?"

Stuart felt nostalgic. He closed his eyes and visualized himself and his sister as children. He recaptured those feelings he had when they played games together. He could almost smell the wonderful aromas that came from the luxurious gardens surrounding that old colonial house. Momentarily, he experienced the happiness and peacefulness of those times. And, the security he felt when he was with Stephanie.

It seemed so long ago, and yet, as if it was just yesterday.

CHAPTER TWENTY: The Flight Home

Julia looked out the window at the parched California landscape, paint-ing the various shapes and muted colors in her mind and wishing she had brought her sketch pad and marking pens. But, she hadn't had time to even think of her art supplies, she had left in such a hurry.

Abruptly the ground disappeared as if someone had waved a wand and all that was left was a smoky screen. Julia strained her eyes to see through the purplish clouds, to catch a glimpse of the majestic Sierra Nevadas far below. A few of the highest peaks had quite a bit of snow on them already even though it was only late October. The snow looked like whipped cream spread over chocolate cones. The Sierras brought back memories of her re-cent trip to Lake Tahoe.

That vast range of mountains had quite a different perspective then. Now, looking down at them from thirty thousand feet was an altogether new visual experience. It seemed as if she could reach out, pick up a scoopful and cup them in her hands. She imagined running her finger tips over the jagged edges of the peaks and wondering if they were as sharp as they appeared to be.

"Ding!" The seat belt sign came on. The plane was swerving from side to side and it began to get bumpy. They were going through that pocket of clouds she had just admired.

She laid her head back, closed her eyes and thought of Andre. He had been so sweet the last couple of weeks, attentive and caring, calling daily to inquire about her. They saw each other almost every night an191 d were becoming inseparable. And, the sex! Well, Julia never had such consistently good sex. She never thought it was possible – multiple orgasms! Explosive ones at that, too! And, every time they made love! Well, almost. Ever since she had forgiven his behavior at Lake Tahoe. Her anger then seemed so silly now.

She was positive she was in love with Andre. She tingled inside just thinking about him. When he kissed her good-bye at the airport they held each other tightly for several minutes. "I love you so much," he said, " I'm really going to miss you."

Andre had such a sad puppy-dog expression on his face when he waved at her as she boarded the plane. He looked so handsome, yet so boyish, his hair tousled from the wind. Julia felt a warm contentment knowing that he was sincere. She fantasized his hands on her, his rigid penis penetrating her. Her underpants became wet and sticky. Right then and there she almost climaxed just thinking about him!

"Would you care for something to drink, Ma'am?"

The interruption startled Julia from her lovely day dream. She looked up into the hollow, icy blue eyes of the stone-faced stewardess, who was wearing flashy bright red lipstick that clashed with the prescribed conservative image required by the airline.

"Oh, ah, yes, of course. I'll have some orange juice please, without ice." Cold drinks made her teeth hurt.

A plastic cup with orange juice and a small bag of honey-roasted peanuts were placed on the tray in front of her.

She thanked the stewardess and in return heard a nonchalant, "You're welcome." As quickly as the intruder came, she was gone.

Julia sipped the juice and tried to recapture her thoughts of Andre, but her mood was broken. She looked out the window again relieved to see the landscape below. They had passed through the turbulent clouds. Glancing down at her Rolex, she was surprised that close to three hours had passed since takeoff. The pilot was announcing they would be flying over the Rockies soon.

Oh, those memorable Rockies. Julia thought about the time she and Ralph and the children spent that awful night in Denver. Every one of them was uptight and grumpy because the car had broken down and they had to kill an extra day waiting for it to be repaired. Denver was a blanket of smog and Bradley, their eight year old, had such a severe asthma attack they had to take him to the emergency room. On the way back from the hospital seven year old Charlie fell and bruised his knee. The way he screamed one would have thought his leg had been amputated. Not to be overshadowed, Sandra threw up all night. Little sleep and too many demands left Julia feeling like a zombie for a couple of days.

They were on an "educational trip" driving from San Francisco to New York City. From sea to shining sea. Julia and Ralph had tried so hard to be "good parents". One of Ralph's requirements for being a responsible father was to teach his children firsthand about the wonderful country they lived in. A family excursion of their star-spangled land was in order. The children could care less about anything that didn't include Disneyland. But, Ralph would not listen to them, or to Julia. He was sure they would all change their minds once they were on the road and saw all the sites he had circled in the AAA tour book.

That was the summer of 1969. A summer Julia would never forget. It was a total nightmare. She could still hear the children's petulant voices.

"It's my turn to sit by the window!"

"No it isn't! You had an hour and my hour isn't up yet!"

"Maah, he hit me!"

"No, I didn't. You're such a cry baby!"

"I am not a cry baby!"

"Yes you are!"

"No I'm not!"

Then Sandra chimed in, "I gotta pee. And, I'm hungry."

"We'll be at the motel in less than ten minutes. Look, we only have about five miles to go." Julia pointed to a road sign on the side of the highway, even though Sandra was barely able to read it.

"I can't wait! I have to pee NOW!"

"Ralph, I think you'd better pull over at that gas station up there. Sandra has to go to the bathroom."

No response. Ralph was oblivious to Julia, the commotion in the car, the fights, the cries, the demands. Julia's heart stopped.

Was Ralph even awake?

"Oh my God! RALPH! Did you hear me? Sandra has to pee –NOW!"

"Uh, ah, what'd you say?"

Julia was furious. Typical of Ralph. Completely "out there" when it came to anything not directly related to his fucking law practice. Julia wanted to hit him over the head with the thermos bottle that was lying on the floor.

"I said ... SANDRA ... HAS ... TO ... GO ... TO ... THE ... BATH-ROOM! PULL INTO THAT GAS STATION RIGHT NOW! THE ONE ACROSS THE STREET!" Julia yelled so loudly that it shocked the children into silence. They put their hands over their mouths, giggling at their mother's outburst.

Yes, that was some trip! Julia was thrilled when it was over. It was probably the beginning of the end for her and Ralph. At home she was too busy tending to the house and driving the children to "sixth and japip", and back every day, which helped distract her from her underlying anger.

After the kids wore themselves out complaining, they fell asleep on a bunch of pillows propped amongst the suitcases in the back of their station wagon. Julia had time to delve into her thoughts about what she truly wanted out of life. Conversing with Ralph was rarely stimulating, if at all possible. He always wanted to tell her stuff from articles he read. He wasn't a good listener. It was always about him and all the knowledge he had stored in his pea brain. Julia preferred silence.

However, one special highlight of that "trip from hell" was memorable. It was when they stopped to eat at a diner in Wapakoneta, Ohio. Inside it was packed with people and it looked like New Year's Eve. Balloons, confetti, and crepe paper streamers were everywhere. The children's eyes lit up. They thought it was someone's birthday. The TV set was blaring and people were glued to it. Then, the astronauts landed on the moon and everyone cheered. Unbeknownst to the Worthington family, Wapakoneta was the home of Neil Armstrong!

A lot had happened in the world since then. It seemed to Julia that her life and world events paralleled each other. War. Quiescence. Eruptions. Calm times. Anger, hatred, murder, love, peace and brotherhood. So much had changed, and was still changing. Wasn't that the cycle of life? Take nothing for granted because tomorrow it might be different, or not even exist anymore. Have no expectations and you won't be disappointed. How easy to say, yet how difficult to live by.

In 1969 the Viet Nam war was still in full gear. Liberals were protesting our "imperialism" in a country we had no business being in, while the conservatives were yelling, "bomb the hell out of those Commie bastards!" President Richard Nixon was sending more troops to Saigon every day. The death toll was rising, and Hippies were burning their draft cards or fleeing to Canada encouraged by Bob Dylan's anti-war songs and Joan Baez's courageous refusal to pay taxes. She protested that her tax money went toward the building of more war machines.

A reprieve from those hectic times were the four oddly dressed, long-haired guys from Liverpool, who had risen to stardom in America since their debut on the Ed Sullivan Show in the early sixties. Julia remembered when she saw that performance and they were introduced as "The Beatles". The Beatles? What were they? Bugs? Or, was that a derivative of Beatniks? It didn't matter. Their songs and lyrics were certainly different. Like Bob Dylan, they were inspirational and made people think.

In spite of the mess the country was in physically and emotionally, people actually liked Nixon. "Tricky Dick" was the name he had earned when he was Dwight Eisenhower's Vice President. Julia couldn't understand why anyone believed in Nixon, especially after his famous, saccharin, fireside chat on TV, called, "The Checkers Speech". Checkers was the Nixon's family dog. Almost every time she saw Nixon on TV she felt vicarious embarrassment for him. She could see in his eyes how phony he was. His voice was melodramatic and it was difficult for her to believe or pay attention to anything he was saying. It baffled her that even after he was defeated when he ran for governor of California, he won the presidential election.

Julia was not a bit surprised, when the Watergate scandal broke out shortly into Nixon's second term. What did surprise her was that people defended him saying, "All politicians are crooked. Nixon just got caught."

She wondered if Bobby Kennedy would have made it to the White House if he hadn't been assassinated. She thought about his battles with J. Edgar Hoover over civil rights and wondered if he really had an affair with Marilyn Monroe.

But, the real hero of civil rights was Dr. Martin Luther King. Through his courage and leadership, black people marched peacefully in protest against the ill treatment they had to deal with just because of the color of their skin. Their rights to equality in terms of education and where they could eat or sleep had been denied them. The right to "life, liberty, and the pursuit of happiness" did not include black people in the South. They had been denied any dignity.

Julia remembered how incensed he became whenever the subject of civil rights came up with Ralph. He barely tolerated "the colored", his name for black people when he was in a good mood. Usually, he was more derogatory. Whenever Julia commented about how sorry she felt for black people, Ralph would snap at her and say things like, "They're an inferior race you know. Dirty, lazy and dumb. And, I for one do not want to live next door to any of them, or have any of my children marry a nigger!"

As if their children were so pure and perfect. Ralph wanted to see what he wanted to see. And, he didn't want to see his own children objectively. He didn't want to see that half the time they were stuporous and lazy watching that god-damned TV. Julia knew from the first year of their marriage that it was impossible to argue with Ralph. He was the attorney in the family and no one ever won an argument with him. Instead, she often bit her lip when he talked about those "scummy jigaboos", or said things like, "we ought to pack all those" jungle bunnies" in a boat and send them back to Africa."

Poor Ralph. Julia actually felt sorry for him now. Sorry that he was such a bigot. Sorry that he was missing out on some of the real joys of life. Ralph went through his life as if in a trance. If he didn't tell people he was an attorney, they would think he was brain-damaged. He talked like a wound-up robot. He had such tunnel vision.

Julia sighed a breath of relief. Thank God she had had Otto Marlton's books to confirm that she wasn't a "nut" as Ralph had condescendingly called her. Thank God she had the wisdom and courage to leave Ralph. Even though her children hated her for it.

Sandra was just a blossoming teen-ager when Julia asked Ralph for a divorce. At least the boys lived away from home at a military academy, so it was easier for them to adjust to a broken home. Sandra had basked in the limelight of being the baby in the family, of having things her way. When Julia and Ralph divorced, it "ruined" Sandra's popularity at school, or so she claimed. She had been one of the privileged few whose parents were "happily married" and the other kids liked to come to her house. Sandra didn't speak to Julia for almost a year and a half after she moved away.

Julia longed for a close relationship with her children, especially Sandra. It was something she had dreamt about when she herself was a young girl, even when her mother mistreated and beat her. Tears welled up in Julia's eyes and she felt a pain in her chest. Her mother ... an alcoholic mess, a disaster. Now, on her death bed.

She dreaded seeing her mother in the hospital attached to tubes and machines. She dreaded seeing the relatives who thought of her as abandoning her "poor mother", to live a "luxurious life" in California. The day before Julia had gotten a call from Aunt Alma, her mother's sister. Alma talked matter-of-factly, with no emotion. Julia never could warm up to her, Alma wasn't easy to be with.

"Julia. I found your mother lying on the bedroom floor unconscious and running a temperature of 103. She's in the hospital, still out of it. Doctors don't expect her to make it through this crisis, to live more than a few days. You'd better come right away. That is, if you ever want to see her alive again." Alma hung up without waiting for Julia to respond.

Alma's tone was so damn sarcastic. "If" Julia ever wanted to see her mother alive again. Of course she did. She didn't hate her mother. She had a lot of feelings for Katherine. It was just, well, Julia searched her brain for the reasons she and her mother had been estranged for so many years. She mulled over the past for so long that she wondered if what she remembered was really the truth. As time went on, however, she felt less critical and more forgiving of her mother's shortcomings. She reasoned that Katherine was an uneducated, unhappy and an immature woman, who, because she had never known love, was not able to give it. This scenario of understanding helped Julia feel more empathetic and compassionate towards her mother which lessened the bitterness of her memories.

Still the pain of feeling unloved by Katherine stayed with her and gnawed at her. It left a huge void in her heart and an emptiness she felt since she was a little girl. That still hurt badly.

Julia began to sob quietly when she realized she might not see her mother alive again. That she never had or would have the kind of close relationship with Katherine she had wished for her whole life.

It also scared her wondering what horrors she might encounter when she arrived back in New Jersey.

## CHAPTER TWENTY-ONE: Mother

The 747 landed in Philadelphia at 3:40pm, ten minutes behind schedule. As it taxied on the runway toward the main terminal, Julia could see through the steamed window that it was raining outside and the wind was blowing. Thankfully, she had packed her warm wool cardigan in her carry-on. She knew from growing up on the East coast that October days were usually chilly.

She had gotten up at five that morning to catch a 7am flight. Andre had spent the night and insisted on taking her to the airport. She wanted to take a cab, telling him, "It's the worst time of the morning to be driving back to the city from SFO. The freeway will be so crowded between seven and nine. Cars will be crawling bumper-to-bumper - half the city will be clamoring to get to work."

But, Andre wouldn't hear of it. He called his secretary the night before and told her to cancel his appointments and reschedule them no earlier than ten. Andre was so sweet and considerate. Julia felt a hot rush as she relived their long, passionate good-bye kiss just before she boarded the plane.

She looked at her watch again and yawned. It was three hours earlier on the west coast. She was exhausted from the five and a half hour trip. She took her blue cloisonne compact from her purse and studied the bags under her eyes in the mirror, then applied a fresh coat of powder to her face. She was uneasy about seeing her family again and wanted to look as presentable as possible.

In a rented car she drove through downtown Philly toward the Ben

Franklin Bridge which crossed the Delaware River. She was headed to Camden, New Jersey, the place of her birth. The place of many memories. The place she dreaded going back to.

It had been only five years since her last visit to the East coast, and, yet, Philadelphia had changed drastically. Expressways were being built, slum neighborhoods razed and renovated. Everything looked torn apart, as if the bowels of the city were being eviscerated.

Julia purposely turned onto Market Street. It was out of her way, but she wanted to see the main thoroughfare again. She had spent many hours in that part of the city going on shopping sprees to her favorite department stores – Gimbal's, Wanamaker's, Strawbridge and Clothier.

Market Street was also where the annual Thanksgiving Day Parade took place, and on New Year's Day, the Mummer's Parade. As a child, Julia looked forward to the Thanksgiving Day Parade the most. Her kind Uncle Joe took her and his three daughters to Philly every year while her dear Aunt Ruth remained at home, preparing the day's feast. Those were some of Julia's most happy memories while she was growing up.

She could still visualize the wonderful, colorful decorations on the streetlight posts during the holiday season – the jingle bells and sleighs outlined in lights, the opulent wreaths of evergreen and holly tied with bows made from bright red and green satin ribbons.

She recalled the exciting window displays, her nose poked up against the panes on snowy days, mesmerized by the mechanical dolls and dancing ballerinas, fairy lands and castles, of Santa Claus climbing the ladder to the top floor of Gimbal's and waving to the crowds. Of Santa's workshop filled with tiny animated elves feverishly making toys. Oh, what toys! They surpassed every child's wildest dreams and imagination.

The old stone and brick buildings on Market Street were still there and life seemed to be going on as if no time had passed. It wasn't much different than she remembered except the area south of Market Street had been redeveloped.

That area surrounding the building that housed the Liberty Bell had become an upper class neighborhood called Society Hill. Formerly, there were old, run-down residences called "row" houses. Now, in their place stood modern "town" houses. The city had cleaned up its historical sites for the 1976 bicentennial celebration. The City Fathers wanted to make a favorable impression. People from all over the world descended on Philadelphia to commemorate our independence from the British.

Julia approached the toll booth on the Ben Franklin Bridge and thought of her life at the University of Pennsylvania. Of those idiotic fraternity parties and how savvy everyone tried to be, each person impressing the next with their phony intellectualism. Although the picnics in the spring along the Schuylkill River were really fun. Somehow the warmer weather and outdoor settings that called for less formal attire created a more permissive mood, perhaps giving the students license to just be themselves.

Recalling her life at the U of Penn., Julia thought of Uncle Roy. If not for him, she might never have been able to afford to go there. She was at least thankful to him for that, even though she could never forgive him for molesting and shaming her.

During those first years at the University Julia was very lonely. Every few months she suffered over a broken relationship, or agonized over a boy she had fallen in love with who didn't know she even existed. She couldn't begin to count the many walks alone when she didn't have a boyfriend, while all her friends were either pinned or engaged. During those vulnerable years she wondered if any man would ever find her appealing enough to want to marry her. She was self-conscious then, thinking she was too skinny. Most of her girlfriends were well-endowed and voluptuous, while she barely had breasts. Now, they probably had sagging boobs and looked like cows, Julia thought and smiled. Time had been on her side and her life had made quite a turnabout. She no longer felt unattractive because she was skinny. Over the years her weight had remained the same, but her bosoms had gotten larger from each pregnancy. Now, her figure was considered perfect because "thin was in".

In spite of her many problems while growing up, Julia recalled how art had given her solace during those difficult times. When she was amongst the masters, many of whom had suffered wretched lives, it helped her to feel she had company in her misery.

Reliving those feelings, she envisioned her many excursions to the Philadelphia Museum of Art where she sat for hours studying the works of Michelangelo and Leonardo da Vinci. And, oh, those Turners, Van Eycks, Monets, Cezannes, Degas, Miros, Kandinskis. She loved them all! She loved art from every period, from every movement, of every style. Somehow she favored Van Gogh and his emotional brush strokes. She could almost feel his agony.

A close second to Van Gogh was the Austrian artist, Gustav Klimt. Julia wondered what he was thinking when he painted so many colors and designs in his representational faces and trees. Klimt's work was truly original and breathtaking.

The Impressionist works by Mary Cassatt were also among Julia's favorites and her biggest inspiration. Cassatt's paintings touched her maternal yearnings. Cassatt was one of the few women artists who received recognition during that time. She lived in Paris, but was born in Philadelphia, which gave Julia a deeper connection to her being from the same "neck of the woods".

Julia often visited the Rodin Museum and remembered her feeling of romance the first time she saw "The Kiss". And "The Thinker". How astounded she was by the incredible workmanship and beauty of these two masterpieces. She appreciated Rodin's labors so much more after she, herself, had made a few feeble attempts at sculpting. That always reminded her of what Paul Cezanne once said, "Don't be an art critic. Paint!" How true that was about everything in life. It is not until a person does something that one can fully appreciate what it takes to do it.

A special treat for young budding artists then was the Barnes Foundation formed by Albert Barnes, a chemist who lived in Lower Merion, a suburb of Philadelphia. Barnes began collecting art in the 30s and 40s, and by the time he died in 1954, he had the largest collection of modern art in the world. It was a collection envied by most museums. Barnes had traveled to Europe often and met and befriended artists such as Picasso and Matisse long before they were famous. He bought many of their paintings and made his home into a museum, but only allowed it to be open to the public two days a week. He had established a policy at the foundation that most days of the week were to be set aside for young art students. Julia was lucky to be one of those students. She loved those special days. It was stimulating to be in the company of other young artists, to study and have discussions about the various paintings in Barnes' collection.

As Julia crossed the bridge into Camden her heart sank. Camden was a squalid mess. It looked like a war zone. Worse than she had remembered. The downtown area had always been old and dirty, except maybe when Walt Whitman lived there so many years before. Now, it was filthy and in a state of complete disarray. Buildings were partially torn down in the process of being destroyed. Store fronts had metal bars over the windows and doors. Litter was everywhere on the streets and the movie theaters were boarded up.

Oh, those movie theaters! How sad to see they no longer existed. Some of Julia's favorite childhood memories were when she went to the movies on weekends, which often featured a vaudeville act, cartoons, and two full length films. She would spend from eleven in the morning until seven at night at the movies, living on candy bars, popcorn, and sodas. Her mother never missed her. Katherine was too wrapped up in her own life. The only week night Julia was allowed to go to the movies was on "dish night". A dish was included with the price of admission and Katherine wanted to collect the complete set.

For a few moments, Julia embraced those fond memories until the garbage that was ankle deep in the gutters and empty cans and bottles lined up by the curbs snapped her back to reality. Poor downtrodden people were walking aimlessly, while others were lying against buildings huddled in shabby blankets to keep warm. Children with crusty bare feet, dressed in tattered clothes, were rummaging through trash cans perhaps searching for their only meal of the day. Julia realized that the slums had expanded into the downtown financial district where City Hall still stood.

She quietly wept as she drove in the direction of Cooper Hospital, the hospital where she was born and where her mother now lay dying. Everything looked awful, even the nice places she had dreamt and reminisced about over the past twenty-five years. She was very disheartened. No carefully calculated expectation could ever match the reality of this situation. It was painful to go back home.

The chaos and destruction of the city reminded Julia of another reality, the inevitable one she was about to encounter. Witnessing the demise of Camden was analogous to seeing her dying mother. She wanted to turn around and flee. But, she knew she had to go through with this ordeal.

In the hospital elevator Julia felt as if she was going to vomit. Hospital smells made her nauseous. They reminded her of her father's death when she was seventeen. It was the most traumatic event she had ever experienced up to that time in her life. She could still picture her father in that same hospital, gasping for each breath of air. Her last memory of him alive was seeing him looking like he was already dead.

Julia heard someone yelling obscenities as she approached the doorway of her mother's room. She chuckled, recognizing her mother's voice. Katherine hadn't changed. She was always crying out to be heard, to be acknowledged. Even on her deathbed she was vying for attention.

When Julia saw the intravenous tubes and the EKG monitor attached to her mother's chest, she felt sick to her stomach again. In spite of being delirious, Katherine was thrashing about, screaming profanities and kicking her legs up in the air.

She walked over to the bedside and touched her mother's arm. Katherine looked up with a fixed, glazed expression on her face. Julia became limp. Her once beautiful mother was lying there looking like she was more than eighty-eight years old instead of sixty-eight. Her lips were blanched and dry, and her jaundiced, weather-beaten skin was wrinkled and shriveled. Like a lemon left out in the sun to rot, Julia thought. Katherine's bright blue eyes, that once sparkled, looked worn, tired and dull. Her sunken-in mouth was stripped of almost every tooth. She laid there looking completely helpless. Whatever consciousness she had left seemed to be pleading for help. And, Julia felt powerless. Their lives had taken opposite paths, their irreparably estranged relationship, and her mother's illness and eminent death were far beyond her control.

The next day Katherine's condition worsened. During the night she lapsed into a coma, though occasionally she would cry out incoherently. She needed 'round the clock care and attention. Julia stayed in the hospital, sleeping in a chair by her mother's side. Katherine died two days later. They never exchanged a word.

Julia wondered if her mother even knew she was there.

Katherine's sister, Alma insisted on a Catholic burial. The funeral was a mockery of everything Katherine despised. From as long as Julia could remember, her mother made fun of religion, the nuns and priests. She hadn't attended church in over thirty years.

It was a downpour the day of the funeral and the autumn leaves on the church steps were soggy and wet. The rain poured on the church rooftop to a rhythm of its own. Julia looked up through the windows and saw that the weather was not likely to change for the better. The sky was overcast with dark, gloomy clouds.

During the funeral mass Julia's eyes wandered around the church, the various shapes and colors captivated her. She was surrounded by yellow, orange, gold and rust chrysanthemums, their pointed petals seemed to be joyously dancing in all directions. Ah, the stained glass windows: How magnificently they were designed and created. She studied the exquisitely carved human-sized marble statues of the various saints and the skillfully painted ceilings depicting biblical scenes. Even though she had been in that church countless times, seeing the art work now was like making a new discovery. How come I never noticed any of this before she wondered? All this inspiration that I took for granted.

Julia knew it was impossible for her to have seen anything in those days as she was seeing them now. As a little girl, she was too afraid of the nuns, too afraid of making mistakes, of not genuflecting properly, not saying the prayers for the sacraments correctly … she had too many fears then to see anything beyond herself.

In the limousine on the way to the cemetery Julia sat between Aunt Alma and Sadie, her mother's first cousin. The two older women were sobbing profusely. Julia wondered why. Alma had treated Katherine as though she was a buffoon. Although Alma was two years older than Katherine, she was very competitive with her. It was difficult for an outside observer to see any love between the two sisters and their cousin. Katherine hated Sadie and they never got along. Suddenly, Alma reached across Julia's lap and clutched Sadie's hand. In a low whisper she moaned, "It's only the two of us now. There'll be no one left to come to our funerals." Julia thought, what am I, chopped liver?

She couldn't help but laugh to herself. They weren't crying for her mother, they were crying for themselves! For their own mortality.

At the graveside, the mumbling sound of voices reciting the "Hail Mary" seemed to be ricocheting from the trees. The last ritual performed by the priest was to sprinkle holy water over the casket as it was lowered into the six foot hole. That was a moment of harsh realization for Julia. Katherine was gone forever. Julia would never have any contact with her again. Feelings of grief clutched her heart and a deep sadness came over her. Because she had never been close to her mother, she somehow felt responsible for her death.

Katherine led a miserable existence. She lived on Camel cigarettes, canned Maxwell House coffee, cheap beer and whiskey. Every time Julia saw her, though infrequently, it was stressful and disturbing to witness how her mother was destroying herself through her addictions and unhealthy habits. Over the years, Katherine's life seemed to have gone from bad to worse.

Still, Julia was plagued with those old feelings of guilt, again – asking herself why had she abandoned her mother. There were also deep feelings of regret, that she had never helped her mother change or discover happiness. But, realistically, what could she have done? How could she give anyone the gift of happiness, which wasn't something to be captured anyhow? Happiness was fleeting.

Julia knew she had to resign herself to the fact that it was not meant to be, that she never would have been capable of making her mother change her life style. From the time she was a teen-ager Julia knew on a gut level that she herself had to change her environment. She realized that it was imperative for her to get away from her mother, that it was necessary for her mental survival. She knew if she stayed in Camden a moment longer she might become just like her mother. Or, end up in the nut house. Physically escaping was her only solution, the only possibility for her own salvation.

Reflecting, Julia now understood that Ralph had been the saviour of the day. Without him she might have been stuck in that horrible, slum neighborhood. When he asked her to marry him, she thought she was in love with him. Now, she wondered if subconsciously he was just an excuse to get out of Camden. Then when Ralph was offered a job in San Francisco, she, as his dutiful wife, was, of course, obliged to be with him. Being three thousand miles away from Katherine made things easier – no one expected her to make frequent visits. Perhaps Ralph was a more important figure in her life than she had given him credit for. Had she underrated his significance?

Still, Ralph was not Otto. Nor Andre - the three most influential men in her life, besides her father.

Andre, oh Andre, Julia pined. If only he was here by my side, this ordeal would be so much easier. With Andre Julia felt strong. It was a different kind of strength than Otto had given her. When Andre was with her she felt courageous, more capable of asserting herself. Otto had planted those seeds, and Andre was nurturing their fruit.

Julia couldn't wait to return to San Francisco safely with Andre's muscular arms wrapped around her. She couldn't wait until they kissed and made love again. She yearned for his warm body against hers, for his large, erect penis pulsing inside her.

Everyone threw a handful of dirt on the coffin and the assembly dispersed into the waiting limousines.

It was time for Julia to go home. She had paid her dues. Now, she had to get on with her own life. There was no looking back. Otto had often remarked, "Guilt and regret are a waste of time."

Otto was certainly right about that.

## CHAPTER TWENTY-TWO: Repressed Anger

"You know Suzie, there are times when you really make me angry, when I don't like you. And, I'm really pissed off at you right now."

Suzie looked at Julia and began to laugh. "Well, it's about time you expressed your anger, 'Miss Goody Two Shoes' , 'Miss Virgin Mary'! So, what's the matter? What's eating you? Let it out baby!"

Julia looked surprised. "Virgin Mary"? "Goody Two Shoes"? Is that how Suzie sees me? I wonder why? I don't think of myself that way.

"Oh, Suzie, you're so god-damn blunt. I mean, you really know how to sting a person, don't you? And, you're so facetious besides."

"You just don't like the truth, Julia. Face it. You like to hide behind your stupid idyllic facade. And, you know, denying stuff doesn't change things. Pretending that problems aren't there, or aren't happening, don't make them go away," Suzie chided.

"Well, why did you have to burst my bubble? I really love Andre. And, now you're telling me he's an asshole. I'm really upset."

Look, Julia, after some of the things you told me about Andre, and then your trip with him to Lake Tahoe, I can't help thinking that he acted like an ass. But, if you want to get married again, go ahead. If you ask me, I think you have marriage-itis!"

"Marriage-itis? I don't understand what you're talking about!"

"It means, Sweetie, that you can't stand on your own two feet. It means you're desperate to be somebody's wife. You're weak alone and need a man to clutch on to."

"That's pretty cruel."

"I'm telling it like I see it. Take my advice, or not. I really don't give a damn."

As she fought back tears, Julia's bottom lip began to quiver. She was not comfortable fighting and found it really hard to take Suzie's caustic remarks. She wanted to hit her where it hurt, but couldn't think of anything to say. Finally, she countered, "Suzie, I think you're still pissed off about Otto, because he chose me over you that night at the opera benefit."

"What? Ha! That's a laugh! I never wanted that old goat. I mean, I sure didn't want to be a nursemaid to some decrepit, ailing 'has-been'."

"Has-been! I resent that. Otto was no has-been! He was an important writer. People from all over the world were reading his books."

"So what? So fucking what! He was still a has-been! His best work was done when he was a young man. It just took him longer to get recognized. And, by then he was on his way out. Poor Otto had lousy timing."

Julia was crimson with rage - a disturbingly unfamiliar feeling. It was bad enough Suzie hurt her by calling her "Goody Two Shoes" and "the Virgin Mary", and then saying Andre was an asshole. And, now picking on poor Otto, who couldn't defend himself. Julia yelled loudly, "Suzie Clemmens! You are a first class bitch!" Then realizing that other people in the restaurant were looking over at them, Julia lowered her voice in embarrassment. With her teeth clenched, she continued, "I will not hear anything more negative about Otto! And, I ... I know you are just saying these things because you were jealous of our relationship."

"Never! Believe me, when we first met Otto I knew right away he had eyes for you. He was always a sucker for a young, pretty, naive new thing."

"Naive new thing?"

"Hold it, before you get your bowels in an uproar ... yes, in case you never observed it, Otto regarded women as "things". He was one of the biggest chauvinist pigs I ever met."

Julia was stunned. She never felt that way about Otto. She thought he loved women.

"Suzie, that's not true! Otto was in favor of women's rights. You just never really knew him."

"Oh, yes I did. I see things very clearly, even from the back of my head. Otto played the part well. He could've gotten an Academy Award, he was so damn fucking good at acting. He knew how to keep women in their place ... to his advantage of course. And, in the most charming, flattering way. He was clever, that old bird. He saw the Achilles' heel on everyone, as if he had X-ray vision. And, believe me, he knew exactly how to monopolize on other peoples' weaknesses."

Suzie hit a nerve in Julia. A nerve, that had been anesthetized for years. Deep down Julia knew Suzie was partly right. One of her gifts was her intuition. But, she never took Otto's chauvinism that seriously. She reasoned it was because he was from an older generation. She also felt a loyalty to her dead husband, needing to defend him. Instead, she decided to change the subject and put Suzie on the defensive for a change.

"Well, if I recall, the last time I heard from you, you sent me a post card saying you were with 'Mr. Right'. Have you become the marrying type now? Maybe you have a beginning case of marriage-itis?"

"God no! I must have been drunk when I wrote that postcard, or else it was one of the few good days with Bill, which didn't last very long. We were at each other's throats before the week was up."

"What happened?"

"Same ole thing. Men drive me crazy. If I didn't enjoy sex so much I'd give up on them for good. That son-of-a-bitch wanted to change me."

"Change you? In what way?"

"Well, at first he seemed enamored with me. Said I really turned him on. He loved my looks, the way I dressed, and my hair. He said I was the perfect woman. That my personality was the right blend of femininity and assertiveness. That I had a wonderful sense of humor and was great in bed. Christ! I believed that line of horse shit! I even thought I was in love with him." Suzie sighed. "That was before we went to Tahiti together. Then after a few days, he started picking on me. I should be more this, or more that. Or, not so much like this, or that. He even started telling me how to dress. And, how to talk. What a drag! As if I didn't get enough criticism as a kid. Then, when I stood up to him we got into some major fights. It really pissed me off. I mean, when a guy acts one way before you go on vacation with him, then becomes the opposite. It's fucking annoying."

"Maybe it was just a lack of communication. Maybe if you didn't get so irritated with him when he criticized you, you two might have been able to work things out."

"Julia, I'm not like you. I'm different. I don't have the patience, or the time. Life is too short to waste on weirdos, or losers."

"So, what did you do? Walk out on him in Tahiti?"

"You bet I did! There was no way I was going to stay there with Bill one more day. He paid for this beautiful room overlooking the Pacific. It was really romantic. At least he was a good fuck, I'll give him that much credit.

But, after he started with his Pygmalion shit, I was out of there!"

"Maybe he wasn't trying to change you. Maybe he was just trying to help?"

"Well, I wasn't askin' for any help! And, what the fuck's the difference? Whatever cloak a guy puts on, it's the same thing. Like I was warning you, with Andre. I'm telling you Julia, he's just like the rest. And, believe me, I know!"

"You don't have to rub it in that you two had dinner together while I was at my mother's funeral."

"Julia, I swear, nothing happened. We just ran into each other in Union Square and began talking about you. Then it started to rain, so Andre asked if I wanted to go for a bite to eat. What do you think? That I'm a sleeze-bag or something? I'd never try to steal a guy from my good friend. But, actually Andre does have some redeeming qualities. So, I take back some of what I said. Still, the way you described him when you were at Lake Tahoe, I couldn't help seeing that he behaved like an ass."

Julia looked down into her plate of food. She picked up her chop sticks and fiddled with the kung pao chicken and chow mein. Was Suzie telling her the full truth? Could she trust Suzie? Her best friend? Her confidante? Julia wondered.

When she wanted to marry Otto, Suzie was very supportive, though she kept telling her to take a little more time, instead of jumping into another marriage so quickly. Otto was never that fond of Suzie, and Suzie sensed it. Julia wondered if that was partly why Suzie didn't want her to get married again. Sometimes friends are just as possessive as husbands. And, if Julia was married, she wouldn't be as available to Suzie, even though Suzie traveled a lot. Perhaps, that was why she seemed to need Julia when she came home. Suzie wasn't in one place long enough to establish other friendships. Or, maybe she was too out front with people which made them a little afraid of her.

Still, she not only came to Julia's wedding when she married Otto, she accepted Julia's request to be her maid of honor. So, how sincere was she?

After the wedding Julia and Suzie remained close. They often talked on the phone and met for lunch at least once a month when neither of them were traveling.

Their outing to Inverness last summer was Suzie's idea. She had an appointment to look at some antiques from a woman's estate, and asked Julia to join her, explaining that she respected Julia's opinions and her taste in art.

Every time Julia thought of Inverness she felt guilty over Otto's death. Many times she wondered if he had the heart attack because she went off with Suzie instead of being home with him. The two always seemed to be competing for her attention.

Julia mentioned to Suzie a few times prior to that trip to Inverness that she was feeling a little stifled by Otto's life style. It was fun to go on book signing tours with him and meet a lot of famous people. But, after a while she felt like a mannequin with a fixed smile on her face. She wanted a few days away from it all. She wanted to feel free to be herself, without pressure.

She thought when she confided in Suzie, that Suzie played the devil's advocate to help enlighten her. Suzie encouraged her to stand up to Otto.

"Don't ask him if you can do something. TELL him!", Suzie would advise her. "You don't need any man's permission or approval for anything!"

Every time after Suzie gave her advice, and Julia opposed Otto, he blamed Suzie, complaining, "You've been spending too much time with that woman, Julia. I warned you she is up to no good. I could never bring myself to be with a woman like that. She's only out for herself. She's not loving and giving like you are."

Julia defended Suzie many times, but Otto never saw Suzie the way she did. Now, in retrospect, she saw that Suzie had a vindictive streak. Both Suzie and Otto were possessive and competed for her. How ironic. Two very strong people vying for her, the weaker one. It seemed to be such a stupid game they were playing. Yet, at the same time, it was flattering.

Suzie poured some green tea into Julia's cup. "So, when are you and lover boy planning to get married?"

Calling Andre "lover boy" annoyed Julia, but she ignored the remark. "Well, we haven't set an exact date. We want it to be after the holidays. Perhaps sometime in January. I'm also in a law suit now. I might have to go to court."

"What kind of law suit?"

"Oh, it's such a headache. Stephanie and Stuart are suing me for the house. They're saying I made Otto sign papers when he wasn't in his right mind. This morning I met with my attorney. A month ago he said we'd probably be able to settle out of court. Now, he's telling me it looks like it's going to be a courtroom case. I can't get married until this is over with. Andre and I want to spend a month in Israel. We're getting married there and will spend the rest of the time honeymooning. I want to have all my affairs in order before we go or I won't be able to relax and enjoy myself."

"What made you decide to go to Israel? Aren't you afraid of those terrorists always crossing the border and blowing up shopping centers?"

Would Suzie ever give up? Why did she always have to throw in a monkey wrench and stir things up? Julia refused to bite the bait. "It was Andre's idea. He has relatives in Israel. His mother is a French Jew, who married a German Jew. She spent a year in Dachau. When she was liberated after the war, she was reunited with her husband. He was never imprisoned by the Nazis. He lived and worked with the allied underground. They lived in Israel for two years, but Andre's mother didn't like being in the army or living on a Kibbutz. So, right after Andre was born they immigrated to the United States."

"Are his parents still alive?"

"Only his mother. His father died a few years ago. A bad heart or something, I think."

"So, have you met Mama Kramer yet?"

"No, I haven't. She's coming to San Francisco in a few weeks and then she's going to Israel with us. She wants to show us the country."

"She's going to Israel with you? What kind of a honeymoon is that?"

"Well, she won't be staying with us, of course. She'll just fly there with us. Then, after the wedding she plans to take us on a tour of the historical sites for a week or so. After that, she'll take turns staying with her brother and some cousins, plus she'll be busy with Allison and Jamie."

"Allison and Jamie?"

"They're Andre's daughter and son from his first marriage. They'll be there too of course."

"Wow, sounds like you're going to have one helluva honeymoon with that troupe!"

Julia faked a smile. "Yes, I can't wait. I'm really looking forward to it."

She resented Suzie's sarcasm.

But, the sarcasm made her question herself. Was she making the right decision in marrying Andre?

## CHAPTER TWENTY-THREE: Disappointment

Andre's kisses were hot and passionate. He embraced Julia tightly, bent his head down and licked her neck with his warm tongue.

"I missed you so much", he whispered, then nibbled on her ear. Her response was cold and distant. She yanked herself from his grip.

"What's wrong Julia? Is something bothering you?"

"I, I'm sorry ... I don't feel very well today, I think it's about that time of the month. I usually get grumpy a day or so before my period. You know, PMS." Julia walked into the kitchen and opened the refrigerator door. Standing there, she pretended to be taking inventory of her staples.

"Wow! Is this thing empty! I'd better get to the store soon." She closed the door, took a few steps across the room toward the round oak table and sat on a bentwood chair. Ignoring Andre's presence, she began writing a shopping list.

"Let's see ... apples, pears, milk, bananas, yogurt ..."

She was afraid to confront Andre. She was afraid what Suzie told her might be true, that Andre was an asshole. It also bothered her that he and Suzie spent time together while she was going through all that emotional turmoil back East. Julia wondered what else they did besides have dinner. What did they talk about? Was she the topic of their conversation? What did they say about her? Was it possible they made love? Did they make a pact not to tell her? Was that why Suzie called him an asshole? To give Julia the feeling she didn't like Andre? To cover up her sin? Or, did Suzie want more from Andre than just sex? Was that Suzie's way of getting her to break up with Andre, so she could have him? Could she trust Suzie? Could she trust Andre? Julia continued to "mind-fuck" herself.

Suppose Andre had slept with Suzie. So what? Julia assured herself that it couldn't have been serious between them. It was probably just a one-night stand. Suzie liked those. That way she didn't have to get involved. Andre had such a strong sex drive, and with her three thousand miles away, maybe he couldn't contain himself. After all, Suzie was beautiful and very seductive.

Andre told Julia he loved her. He wooed her with words of love and passion. He told her she was all he ever wanted and he loved her with all his heart. She made him happier than any other woman ever had. Julia felt secure with him and was convinced that he really cared for her. At least that was before she went away.

But ... now what? Had Andre been telling her lies? Could she believe him, or trust him again? Would he be faithful to her after they were married? Was he, underneath his loving facade, a womanizer like Ralph? What did Andre really feel?

"Julia, you're evading me. Are you sure you're just premenstrual, or, is it something else?"

Julia laid down her pencil and looked up at Andre. "Well, yes, it's, a ... a ..." Her eyes began darting about and she stuttered searching for something to say. She wanted to tell him how insecure she felt. She wanted to say she didn't like that he and Suzie had dinner together. She wanted to ask him if they slept together. And, if he said yes, she wanted to tear him to shreds and tell him how hurt and angry she was.

Instead, she quietly said, "It's the law suit. And I'm really worried about losing the house."

"What's going on? What does Valenti say?"

"We're going to have to go to court."

"What! I thought he told you it would be settled out of court?"

"I know, but, now Iz ... uh, Valenti says there is a new development. He wouldn't tell me exactly what it was over the phone. I'm really upset. I couldn't sleep last night."

Julia avoided making eye contact with Andre. She worried he would detect she was lying. Partially. Actually, there was a new twist to her case.

Valenti had previously told Julia that Stuart had pneumonia. That Stephanie was going to fight her "tooth and nail" for the house. According to Valenti, "Stephanie told her attorney she would only settle this case in court". Their attorney, Bob Fredericks, however, was unaware that Stephanie intended to use Stuart's condition to intimidate Julia and play on the judge's sympathy.

"It's not just that I have to go to court. I'll also have to postpone our wedding, maybe for as long as a month."

"Why? You can't do that! My mother has it all planned."

"Your mother? Andre, this is our wedding. Not your mother's!"

"I know, Julia", he said sheepishly, "but, it really means a lot to her. She wasn't able to be there when I married Lauren and that was important to her. Allison was almost two years old and my mother wanted her granddaughter's parents to be married. But, she was in Israel then and the Six Day War was going on. She wasn't able to leave then. So now, see, she and the relatives in Israel made all the reservations for our wedding. They put a deposit down on the hotel, paid half the cost to the caterer and the rabbi, too. She'll be so upset if we don't show up as scheduled."

"Andre ... Valenti said Stuart hasn't been well for several weeks. He's in the hospital. They're still doing tests on him. We'll have to wait until he gets out of the hospital before we can make a settlement. I can't go to Israel until all this is over and taken care of. I wouldn't be able to relax or enjoy myself if I was still worrying about everything."

"Well, if it's because of Stuart, forget it. He's not gonna get well. He's got AIDS, which I hear is fatal. You won't have to worry about him anymore. He's a goner. So, concentrate on fighting Stephanie, and get it over with fast."

Julia was shocked. She felt like a bolt of lightening had struck her. Valenti didn't tell her Stuart was dying. She looked at Andre in disbelief, then annoyance. How could he treat such a tragic situation with so little compassion?

She began to cry. "Oh, my God!" Julia put her head down in her hands, elbows on the table. "I had no idea. Poor Stuart. Poor, poor Stuart. It can't be. He's so young.“

Julia always liked Stuart. They had many conversations over the years, and she felt close to him in spite of the law-suit.

"Andre, how do you know Stuart has AIDS?"

"News gets around. Actually, one of my friends told me. He works at the hospital. I hear those gay guys are gonna start dropping like flies. You know Stuart's lover died of AIDS, don't you?"

Andre's words stung. "Andre! You're so callous, so insensitive!"

"Well, what do you want me to do? Cry, too? After all, if you play with fire, you're gonna get burnt. And, those fags play with fire. They brought this on themselves."

"That's not so! How can you speak that way Andre?" Julia felt like hitting him. She began to shake as tears streamed down her face.

"Aw, look Honey, I didn't mean to sound like I don't care, but ... " He leaned over and put his arms around her. She shoved him away.

"But what? Of course you don't care! Because Stuart is gay! Does that mean he deserves to die?"

"No, ah, ah ... " Andre couldn't find the right words to express himself. He felt cornered, so he kept quiet.

"You, you ... I hate you! All you care about is yourself! I should've known from the time we went to Lake Tahoe."

She knew that she was being irrational, but she couldn't control herself. A lot of her anger was related to what Suzie said. The sad news about poor Stuart was just the catalyst rendering her more vulnerable.

"Now, wait just a minute, Julia. Hold on ... You're hitting below the belt bringing up old shit. I told you I was sorry for being late that day, and ... "

"Andre, I am sick and tired of your bullshit! I'm sick and tired of your lies and lame excuses!"

"What lies? What excuses? What are you talking about?"

"You know what I'm talking about." Before Julia realized it, she was blurting out her fears about Andre and Suzie spending time together. Maybe even having sex while she was back East suffering.

"Oh, Julia, we just went for a drink and appetizers over at Scala's. See, I ran into Suzie, and, to tell you the truth ... " Julia's heart began to beat as she was about to hear what she dreaded, what she wasn't so sure she wanted to hear after all. Andre continued, "I was at the jewelry counter at Saks and Suzie happened by. She saw me and stopped to say "Hi". I was trying to make a decision between several bracelets. I wanted to buy you one for Christmas. I wanted it to be a surprise, but now that you're putting me on the spot, I have to explain. Anyhow, I asked Suzie to give me some input, figuring she knew your taste. I'm not very good at buying things for other people. So, Suzie helped me pick one. Then, we began talking. I didn't realize how lonely I was with you gone. So, when we were both leaving Saks it started to rain, and, it was kind of impulsive, I thought it would be nice to treat her to a drink at Scala's. You know, it's real close to Saks. I wanted to show her my gratitude for helping me. Believe me, Julia, it was all completely innocent."

"And, you never slept with her?"

Andre turned red with embarrassment. He squirmed in his seat and looked away from Julia. He felt trapped. He couldn't deny that he and Suzie had slept together.

"No! No way! Not then! But, I must confess that years ago we did."

"You did? How did that happen? When did you meet her?"

"Julia! She was the one who recommended me to Otto, remember? Suzie often had a stiff neck after sleeping on planes and she was a patient of mine."

"You never told me, and neither did she, that you were a twosome". But, then, Suzie never mentioned names of guys she was sleeping with, whenever they talked about sex it was very casual.

"Well, first of all, Julia, our short-lived affair happened at least five years ago. And, besides, it would have been unethical for me to say anything about her. Or, for me to even mention she was a patient."

"Unethical to say anything! What about sleeping with your patient? Isn't that unethical?"

"OK, it was, but ... well, it just happened so quickly and I really regretted it. It only happened once."

Andre felt he had to focus on Julia and reassure her that he loved her. "I swear, Suzie means nothing to me, she never did. I love you. Only you." He took her hand and clasped it in his.

Julia pulled away. "Did you love Suzie when you slept with her? Is she still your patient?"

"First of all, she's no longer my patient. I adjusted her back and neck so well in a few sessions that she didn't need to come back. And, secondly, no, I didn't love her. It wasn't what you think. You see, Suzie seduced me.

"Suzie? Come on Andre. You can do better than that. Why not tell me Suzie raped you? That would almost be more plausible."

"Actually, it was kind of like that. See, she came to my office with a sore back, and while I was working on her she began to run her hand up my thigh, and, well, I got horny. I hadn't had sex in months. It all happened so fast I didn't think."

"You mean you two had sex in your examining room?"

"Yes, well, I mean, no, ah ... ah ..."

"Well, what is it? Yes or no? Did she at least get off the table? Did you do it on the floor, or what?"

"Uh, no, uh ... we went upstairs to my bedroom, but ... "

"Your bedroom? That doesn't sound to me like it was all Suzie's prompting. She's too thin to lift you up, or force you into the bedroom!" Julia's voice weakened as she shouted. She could almost hear her heart pounding, and she felt nauseous at the thought of her best friend and her fiance' in bed together ... but, it also titillated her.

"I told you, Julia, Suzie meant nothing to me. She was good for a great lay, and to let off some steam. Suzie really has the makings of a hooker. She knows how to get a guy worked up. And, when it's over, she has nothing else to offer."

Makings of a hooker? Nothing else to offer? That incensed Julia. She screamed at Andre, "That's not true! Suzie has a lot to offer! She's beautiful inside and out! She's smart, she's sharp, she's intuitive, she's worldly, she's loving and caring – usually. And, she has a great sense of humor! Suzie Clemmens is my best friend and I will not listen to you say these things. I will not have you denigrate her with your male chauvinist viciousness!"

Before Andre could defend himself, a ceramic vase from the windowsill came flying towards him. He turned to dodge it, but it skinned the top of his head and he sustained a gash near his hairline. Stunned, he looked down at the lethal weapon lying on the floor in a hundred pieces.

"Holy shit! That hurt!" Andre ran over to the sink and put his bleeding head under running cold water. He grabbed a towel and held it tightly on his wound, hoping to stop the gushing blood with pressure. "Jesus Christ, Julia! You don't have to murder me over something so, so ... "

Andre was just about to say the word, "trivial", but caught himself. He was already in enough hot water and knew whatever he said would only get him in deeper. Women! They're impossible to read or understand.

First, Julia was angry with him for having dinner with Suzie. And, not telling her previously that they had once slept together. Now, she's defending Suzie, and he's the "dirty bird" taking all the blame. What could he do or say to her?

He didn't have to speak. Julia was nervously putting ice into a plastic bag. She felt guilty that her temper had gotten the best of her. It scared her to realize she could have killed Andre.

"I'm sorry Andre. I didn't mean to hurt you. I was just pissed." She was crying as she applied the ice pack to his forehead. Then, with a clean cloth she wiped the blood from his face.

"I'll live, don't worry, and, I promise I won't sue you. You have enough legal battles to deal with." Andre felt the swelling on the top of his skull. "That's some goose egg you gave me. Remind me to keep my trap shut if we ever get into an argument again. You're dangerous!"

They looked at each other and burst out laughing. Then he grabbed Julia and hugged her. "I love you so very, very much. And, I would never do anything to hurt you ... not intentionally anyway. I am truly sorry if I said or did anything. Will you please forgive me?" As he was asking for forgiveness he was still confused about what he did wrong. But, he didn't know what else to say to put Julia back into her usual good mood.

Andre sounded so sweet and sincere at that moment and Julia felt like putty in his arms. She also felt afraid to let go of him. She had known enough men in her life to see that Andre was a prize. So, he wasn't always perfect. Big deal. "Of course, Darling, I forgive you. And, will you forgive me for being so violent?"

"I could never stay angry with you, Julia. I love you too much."

He squeezed her, kissing her lustfully. She opened her mouth to let his tongue in, as she melted to his touch. She wanted to believe him and she wanted to believe Suzie. She loved them both and decided then that she was being silly and jealous, acting like an immature teen-ager. And, paranoid and insecure for worrying that they cheated on her. She promised herself to never mistrust either of them again. She also decided she really loved Andre and wanted to marry him. And, after they got married, she wanted to live "happily ever after" with him for the rest of her life.

Was that too much to ask for? Was it too much to hope for?

## CHAPTER TWENTY-FOUR: The Surgery

Stephanie sat in a gray metal chair next to the large window overlooking the city of Palo Alto. It was high noon. A warm, bright day. A gorgeous array of magenta and deep purple pansies glistened in the sun on the lawn below. The colorful blossoms reminded her of the gardens where she and Stuart once played, when they were children, when they were young, innocent, carefree, and happy. Momentarily, Stephanie felt a little happiness.

Ever since Stuart contracted AIDS Stephanie felt wretched. She thought he could be treated and cured. She didn't know that much about this horrible new disease that was spreading throughout the San Francisco area. Everything seemed to be happening so quickly.

First, Stuart began to cough a lot. Then he complained of severe headaches. Then came the lethargy and drowsiness, the weight loss. When his body started to deteriorate rapidly over a short three weeks, Stephanie knew she had reason to be concerned. Nevertheless, when the doctor told her that Stuart's condition was terminal, she refused to believe he wouldn't get well.

Three weeks to the day after the dreaded diagnosis was made, Stuart developed pneumonia. When Stephanie rushed him to the hospital, he was gasping for every breath of air. She remembered how terrified she was, almost certain he wasn't going to make it. Thank God for antibiotics and modern medicine!

During his week-long stay at San Francisco General, Stuart had a grand mal seizure. An electroencephalogram was immediately performed and to

Stephanie's dismay, a small intracranial lesion was discovered. It was a nightmarish day. The unemotional doctor only added to her despair.

"Sorry Miss, ah, Marlton, your brother has a brain tumor. Chances are it's probably malignant. He'll be lucky if he lives six months." And, with his death sentence declaration the doctor hastened out of the room, not even waiting for Stephanie to respond, or allowing her the opportunity to ask questions.

It seemed the great "White Knight" could care less. Why should he? Stuart was just another number. And, a gay one to boot. Who cared if another homosexual "kicked the bucket"? That was an expression her father had often used when someone died.

Stephanie immediately had Stuart transferred to Stanford Hospital where she felt he would be given better care and treated by the top doctors in the world. She was determined to do everything she could to help her brother, vowing to him that he would get well, and telling him, "If it's the last thing I do … if it takes every dime I have."

Now, Stephanie sadly realized it wasn't a matter of money. It was fate. And, there was nothing she could do. How unnerving it was to wait … and hell trying to be hopeful.

She looked across the room at Stuart. His surgery had taken more than five hours. He was asleep, but his breathing was laborious even with an oxygen mask. After returning from the recovery room he lapsed back into a deep sleep. A bandage was wrapped around his head and his body looked gaunt and frail. An intravenous line was attached to his arm and there was a catheter connected to a urine bottle strapped to the side rails of the bed. The surgeon had not come to Stuart's room yet, so she still didn't know the results of the biopsy.

Stephanie anxiously twisted her scarf, fretting the tumor was malignant, and if it was, wondering how long Stuart had to live. Would he fully recover from such a major operation? And if he did, would he be able to function normally? Would his life have any quality? What would she do?

Their mother Estelle was in Europe traveling with her new beau, so Stephanie had to deal with Stuart's condition alone. There was no way to reach Estelle, but even if she was still living in California, Stephanie wasn't sure how she would tell her judgmental mother that Stuart was homosexual. He and Marty had cleverly kept it hidden from both sets of parents.

For the first time in many years, Stephanie felt completely out of control and sick to her stomach. She walked over to the adjoining bathroom, quietly closing the door and turned on the fan. She reached into her purse and took out a pack of Marlboros. She needed a nicotine fix to calm her frazzled nerves. But, when she lit the cigarette, took a long drag and inhaled deeply, she gagged. Even smoking had lost its appeal. Feeling nauseous, she threw the partially smoked cigarette into the toilet, bent over the bowl and vomited.

She sensed the presence of another person as she stepped out of the bathroom. A slight shadow was cast across the floor. Feeling guilty for smoking in a hospital, she expected a nurse to reprimand her any minute. She looked up sheepishly and was shocked to see Julia standing in the doorway. Of all people. The "bitch".

"Stephanie, I came as soon as I heard. I am so sorry", Julia whispered. Her bright blue eyes were so misty they almost looked gray.

Stephanie was taken completely off guard. Julia was the last person she cared to see, or confront face to face. Especially, under these circumstances. "Uh, yeah, it's a bummer, ain't it?" Stephanie scarcely replied, averting her eyes, she needed to be in control of the situation.

"How is Stuart? Why is his head all bandaged up?"

"He has a brain tumor, or, I should say had a brain tumor. They removed it today." Stephanie's voice was cold and insolent. She turned her back to Julia and walked over to the window. She didn't want Julia to see how weak she was truly feeling.

"Oh, my God!" Julia gasped, putting her hand up over her mouth. Then she began to cry. She followed Stephanie toward the window and put her arm on Stephanie's shoulder.

Stephanie stiffened when she felt Julia's hand, but before she could move away, Julia had both arms around her. Tears were streaming down Julia's face.

"Stephanie, I know how you feel about me, and I'm sorry. I am truly sorry that we couldn't be friends. I'm sorry we couldn't have worked something out without our attorneys, but now, I don't care about the house."

Stephanie pushed Julia away. "The hell you don't! You bitch! You only married my father to get what you could. You're a gold-digger. I bet you and that, that, sneakin' boyfriend of yours, that charlatan, who has the nerve to call himself a doctor, bumped off my father!"

"Stephanie!", Julia exclaimed. "I can't believe what you're saying! I can't believe you would even think such a thing! I loved your father dearly. More than you could ever imagine. And, I never needed your Dad's money ... what little he had. I paid my own way, and then some. And, as far as Andre is concerned, well, we never, I repeat never did anything while your father was alive. Andre deeply respected Otto and wouldn't have done anything to hurt him."

"Yeah! Tell that cock n' bull story to the judge! I'm sure he's heard that shitty melodrama before!"

Julia felt like a raging bull. She wanted to strangle Stephanie for being so heartless. So, untouchable. "Stephanie, you are the absolute coldest person I have ever known!" Julia shouted. "You are impossible! And ... and, you, you can go to hell!" Julia abruptly turned to leave.

At that moment Stuart's surgeon walked in. His expression was grave as he extended his hand toward Julia.

"Hello, I'm Dr. Gartner, J.G. Gartner."

Julia shook his hand and responded, "I'm Julia Forrester, I, I'm Stuart's, I, ah, was married to Stuart's father."

"Oh, Mrs. Marlton then, eh?"

Julia ignored Dr. Gartner's rudeness for not paying attention to her after she had just told him her name was Forrester. "Well, no, I, ah, never changed my name. I go by Julia Forrester."

"Oh, hmm, well, as I was telling your, a, daught ..." Seeing that the two women looked close in age, it seemed odd to refer to Stephanie as Julia's daughter. He rephrased his sentence, "As I told Miss Marlton before the operation, Stuart had a neoplasm, a frontal lobe meningioma. It turned out to be bigger than we expected and it had invaded a large portion of his brain. That's why the surgery took so long, and, I'm sorry to report, it was malignant."

Julia let out a wail while Stephanie stood there looking bitterly at the doctor. The bad news did not seem to affect her when she matter-of-factly asked, "Well, did you get it all?"

"Ah, yes, we did, but ... "

"But, what?" Stephanie demanded.

"We had to cut out a lot of the surrounding tissue to make sure none of the cancer was left. Stuart might have some side effects."

"And, what does that mean?"

"It means, that, of course, with each patient it is different, but your brother may have expressive aphasia. A tumor on the medial surface of the frontal lobe may precipitate uncontrolled urination and personality changes. Also, an ataxic gait is common when a tumor has spread. And, the optic chasm could be compressed, which could affect his sight. And ..."

"Hey, knock it off! What are you some kind of joker with all these fancy words and ivory tower medical jargon? Can't you speak English? Look doc, is Stuart gonna live, or not?"

"Well, ah, it's very hard to predict. But, his prognosis is not looking favorable."

"What are you saying?"

"Miss Marlton, Stephanie, we did a CAT scan which revealed that the tumor in Stuart's brain was a metastasis from his lungs. We also biopsied several lymph nodes and it seems that ... well, that, it has probably metastasized to other parts of his body, too."

"Oh no!" Stephanie's legs wobbled. She had to sit down. Julia, crying uncontrollably, asked, "What is Stuart's prognosis?"

"Perhaps six months, at most, that is if he responds to treatment, Mrs., uh, ..."

"Ms. Forrester. What kind of treatment?

"Mrs. Forrester, we're going to try chemotherapy and hope for the best.

Right now we're concerned about Stuart's recovery from this surgery, which took longer than we thought it would. He was under anesthesia for a couple more hours than we expected. We might also try radiation if the chemo isn't successful. We'll try everything possible and do everything we can to make him comfortable."

And, that was that. Dr. Gartner said he had to hurry back to the operating room for his next surgery. He handed Julia a card with his name scrawled on it. "Call me if you have any other questions."

Julia stared at the card in her shaking hand. She was still crying. Stephanie was quivering, slumped in a chair, holding her head in her hands.

Julia walked towards Stephanie, then hesitated. It was apparent Stephanie didn't like her, but so what? Julia cared about Stuart and wanted to help in any way she could. She decided to risk Stephanie's animosity and wrath once more.

"Stephanie ..." she said remorsefully, "I'm sorry if I hurt you in any way. I never meant to." Then swallowing her pride, Julia asked, "Can you forgive me?"

Stephanie looked up into Julia's eyes. "Why should I?"

"Because, because of Stuart. He needs us both now."

"The hell he does! He doesn't need you! I'm the only one he needs!"

"Stephanie, Stuart needs me, too. He needs all the help and support he can get. I just came back from my mother's funeral, and ... ah, a dying person can be a strain on the people around them, the people who care. I want to offer my assistance in any way I can."

"And, just what can you do? Do you think that, that you have the power to make Stuart well? Or, perhaps that boyfriend of yours has some magic potion, or voodoo cure?"

"No, I don't! And, leave Andre out of this! Look ... " Julia clenched her teeth, "Look, Stephanie, I care about Stuart. I've tried to get close to you to show you that I care about you, too. But, you would never let me. So, for Stuart's sake, let's forget the past and join forces. If you need money, I will give it to you. And, if you and Stuart want to move back into the house after he is released from the hospital, you may do so. I'll move into the guest house until I find another place. And, I intend to call my attorney as soon as I get home and tell him that fighting you for the house is no longer important. If the house means that much to you, you can stay there for a while, until Stuart is better. Call me after you think things over. Stuart may need 'round-the-clock care and attention, and you can't do it all yourself." Julia picked up her jacket and purse and briskly walked toward the door.

Stephanie was stunned, shocked at what she had just heard. She looked up, "Wait! Julia, please, please ... don't, don't leave", she called out.

Julia was gone.

## CHAPTER TWENTY FIVE: The Break-Up

"I can't believe you, Julia! I just can't believe you!" Andre shouted. His arms went up into the air as he threw himself down on the faded burgundy sofa in his living room. "That was the stupidest decision you could've made!"

Julia cringed then looked away towards the foyer. She hated to get hollered at. It reminded her of the awful years with Ralph when he yelled at her or blamed her for doing something "stupid". It was also a reminder of her mother. Katherine's accusing tone echoed in Andre's words.

"Julia, you naughty little girl. You should know better. Why do you always do such dumb things?"

Julia never remembered doing anything "dumb". Her actions made sense to her. Especially one incident when she was five years old. It was the time she had tried to be "good" by cooking dinner for her mother. That horrible day was still vivid in her mind.

Julia felt sorry for her mother who was vacuuming the upstairs bedrooms. She wanted to do something to help her "poor mother" who was working "her fingers to the bone". At least that's what Katherine always complained about when Julia's father, came home from work.

Julia had noticed a chicken on top of the kitchen counter. Katherine said she was going to make it for dinner that evening. Julia had often watched her mother prepare chicken, so she wanted to cook it and surprise her. She wanted to save her mother the extra work. She moved a chair over to the gas range and began to singe the feathers off the chicken, just as she had seen her mother do countless times.

In those days, stores displayed live chickens in cages and when a customer pointed to the hen she wanted, it was taken into another room and killed. The head was chopped off and the insides removed. Then the body, held by its feet, was completely immersed in scalding water to remove the feathers. Later, at home, any remaining feathers that hadn't fallen off had to be singed over a flame on the stove.

When Katherine smelled the burning feathers she rushed downstairs and reprimanded Julia for "playing with fire". Julia tried to explain what her intentions were, that she was only trying to help, but her mother kept screaming, "You stupid little girl! You stupid little girl!" She shook Julia, then took her hand and put it on the hot range to "teach her a lesson".

That night Julia lay awake in bed crying. She was only trying to do a good deed, and instead, she had a scorched hand throbbing in pain. She hated her mother for being unjust and vowed never to give Katherine any of her love ever again.

Life with Ralph had not been much different. He treated Julia as if she was a child who didn't know anything and had to be directed. He rarely gave her credit for having the intelligence to make up her own mind. He often criticized her claiming that she was not experienced enough to make wise decisions. Ralph's voice rang in her head.

"Julia, why are you so forgetful? Are you just plain dumb? I told you a million times that I needed my suit dry cleaned by the weekend. Is there something wrong with you? Can't you remember anything?"

"Julia, you balanced the checkbook wrong. Don't you know how to add and subtract?"

"Julia, you didn't buy enough raisins this week. Didn't you check the cupboard before you went to the market?"

"Julia, you put the wrong kind of gas in the car. I told you to get Exxon not Shell, it's five cents cheaper. Why can't you pay attention and listen?"

"Julia, that was an incorrect way to write that letter. What's the matter with you? Your logic is weak, and your spelling, well, it's so bad, you ought to go back to school."

"Julia … Julia … Julia …"

Ralph found fault with everything. He never let up. Julia felt trapped with no way out.

Except one time. The only time she trumped him. It was a minor victory over his relentless demands and criticisms. Nevertheless, it made her feel really good when she proved him wrong.

Julia had written "raspberries" on her grocery list, and when Ralph saw it taped on the refrigerator door, he laughed and said, "Who ever heard of a 'P' in rasberries?" He said the word loudly and clearly emphasizing the "S" and "B". Then he exclaimed, "Julia, I told you, you were awful at spelling. You really need to study words better. If you can't spell something why don't you use the dictionary?"

Which is precisely what she did. Ralph practically turned the color of a rasPberry when she got the Webster from the book shelf and showed it to him. She was right! That kept him quiet and humble for a few days. Julia glowed remembering how wonderfully vindictive she felt watching him squirm.

It took her a long time to honor her anger towards Ralph. Right after he put her down, he'd then give her a warm hug and say, "You know I love you.

I'm just trying to help you be a better person." And, each time Julia believed him and forgave him.

Otto never belittled her. In spite of his genius, Otto respected her, her opinions and what she had to say. Those three years with him were golden years. Years that could never be recaptured except in memories. Thinking of Otto gave her a surge of strength.

Andre's criticism of her generosity with the house felt like a dagger stabbing directly into her heart. His words were too much of a reminder of her mother and Ralph, who both professed their love for her, while their actions contradicted their words.

Julia was furious with Andre. "Don't you ever call me stupid!"

Andre's mouth dropped open. He raised his hands as if to protect himself and backed away. "Look, Julia, I didn't say that you were stupid. I was just saying that you did a stupid thing – telling Stephanie they could have the house."

Andre looked around the room at his inexpensive furniture and at the shabby way his house was decorated. He was disappointed to think that after he and Julia got married they might not have that gorgeous mansion to live in. He had fantasized about living there. When he first began taking care of Otto, he wished he could someday live in such a palatial home. It disturbed him that he had to reside in a small two-bedroom flat in the city. He hated the pollution and all the noises. Horns honking, sirens screaming by constantly, and trolley cars clanging. He hated everything about living in the city.

Though Saint Francis Wood was a section of the city, it was away from all that racket. It was still within minutes of downtown San Francisco and close enough to take advantage of all the city's cultural events. It was like a country retreat with magnificent homes and lush foliage. And, decent neighbors. Even the mayor resided there. With armed guards. No one needed to be fearful of crime in an area like that. Andre had been counting the days until he could go to sleep every night unafraid of burglars ... maybe even murderers.

When Julia accepted his proposal, Andre dreamed of their wedding on the emerald green lawn that surrounded the house. He imagined the rich and famous witnessing his marriage to Otto Marlton's widow. He greedily thought of all the expensive wedding presents they would receive. It made him feel proud to think that he and his new bride's photo would appear in the social section of the San Francisco Chronicle.

It was a disappointment when his mother insisted that they get married in Israel. Seeing how much it meant to her, Andre gave in. He decided after they returned to California, they would throw a party to celebrate their marriage.

Living in such an opulent home would also make Andre's future brighter. He would be living in luxury, no longer struggling to make ends meet. He visualized himself in a black silk dinner jacket with a cummerbund greeting the elite of the Bay Area. He always wanted to be part of the upper echelon social circle, but never had the required collateral.

It wasn't that he was materialistic, or shallow, he reasoned, it was simply good business sense. Marrying into wealth was a lot easier than marrying someone he had to support, like Lauren. She and the children were still a financial drain on him.

Besides, his practice might flourish from all the celebrities he would meet through Julia. After all, the rich were better paying clients than the poor. Perhaps he could even retire in a few years.

"It was not stupid!", Julia yelled back. "I care deeply about Stuart, and, he's dying, for pity sake."

"That's just the point. Stuart won't be around much longer, so Stephanie will get the house and she doesn't deserve it."

"Andre! I don't know how long Stuart has to live, and neither do you! But, I do know that if he moves back into the house where he grew up, where he has happy childhood memories, it might make him feel better, be more comfortable and it'll make his last days more enjoyable."

"I think you're just reading your own feelings into it, you know, projecting. How could you know what would be more enjoyable for Stuart? After all, his kind of sex is enjoyable for him, but not for you."

"Look, Andre, I've made up my mind. Stuart needs that place more than we do. He'll have the grounds to stroll around on, room in which to breathe. His townhouse in the Castro is depressing, especially with Marty gone. I was there once and couldn't wait to leave, even though he and Marty had it artistically decorated it was claustrophobic and stifling."

"Then, where will we live after we're married?"

Julia was incensed. So, that's it! Andre's not concerned about me, just about the house ... and himself!

Andre's reactions to Julia's decision only added to her mounting feelings of discomfort with him. She had several restless nights during the past few weeks. Upon awakening, all she could remember were dreams about being a helpless bird in a cage, or locked in some sort of prison. It seemed more and more obvious to her that her decision to marry Andre was, well, a hasty one.

Doubts were flooding her heart. Now, more than ever, she was positive she couldn't go through with this marriage.

"That's something I wanted to talk to you about, Andre. I'm not sure I'm ready to get married again. At least not right now, I ... "

"Julia! If it's about Suzie, I told you the truth, exactly what happened between us while you were away. What else can I say?"

"It has nothing to do with Suzie. It's me. I'd like to postpone our wedding for a while longer."

"Are you insane? You already postponed it a month. I can't believe what I'm hearing. We've talked about this so many times. My mother already rearranged everything in Tel Aviv. I can't tell her to do it again. She'll be upset, and so will the rest of the relatives. And, my kids have taken off time to be there, too. Now you're telling me that you're not ready to get married!?"

"Andre, I ... I'm sorry. I really am. I don't want to hurt you, but my feelings have changed and I'm really confused. I can't help it ... "

"Well, when do you think your feelings will change again? When do you think you will want to marry me?"

She resented Andre's pushiness. She resented feeling pressured and put on the spot. She hated it when people tried to make her feel more guilty than she already felt. She gritted her teeth. "I, I don't know, Andre. Perhaps never."

"What! So, you've been leading me on? So, you were never serious? Never really intended to marry me?"

"No, that's not it at all. I loved, ah, I do love you, Andre. But, so much has happened to me recently, that I'm, well ... overwhelmed and confused."

"Confused? About what? If you love me, then that's all that really matters."

"No, it isn't. Love is one thing. Marriage and commitment is another thing all together."

"Oh, so you want to go out with other men then?"

"No, I don't. I want a close, loving relationship with only one man. But, the thought of being married again makes me feel restricted."

"Ha! And, you think that being alone is better?"

"Actually, yes, and no. And, that surprises me. I never lived alone before I married Otto. Then when he died and I was alone, it wasn't so bad after all. In fact, I kind of liked the freedom."

"That's because it's only been a few months. It gets pretty lonely being by yourself. All the single spinster patients I have are begging to get married. Look at all the ads and lonely hearts looking for mates in the newspapers. You know, Julia, you're not so young anymore. I think you're making a big mistake. You'll be sorry."

"Well! I'm hardly a spinster! I have quite a few good years left. And, I have lots of friends for company ... when I want them."

The more Andre baited her, the angrier Julia became, and more sure of her decision. And, more disillusioned about Andre.

"Look, Andre, I don't need your permission, or approval for anything I do, think, or feel! I might be making a mistake, but as my art teacher once said, "There is no such thing as a mistake. Only an opportunity to learn. So, I'll take my chances."

Julia felt like her head was going to split. She couldn't stand another minute arguing with Andre. She picked up her suede jacket and walked toward the door.

"See you around," she said, and left.

## CHAPTER TWENTY-SIX: The Cruise

A month passed since Julia had last seen Andre. She could still visualize his perturbed expression when she told him she was going to let the twins live in the house. She could still hear his angry voice.

It seemed he was more interested in the house than he was in her. Yet, she wondered if she had not given him enough credit. Was she too harsh on him? She wondered if her feelings about him were valid.

She relived that last time trying to remember what it was that made her so mad at him. She was now feeling she had to justify her anger. After all, she had never felt entitled to be angry with anyone.

"But, Julia, where will we live?"

"It doesn't matter. I could move in with you until we find another place. It's being with you that's important to me. Not where we live."

"But, my flat is crowded, and not that nice for entertaining."

"My friends don't care."

"But, your house is so much more impressive."

Julia looked at him in surprise, "And, who exactly is it we have to impress, Andre?"

Andre blushed and stammered. He had blurted out his true feelings before he had time to analyze what he was saying, and his words didn't put him in the most favorable light. "Well, ah, you know, I'm not trying to climb any social ladder or anything. I'm not like that. But, there are some really important people in this city, and it could help my practice – and your art career – if, if we threw a few big parties in your beautiful home."

"Andre! You're despicable! I'm shocked. I thought you were above all that … that bullshit!"

Julia thought about how vulnerable she felt that first night with Andre when they made love. He was understanding, tender, and caring. And so sexy. There was no doubt her hormones ruled her mind when she was with him. She had been love-starved, and, previously, sex for her had not been fulfilling. Could she have been desperate when she began seeing Andre? Unfortunately, the excitement of those first several weeks, gradually diminished.

Over the past few months Andre's shining armor had worn transparently thin. Beneath his confident, sometimes haughty facade, Julia slowly began to see another scared human being. Though she never lacked empathy, she began to feel contemptuous of his ignorance. Instead of being honest, he played games with her. To compensate for his own insecurity, he tried to manipulate her and her vulnerability.

Andre's tactics had blinded her in the beginning. Now everything had changed. Julia felt … independent. She was learning to trust herself and act on what was in her own best interest. She didn't want to be with a man who made life more difficult than it already was. She didn't need anyone's permission, or approval anymore. She wanted to do exactly as she pleased.

So, what if she never got married again? So, what if she grew old alone? What if … ? Hell, she'd cross that bridge when she came to it.

It had not been easy for her to arrive at this conclusion. It happened an inch at a time, then in a rush. Now, with a taste of personal power and entitlement, there was no turning back. As frightening as it was, in an odd sort of way, her new found freedom was also the beginning of an exciting new journey. And, marriage didn't seem to fit in to the agenda – at least not now.

Julia worried if Andre's daughter Allison would be able to understand. Before Allison knew the wedding had been cancelled she had written Julia a warm, touching note saying she couldn't wait until Julia became her stepmother. Julia sighed. She remembered how flattered she was when she read that note. It hit her maternal nerve and helped alleviate her guilt about what she considered being a failure as a mother to her own children. Nevertheless, she was not flattered enough to make any sacrifices to spare Allison. Unfortunately, accepting disappointment was one of life's lessons. Julia knew the pain well.

Especially the excruciating painful disappointment of losing a loved one. All plans, hopes and dreams snuffed out in an instant. Gone! Julia relived the pain she felt when she found Otto dead. The instant emptiness. The awareness that a part of her had died with him. She realized on the night of his funeral, her total aloneness hit her. With Otto gone who would guide her? Encourage her? With whom would she share her life now? Who would take care of her? No, her life would never be the same again.

Similar feelings surfaced when she was with her dying mother. Seeing Katherine deteriorated forced Julia to imagine her own death. She remembered sitting by her mother's bedside with thoughts of growing old and sick, with thoughts of lying on her own deathbed, like her mother.

That was when she made a promise to herself to make every moment of her life matter. To experience all of life, in all its facets, before it was too late. Before it was all over.

This awareness helped diminish her feelings of guilt. It helped her to better understand her estranged relationship with her mother. To live, she decided, was to die to the past, without expectations of the future.

Expectations only set people up for disappointment, anyhow. Few things ever turn out the way one expects.

Stuart's illness shed a new light on Julia's perspective, too. Though not old, he was at death's door. That harsh reality reminded her that one doesn't have to be up in years to die. At the snap of a finger, life could be over. She had no control over fate, or her final destiny. But, she did have control over how she chose to live her life.

When Julia saw Stuart in that hospital bed, half delirious, hooked up to tubes and machines, she suddenly became acutely aware that fighting with him and Stephanie over the house was ridiculous. How important was a house anyway in the scope of eternity? She didn't have to reside in a mansion to be happy and she had plenty of money to live comfortably the rest of her life. She still had a sizable sum of money left from her divorce settlement, still had a savings account from the paintings she sold, as well as the money from Otto's insurance policy and will.

No, it was becoming clear to Julia that tangible possessions were not important. Sure, she enjoyed the good life and she liked expensive things, but she could be just as happy without them. She also loved living in a beautiful home, but that wasn't what made her life a fulfilling one. It was Otto, the man, who loved and adored her.

Isadore Valenti was infuriated when Julia called to tell him she was letting Stephanie and Stuart live in the house.

"After all the work I did!" he yelled.

"I paid you for your time," Julia firmly replied.

"But, Julia, I'm thinking of your best interest, and ... "

"I've made my decision, Mister Valenti."

"Well, it was made too hastily. You should have consulted with me first and I would have advised you."

"I didn't need your advice. I know exactly what I'm doing."

"Well, it was too impulsive. You've made a grave mistake, little lady." Valenti continued to rant and rave like a maniac shouting at Julia as if she was his subordinate. He even implied that women were not equipped to logically deal with legal matters.

Not feeling the least bit intimidated, Julia simply reiterated that she had made up her mind. Being in total control of her decisions and actions was a terrific feeling. Screw Isadore Valenti and his greedy ambitions!

"Perhaps I have, but I am willing to pay that price. I appreciate your services. Thank you. I sent you a check for a thousand dollars. According to my calculations, that's what I owe you. If it's more than that, bill me, and itemize your hours."

Before Valenti could say another word she hung up the phone.

She was nostalgic thinking about the house. It also made her feel a bit uneasy. What would she do now? Where she would live? That house had been her life. It had monopolized most of her time when she lived there with Otto. She oversaw all the maintenance and the expenses, keeping that house was a constant job. Now, without it, her physical and financial burden was tremendously reduced, which actually felt good. She was sure she was making the right decision. The twins would benefit from living there more than she would.

Just seeing the expression on Stuart's face when she announced that he could move back into the house was worth any inconvenience to her. Maybe it was enough to give him an extra boost of hope. Who knows? Perhaps hope would put him into remission until a cure was found.

Stephanie didn't show the same appreciation. She acted as if Julia should have known all along that the house rightfully belonged to them, not Julia.

"It's about time you came to your senses," she barked sarcastically.

Julia's jaw tightened. "Stephanie, I am only doing this because of Stuart. Otherwise, I would be fighting you in court."

"So, aren't you the generous one. Seeing poor, helpless Stuart sick and dying pulled on your heart strings?"

Julia felt like strangling Stephanie. At that moment she never felt such hatred for anyone. It took tremendous self-discipline for her to not change her mind and retract her offer.

"I'm not being altruistic. I need time to myself and since I'll be gone for a while I figured you two could house sit."

"House sit! So that's it! You don't really have any sympathy for Stuart! You just want your fucking plants watered! Well, let me tell you, you'll never get us out of the house when you come back. You'll have to fight us for it."

Julia retorted, "I think, Stephanie, you should put your energy into helping Stuart, not fighting me. I'm hoping that when I return in six months you will have simmered down. If not, well, I guess I will have to fight you in court. And, I'll win. Because I paid the mortgage, the taxes, and the maintenance most of the time while I was married to your father. I have all the receipts to prove it. And, I also spent my money remodeling and decorating the house, for which I also have receipts. So, Stephanie, save yourself unnecessary time, energy and money and don't file another law suit. And don't worry, I'll give you enough notice when I want you to move out. Now, I want your signature on this contract."

Stephanie was speechless. She never realized Julia had her own income. She had been positive that money was the only reason Julia married her father.

In the same mail with Allison's note was a postcard from Stephanie. Julia was almost afraid to read it, fearing the worst about Stuart. To her surprise, Stephanie wrote:

Dear Julia,

Stuart and I are in a support group and it is helping us both. We are grateful to be back in the house, especially at this time. You made it so much more comfortable and enjoyable than we remember. Stuart is regaining his strength and his spirits have picked up. Now only time will tell.

Enjoy your cruise to Mexico.

Bon Voyage, Stephanie

Julia was shocked that Stephanie had taken the time to write to her. Especially with such a warm tone. Was it possible she wanted to be friends? Stephanie was still impossible to figure out. She was covered with too many layers of pride.

She laid her head back on the blue and white striped deck chair. She closed her eyes, swallowed hard and took in a deep breath of crisp clean sea air. It felt healthy seeping into her lungs. It restored her energy. She opened her eyes again and gazed out at the shoreline covered by a thin gray mist which made it barely visible. Although one could view the morning sun peeping up behind the mauve-colored mountains, the ochre and pink sky was calm. There wasn't a cloud in sight.

She loved this time of the morning, when everything was quiet, when life was beginning again. Sea gulls were flying overhead croaking at each other. She wondered what they might be saying. Did the sea gull society imitate humans in any way? Then, as if someone directed them, the birds flew off en masse.

Suddenly, the ship rocked to and fro. Waves could be heard crashing and breaking below. The jagged cliffs and majestic rocks off the California coast were not easy to maneuver. The ship abruptly turned west and moved further out to sea where the water was calmer. Julia hoped they wouldn't encounter any more turbulence before arriving in Ixtapa, Zihuatenejo. She hated getting sea sick, especially, being all alone.

Her eyes were fixated on the deep blue water. The early morning sun's golden rays created an effect of sparkling diamonds that was hypnotizing. Almost instantly she forgot about being sick. Feeling the urge to paint, she wished she hadn't left her art supplies in the cabin.

Painting relaxed her. It had always been therapy for her. It had given her more strength than anything else in her life. Even, more than Otto's books. Only in the past few months did she realize it and made a promise to herself that she would never give up painting again.

As if sitting by her easel, she began to paint the spectacular scene in her mind. Anxious to begin her "masterpiece" she studied the exciting spectrum of colors on her imaginary palette. Which color should I start with? They all look so delicious. She dipped her pretend brush into the vermillion red. One of her favorite colors. It was difficult to paint anything without using vermillion red. She slapped thick gobs of it on her imaginary painting. With another large square-tipped brush she reached for the cobalt blue. Painted right next to the intense red, the ordinary blue screamed out. The breathtaking duo portrayed her sunrise. Now for the mountains. Ah, purple, of course. Yes, dark, rich purple. It seemed the most natural hue to create the valleys on the peaks — of what color? Yes, yellow-green peaks.

CHAPTER TWENTY-SEVEN: Tempting Invitation

"Good morning! May I join you?"

Julia spun around, startled from her painting fantasy. She hadn't expected to be interrupted this early in the morning. When she crept outside she was sure everyone else was still asleep.

She looked up to see the pleasant face of a handsome, olive-skinned man. Although his English was spoken flawlessly, she detected a Spanish accent. Still in a daze, she studied his face for a familiar sign.

"Uh, well, sure." Julia's heart began to race. She felt nervous and uncomfortable, not knowing quite what to say to this seemingly debonair stranger who was sliding a chair beside her. He was casually dressed in a Ralph Lauren sweat suit. He also wore a pair of white Nikes that looked brand new.

"I'm Javier Lopez," the stranger announced, as he extended his hand. He didn't look as though he was much older than forty.

Julia smiled, saying, "Uh, Hi, I'm Julia Forrester."

As they shook hands Julia looked up into his seductive black eyes. They seemed to have a sadness. She searched Javier's face more intently. There was a story carved into the deep furrows and lines that she longed to know. She wished she could make her intruder sit down and pose so she could do a portrait of him.

"The turbulence woke me. I'm a light sleeper anyhow." Javier's bulging muscles showed off his sensational physique.

"Oh, ah, yes, the ship did get a bit rocky, didn't it? It woke me too, and I couldn't fall back to sleep." Julia had completely forgotten the turbulence while she was involved in her imaginary painting.

"Are you alone?"

"Um, yes, I am."

"And, what may I ask is such a beautiful young woman doing unescorted?" Javier's eyes glanced down at Julia's chest. Her cleavage was peaking out from her lavender V-neck sweater.

Julia blushed, "Well, I, ah, my husband is dead. He just died about six months ago, and, I needed some time to think."

"That's quite a coincidence. My wife also passed away recently."

"Oh, I'm sorry."

"I wasn't. My wife, though I loved her very much, suffered too long. She was a severe diabetic and was never able to lead a full life. Her day-to- day existence was a nightmare, a horrible tragedy."

Javier seemed to be the epitome of impeccable etiquette and graciousness. There was a clarity about him. Pride and dignity. Even though he seemed genuinely sad, he comfortably related his tale.

They continued to converse politely, as they became acquainted. Julia learned that Javier was a businessman in San Francisco. He said he had always dreamt of going on a cruise back to his native land, but his wife had been so ill, or was in the hospital so often, that it was never possible to travel for long periods of time. When she died, he promised himself a cruise. He hated to fly.

"Let me guess," Javier announced suddenly. He didn't want to dwell on the past, "I bet you're a model?"

"No but thank you for the lovely compliment. Actually, I'm, I'm an artist. A painter."

"Is that right!" he exclaimed. "I love art. In fact, I collect art."

"You do? What kind of art do you collect?"

"Well, I have several Leroy Neiman's ... "

Julia frowned. She disliked Neiman's work. Not because it wasn't skillful, but because it had become so commercialized. Once she had been in three homes in one week and every one had Neiman's "Satchmo" hanging over the fireplace.

Javier noticed Julia wince when he mentioned Neiman, "Of course, Neiman is not my favorite. I bought his work a while ago as an investment."

"Yes, I know, his prints have gone up several hundred dollars a year. I suppose they are a good investment. Do you like his work?"

"Well, yes and no. You see, when I first bought a Neiman I didn't know that much about art. The salesman sold me on him saying that not only was Neiman good, but his work would go up in value, and the salesman was right. After living with Neiman's painting for several years I began to appreciate art in a new and different way. His use of color is magnificent. And, I learned a lot about modern, abstract art, which prompted me to buy an original Peter Max. Then later a Jasper Johns."

"You have a Jasper Johns? Where did you get it?"

"At an auction. Once, when I was on business trip to New York City, a friend took me to Sotheby's."

Julia was impressed. John's work was selling for millions of dollars. "My gosh, how much did you pay for it?" She realized it was rude of her to ask, but her curiosity got the best of her.

"A million dollars. It was a real bargain."

"Which one of his paintings do you have?"

"One of the American flag."

"You do!? Wow!" Julia knew that a million dollars was a lot of money to pay for a painting. Though, not for a Jasper Johns. She had read in Time magazine some of Johns' work commanded more than a million dollars.

Javier seemed slightly embarrassed. He was not a pretentious person. He again wanted to change the subject.

"Tell me more about you," he asked as he looked into Julia's eyes. "Your eyes intrigue me."

Julia looked down and nervously twirled the end of the towel she was sitting on. She smiled, as she said, "I was thinking the same about your eyes. They, they, are, ah, very mysterious." She almost said "seductive" but caught herself.

Within an hour they were giggling and chatting like old friends.

"Hey, you know, breakfast is being served." Javier was looking at his gold watch. "Would you care to join me?"

"I'd be delighted. But, first I'd like to freshen up. Meet you in the dining room in half an hour."

"Wonderful. See you then."

For the next three days Julia and Javier spent most of their time together. When the ship docked for a couple of hours at various ports, they shopped and explored the towns. Back on ship, they ate every meal together, swam in the pool in the afternoons, and at night they strolled on the deck holding hands. There was so much to say, they talked non-stop. By the fourth night they slept together.

Julia was in a dither. Javier was such an open and charming man. He kept her entranced with stories of his poor, deprived childhood growing up in Mexico, and of his awkward adolescent years as an immigrant in the United States. He brought tears to her eyes as he spoke of the prejudices he faced in high school. When he tried to date "white girls", they didn't want to have anything to do with him, calling him a "wetback". He talked about working his way through college, holding down two jobs while going to school full time.

After his MBA from UC Berkeley, he got a job as an appraiser for almost a year. His boss was a complete tyrant who worked him sixty hours a week and yelled at him every day. When Javier was offered an executive position with a large investment firm, he quit that job. His stock market acumen and expertise helped the new company expand from ten employees to a hundred in just two years. Within five he became president of the firm.

It was a ten-day cruise and the day before they were about to dock in Ixtapa, Javier made a proposal. "Julia, I have a lovely villa overlooking the water. It has a pool and is in a perfect location. Secluded, yet near everything. I would love it if you came and stayed with me. You won't have to do a thing. I have a staff of several servants."

Julia thought of the photograph she had in her purse, of the tiny house she had rented through an agency in San Francisco. She had gotten it at a very economical rate since she planned to stay for six months. She wondered if the facilities were modern. What kind of plumbing did it have? Was the electrical wiring safe? She thought about how weak and frightened she still felt, especially in a foreign country where she wasn't very fluent in Spanish. How, being with Javier had eased some of her fears.

She flashed back on the last time she saw Andre, and how he had played on her fear and insecurity, saying, "I can't believe you, Julia. I just can't believe you cancelled our wedding again! You know time doesn't stand still. You're not getting any younger, you know. If you wait too long, and I'm no longer available, you might end up all alone! Try it for a while. Try zipping up your own clothes in the back. Try slapping yourself on your back when you're choking."

"Andre! You've got to be kidding! I can't believe how neurotic you are, thinking of these stupid scenarios."

"Ha, well give it ten years or so, when your prospects will be fewer. There aren't too many guys out there who want to take care of an old lady."

"An OLD LADY! In ten years I'll only be in my fifties! And, what makes you think I'll need to be taken care of? Is that why you think I wanted to marry you? So I'd have someone to take care of me?"

Andre stammered, "Well, I, uh, I mean, I was thinking about the future. Someday if you're sick and, and, perhaps dying ... "

"Andre you're being so manipulative playing on my insecurities. And, you know what? I think you're projecting. I think you're the one who's afraid to grow old alone! You're the one who needs ME to take care of YOU!"

Julia remembered how furious she felt then, as she picked up her bag and stormed out of Andre's house.

Well, Javier had proven Andre wrong. She was not an old lady whom no one wanted. Javier helped her see that she was still quite appealing to men. Even, younger men. Javier was only thirty-six. Eight years her junior! Her age didn't bother him in the least. When she told him she was forty-four, he merely replied, "I would never have guessed. I thought you were about thirty. Ah, that must be why you are so mature. You are like a fine wine that gets better with age."

Ever since Javier came into her life Julia had mostly forgotten her past. He was the best companion a single woman could ask for. He was entertaining and intelligent. And funny. His spontaneous sense of humor often had her laughing until tears came to her eyes. And, as a lover he was even better than Andre. More gentle and tender. And, he never passed out afterwards. Instead, they would lie in bed and talk, locked in each other's arms, sometimes for more than an hour. Then they'd get up and chase each other around the deck, return and make love again. They made love more than once on many days.

Javier's invitation was a wonderful one. Too good to be true.

"Javier, I ... yes, I would love to stay with you at your villa."

"It's settled then. I will tell the steward to have your bags delivered there."

That night Julia was very restless, tossing and turning in her sleep. She was still plagued by the same doubts and fears. Javier was a wonderful man and she loved being with him. He taught her so much in the nine days they were together. Especially, that Andre was not the man she wanted to marry.

But, she had gone on the cruise to think, to be by herself. To paint. That promise to herself had not lasted a day before Javier came into her life. Now, she was in the same position she had fled. Belonging to a man. Putting her life on hold again. It was not that it didn't feel good being with Javier, because it did. But, she didn't want to rush into another relationship so quickly. She needed time. She needed time to test her single status. Javier would only postpone that test.

She also thought of her children, who had promised to visit her in Ixtapa during their spring break. Her sons were in their junior and sophomore years in college. Sandra was just graduating high school, and in the fall she would begin her first year at Smith College, in Massachusetts.

After living with Ralph and his new wife for several years, Sandra began to appreciate her mother. Compared to her stepmother who was self-centered and often tried to exclude her, Sandra thought Julia was so much easier to be with and she no longer felt any animosity towards her mother. After her parents' divorce, Sandra became closer to Julia which enabled the two of them to resolve many of their past issues.

Julia was looking forward to seeing her sons and daughter again and spending quality time with them. If she was living with Javier it would not be the same. It would dilute her visit with her children.

She jumped out of bed, pulled an embroidered caftan over her head and stepped into a pair of thongs. She ran all the way to Javier's cabin. The door was open. He was sitting by the porthole reading.

Out of breath, she said, "Oh, Javier, I loved every minute being with you, and I adore you, but I really need time to myself. I came to Mexico to work, to paint, to think. So, please don't take this the wrong way, but, I, I can't accept your generous offer."

"Are you sure?"

"Yes, positive."

"Will we ever see each other again?"

"Perhaps."

"May I take you out to dinner one night in Ixtapa?"

"That would be lovely. But, not for a few weeks. I have to get settled." She handed him a small piece of paper. "I'll be at this address."

They hugged each other tightly. Julia waved good-bye as she left Javier's cabin. "Thank you for a wonderful time. I'll look forward to seeing you again and having dinner with you."

"Me, too. Adios, and good luck."

"Thanks, I'll need it."

## EPILOGUE ... CHAPTER TWENTY-EIGHT: Ixtapa

The cruise ship docked at the port of Ixtapa, Mexico. Julia looked out the porthole of her cabin anxious to get a glimpse of her destination. Palm trees swayed in the breeze, the white sandy beach glistened and sparkled like diamonds. It was a welcoming sight for a tired traveler, especially on this warm, sunny day. Her heart beat rapidly anticipating the adventures awaiting her.

Taxi drivers were lined up waiting for the passengers to disembark from the ship. Julia examined their faces, wondering which one to choose to take her to the house she had leased.

Javier Lopez suddenly appeared and asked her if she'd like his chauffeur to drive her to her new home. Politely, Julia refused. Javier was too much of a temptation. His invitation to stay at his villa was very intriguing. As much as she wanted to be with him, she knew it would put her life on hold once again. Even allowing his chauffeur to drive her might challenge her resolve.

The main reason she decided to come to Mexico was to spend time alone – painting, reading, writing, thinking, introspecting. So much had happened to her during the last few months which was still confusing. She needed to be by herself for a while to figure things out. Even allowing herself to have that thought was something new for Julia. She needed to listen to herself for once.

Her beloved husband, her love, her Otto had only been dead for a little more than six months now. She was surprised to realize she was still affected by the shock of his death. Six months! It seemed like only yesterday when she was married to him. And yet, so much had happened to change her life.

Otto's death had traumatized her more than she understood at the time leaving her with a deep feeling of abandonment. One she was all too familiar with from her childhood. She had been totally dependent on Otto and, now, truly for the first time in her life she was alone. It was scary.

Julia was beginning to understand how she had sought refuge with Andre Kramer. At first it seemed as if he'd make a perfect partner – handsome, intelligent, caring, and adoring of her. Then there was the sex. Her mind wandered, remembering how life with Ralph had been unfulfilling in many ways. With Otto, sex was only occasionally satisfying. Andre had awakened something in her.

Looking back on those few months with Andre, Julia thought she might have fallen in love with him. Were those feelings driven by her fear of being alone? Or, was it her desire for sex? It was scaring her now to admit that her new-found sexual appetite could have dominated her behavior. Even more scary was that she had almost married him. Fortunately, the more time she spent with Andre the less attractive he became.

Andre was a different person in private than the persona he presented to the public. He was very self-centered, selfish and controlling. Thankfully, Suzie was a good catalyst for Julia and gave her a lot to think about, "food for thought" she'd say. Especially when Suzie accused her of having "marriage-it is", candidly pointing out Andre's obvious faults. Julia was nostalgic about those talks with her friend and wished Suzie was there with her now in Mexico, even if she didn't always agree with her.

She thought of the chain of challenging events after Otto's death again, and how Stephanie and Stuart made her transition into widowhood even more difficult and traumatic. Their law suit had allowed her little time to grieve. They were so sure of the reality they had created in their minds. How does one develop such a strong sense of self-righteousness?

Thinking about the twins made her feel sad for Stuart. Picturing him the last time she saw him and Stephanie at the hospital brought tears to her eyes. Was he in pain now? How much longer did he have to live? Would she ever see him again? Somehow in her "new growth" their behavior became a curiosity to Julia. Her sadness thinking of Stuart was genuine.

Then there was Isadore Valenti – she was glad to be rid of him. His anger with her for dropping the lawsuit was contemptuous. Looking back at that last meeting with him made her laugh. His chauvinism and pompousness convinced her she had done the right thing. What an ass!

Julia was distracted from her memories when a short, toothless man approached her and asked, "Senorita ... you want ride?"

Senorita! Wow! Julia smiled. Did she really look that young? Or, was he being flattering to the turista? Remembering the few Spanish words she knew, she replied, "Si, Senor, muchas gracias."

The little taxi driver introduced himself as Pedro Juarez. He quickly picked up her suitcases and put them in the trunk of his cab with such ease his strength defied his physique.

The other cabbies looked at him with envy. They had all been studying this lovely blonde lady, whispering to each other, "Muy guapa" (pronounced "wapa", a common remark in Spanish describing a very sexy woman).

It was a short drive to the house Julia had rented. The photo made the house look charming and it was on the beach which was her main requirement. She always loved being by the water, especially the ocean, where the sound of the waves gave her a feeling of tranquility. She imagined sitting on the beach gazing out at the sea, thinking about her life. The warmth and quietness would help her to relax and to be more in touch with herself.

Being at the beach was important to Julia, but it made her wonder if she had overlooked other important aspects of the house: Would it be furnished nicely? Would it have any modern conveniences? Hell, would it have electricity? Running water? Would the water be safe to drink? What if she got sick? Who would she call? Was there a qualified doctor nearby?

Suddenly, she was filled with fear and anxiety again. She didn't know a soul in Ixtapa except Javier. She adored him, but was cautious to call on him. Javier seemed like a wonderful man. They had a lot in common and were very compatible. Having second thoughts, she wondered if her refusal to accept his invitation was too hasty. With Javier she would have felt safe and unafraid. Now, she was all alone.

Paradoxically, being alone was her initial intention. Her "tough side" was sure that was what she needed to grow as a person. Unfortunately, she was not that tough, and the "frightened child" deep within exposed her insecurity and vulnerability.

Thankfully, these thoughts were lost when Pedro pulled into a driveway abundant with beautiful, colorful flowers. The stucco adobe exterior of the "casita" was equally impressive. Julia couldn't wait to jump out of the cab and see the inside. Much to her delight it was also lovely, though small and compact. Whoever owned it had excellent taste. It reminded her of something the Mexican artist Frida Kahlo might have decorated. For a few moments Julia relished the decor. Bright, complementary red, yellow and blue colors painted on the walls, cabinets and counter tops jumped out at her, satisfying the artist in her. The Spanish-style furniture and touches of black wrought iron which she always loved added to the charm, as well as the interesting turquoise tile that enveloped the kitchen. Large paned-glass windows faced the ocean and a cool breeze was blowing in. A special addition, an air-conditioner! Thankfully. Julia heard that Ixtapa could get very hot and humid. And, much to her delight there was a "telefono" attached to the wall in the kitchen. Not many people owned or could afford a telephone in Mexico, but because of all the new construction of condos happening nearby there was easier access to the outside world.

"Senorita ... where Usted want bags?" Pedro asked. Julia was so deep in her thoughts she was startled when he spoke. She smiled and explained where each suitcase should be put, and without asking what she owed she handed him a crisp twenty dollar bill. She hoped it was enough for the taxi plus a tip. Pedro's face lit up when he saw the American currency and, even without his two front teeth his smile glowed.

She had guessed correctly. Julia had no idea what the exchange rate was in Mexico, but later found out that an American dollar was equivalent to 150 pesos. No wonder Pedro was ecstatic. Twenty dollars was equivalent to 3000 pesos! She felt pleased to have made a small difference for this kind man.

The following day Pedro was at her front door presenting her with a pan of hot chile rellenos and enchiladas prepared from scratch by "mi esposa" Maria. They were the very best Julia had ever tasted. More importantly, she felt welcomed and less afraid in her new home.

Over the next few days Pedro and Maria called on Julia frequently to inquire how she was doing, and within a short time they became her Mexican "familia". Even though their verbal communication left much to be desired, Pedro and Maria's warmth gave her a sense of belonging which helped ease her anxiety. They barely spoke English and Julia hardly knew Spanish, yet caring feelings were always present.

Julia also befriended their three children. Emilio, who was eight, liked to visit her and ask questions about the Estados Unidos. He was a big help when he accompanied her to the market. Knowing so little Spanish she might have ended up buying weird things. Julia always gave Emilio a dollar tip for escorting her and helping her learn a new language.

Teresa, the little five year old girl, loved running her hands through Julia's honey-colored hair, curious why Julia wasn't a brunette. All the other women she was knew had dark hair. She enjoyed studying Julia's jewelry and was thrilled when she was allowed to wear her necklaces, bracelets and earrings. Julia delighted in Teresa's giggles as she watched her dress up like a "mujar". It reminded her of Sandra who did the same as a little girl.

It also hurt Julia knowing Sandra was thousands of miles away and they wouldn't be seeing each other for several more months. She also thought of her two sons, Brad and Charlie, wondering how they were and when or if they would come to Mexico for a visit. The Juarez "muchachos'" brought back so many memories for Julia. Her heart-broken, maternal instincts surfaced every time she visited with her new Mexican friends.

Jesus was the six-month old baby. He was named Jesus because he was a "miracle baby". Maria had four miscarriages before she got pregnant with him. At first Julia thought he had a Greek name, because his parents called him "Hey Zeus". When Julia questioned their choice of a name, they laughed and explained that Jesus was pronounced "Heyzeus". It still seemed odd to Julia to call a baby "Jesus". She decided to call him "Chico", which was how his siblings addressed him.

Chico seemed different than the babies she knew in America. He seemed happy and smiled most of the time. Never colicky and was usually a pleasure when he was awake. Maria breast-fed him on demand. That was so unlike many young mothers in the states who fed their babies formula. Julia observed the love and attention everyone in the family gave Chico, and wondered if that had anything to do with his easy-going personality. Maybe he was born with that kind of temperament ... or was it his Karma?

Though younger than Julia, Maria was like a mother to her. She offered to clean Julia's house once a week, and each time she brought a pan of home-cooked food. It made Julia's mouth water in anticipation, wondering what delicacies Maria would bring next. She looked forward to Maria's company every week and often worked with her. Cleaning was actually a fun time together, plus it included a Spanish lesson. What really impressed Julia however, was how Maria took pride in whatever she did, enjoying her work with no complaints.

Yes, Ixtapa was a new beginning for Julia, learning something each day. Besides becoming more fluent in Spanish, she was starting to see that it was possible to live an uncomplicated life, taking it one day at a time with few expectations.

She compared their vastly different cultures, so different from what she had known while growing up and later as an adult. People in Mexico seemed more appreciative of simple pleasures. Happiness was evident on their faces.

Happiness! It's what everyone seeks, yet is difficult to capture. Maybe, because we seem desperate to be happy, it evades us, Julia thought. Her Mexican friends went through each day matter-of-factly with purpose and contentment - an enlightening experience for Julia.

It was an inspiration for her to see life from a simplistic perspective, which gave her an indescribable sense of security and peace. A similar feeling she had on the day she married Otto at Big Sur. With him in mind, almost every night she would hold on to her sapphire ring with a satisfied smile, and usually fall into a deep sleep.